# SOMEONE'S DAUGHTER

By

David Fettes

*For Tim, Anna and Kate*

*Who taught me how to be a father*

*And what it is to be loved*

# CONTENTS

# ACKNOWLEDGEMENTS

Acknowledgements are usually at the end of books, but I've never been one for 'usual' or convention. Anyway, I'm always a little suspicious that not many people read them because they can be like an acceptance speech at the Oscars. It brings to my mind Spike Milligan's acceptance ad lib for his Lifetime Achievement Award when he said he wasn't going to thank anyone since he did it "all by myself".

Good old Spike, but I cannot claim the same for *Someone's Daughter*. I did seek and was given help by some amazing and brave women who offered to speak to me about their own experiences of having a father, and who I don't think deserve to be mere footnotes at the end of the book.

You each know who you are, but your true identity stays with me, so Danielle, Julie, Tracey, Kate – thank you. You have no idea how much you each helped me, and just how you made me examine my own conscience about being a father. You, or aspects of you and your words are all in Jamie's story. You may spot yourself and if you do, know that I was thinking of you as wrote those words.

Anonymous girl. Your name I didn't hear when I listened to you being interviewed on the radio over thirty years ago, but your story so moved me as a father, as a man and as a hopefully compassionate humanitarian that I resolved to tell it one day. That day is here and I hope I have done you justice, and that you have found peace and a partner in life who has loved and cared for you as you deserve to be.

Evie Bowes, your insight and advice about damaged women was powerful, emotive and a pathway to veracity.

Freddie and Evie, thank you for agreeing to 'share' your moment on the beach on the front cover, for me the epitome of what fatherhood should be.

Anna England, yet again you encouraged, guided and helped in ways you cannot imagine - and have forgiven your father for so much.

And finally, Nicola. How many times have you read and lived Jamie's story?

Thank you all. It is a privilege to know each one of you and to see and know your strength.

To anybody I have missed out, know that you were no help at all.

# CHAPTER 1

## LONDON, OCTOBER 2014

Jamie took the proffered money, counted it quickly with well-practised flicks of her fingers and stuffed the folded notes into the pocket of her tightly fitting jeans.

"Thank you," he said, tucking the tails of his white business shirt into the top of his trousers and pulling up the zip. Jamie noticed how his expense account belly hung down, a fleshy Roman blind hiding the buckle on his black leather belt, the thick hair covering his blotchy pink skin now hidden by the shirt. She wondered if the belt had been a birthday present from his wife, or perhaps a loving gift for Christmas from his children. His wedding ring, burrowing into the pudgy flesh of his finger, shouted 'married' and she marvelled that he made no attempt to hide this from her. She was no more than a piece of meat for him to buy and enjoy, like a steak at the butcher whose sole purpose is to give selfishly taken pleasure. Revulsion overwhelmed her as she turned for the door. Suddenly she was desperate to get back to her flat and a shower to wash off the touch of his damp flesh on her body.

"Can I see you again tomorrow?" he said. "You're good. I'm in London for a couple of days. Nine o'clock?"

"Sure," she replied as she turned the door handle and walked away from his fetid breath, with its top notes of open Lagos sewer on a hot summer's day. "You have Steve's number. You need to arrange it through him."

She quickly closed the door behind her to kill the chance of further conversation. She had learned the essential art of emotional detachment, the skill she desperately clung to for the preservation of her sanity.

As she stood at the lift waiting for the ring of its arrival, Jamie's thoughts turned to her apartment in Earl's Court, and more pressingly to the revision for her exams that awaited her there. She longed to be out of the building, to escape the punter and his sweaty, hirsute, corpulent body. She needed to wipe the memory of him from her mind and get back to her work and focus on her future, the key to her escape from the humiliation of the revolting trade she endured. She knew her three flatmates would be sitting around the candle-lit kitchen table, having supper together in the soft gloom, blissfully ignorant of what her evenings in the University library really entailed. She could see their glasses of wine glinting in the flickering flames of the candles, and hear the chatter of their voices as they compared their stories of the day, discussed their boyfriends, dreamt aloud their dreams for their futures. They each worked and had real jobs, whilst being supported by their families, giving them easy access to money. She was now a third of the way through her second year at university, the outsider in the quartet whose only access to money was through the enforced sale of her body. She liked to think it more as hire than sale, fiercely clinging to possession of her soul, her last tattered shreds of dignity, detaching her mind from what was being done to her body, which had somehow become a business asset rather than part of her being.

Jamie had never admitted to the others, nor anyone else, how she was funding her way through her university course. At the beginning, when she first moved up to London, she had tried the usual suspects of casual jobs that are open to impecunious youth who are in full-time education and unable to commit to full-time employment. Waitressing had been her first foray, enduring the groping hands of drunks who were convinced they were attractive in their drooling alcohol fuelled stupor. It was the price she had paid in the hope of enhanced tips until one final hand up her skirt proved to be the hand too far. She had worked in bars filled with men whose wives didn't understand them, but were convinced someone young enough to be their daughter would. She had babysat obnoxious, spoilt children suffused with a sense of entitlement in their egocentric lives whilst being devoid of even the most basic manners. Indulged by their guilt-ridden parents, each pursuing their individual careers, the 'entitled little shits' as Jamie thought of them became masters of manipulation in their craving for attention and affection. Many of those emotionally impoverished children had never eaten a meal at a table, rebelling when Jamie insisted that they should. Having cutlery thrown at her by an enraged six-year-old brought down the curtain on her child-minding career.

Eventually Jamie came to realise the earnings from the rare part-time work opportunities available to a full-time student could never meet the cost of living in the capital city, even though she felt she had adopted the social life of a closed order nun. Perhaps it was desperation Steve saw in her face when she served him his meal in the classy wine bar in Beauchamp Place. When she saw the bar had a vacancy for a waitress she had hoped it might be the one place in London where men went to with their wives for dinner. She hoped these would be the wives who did perhaps understand their husbands, even if it was only well enough to chaperone their wandering eyes and hands through dinner. Steve had come in as part of a group of four men and had slipped a card into her blouse pocket as he took his coat from her at the end of his meal, gently brushing her breast with his hand as he did so. He leaned forward and whispered in her ear to call him if she wanted to earn money modelling. Tall, slim and good looking, with swept back blond hair, his blue eyes locked onto hers and he smiled gently before turning to the door to leave with his companions.

The card revealed nothing of him or his work, confining itself to giving his name and telephone number. Jamie put it into the pocket of her jeans and forgot about it until the arrival of a credit card bill a few days later on rent day resurrected the cold hand of panic that gripped her heart. The monthly payments she was making were no longer making headway against the unassailable forces of compound interest, and the outstanding amount was now growing, seemingly exponentially. Despite her relative innocence about all things financial, she was aware of the usurious rates of interest that credit card debt attracts and that unless she stopped using the card, there was only going to be one outcome. She knew that in a different era she would have been a few short steps from the debtor's prison. And yet, resorting to credit was her only way of surviving, of even feeding herself. The card was her lifeline, one slipped to her by her mother the day she left home to go to London to start her course.

"I've got a second card to my credit card for you," her mother had said. "Don't tell you father, he doesn't know and I don't want him to. He wouldn't be happy about it. It has a limit on it but it might help you when you need anything. I can pay for it out of my allowance he gives me and he won't know."

Jamie's relationship with her mother was somewhat distant, because her mother had always been a detached person in her life, a wife to an overbearing husband before she was a mother and so this thin sliver of love was a sign of a protective shield for her.

"Thank you, Mum," Jamie said. "That's amazing. I'll be really careful with it and only use it when I have to."

With no allowance to support her she had no option but to maximise student loans and take on part time work, but the cost of living in London, even living very frugally as she did, was beyond the capabilities of casual work's meagre rewards. Jamie's high living costs were compounded by the essential but always expensive books she had to buy for her course. The constant, corrosive stress of what was becoming an insurmountable problem, with its inevitable consequences, had become a Damoclean cloud that hung over her, invading her thoughts at all hours and making any flow of creative thinking impossible. The marks for two recent pieces of work she had handed in were poor, a departure from the usual high standards she set for herself, and she knew instinctively they were a reflection of the destructive distraction of her mounting debts. A good degree was her passport to a new and fully independent life and the threat to this was almost too much for her to bear. An added stress was the need to protect her mother from her father finding out about the debt she had accumulated, increasing the sense of desperation she felt.

As Jamie put the credit card statement on the chest of drawers in her small bedroom, she noticed the business card she had been given in the restaurant. She picked it up and studied it, turning it over to see if there were any clues on the back but it still remained obstinately silent about what Steve did. She remembered he had said something about modelling and felt slightly flattered he had felt she was good looking enough to be considered for that. Slim waisted and of medium height, her naturally wavy auburn hair that she kept cropped to just above her shoulders framed a pretty elfin face, with its full lips and large clear blue eyes.

Seizing the moment, she picked up her phone and dialled the number on the card. After ringing for a while the phone went through to an anonymised, pre-recorded voicemail, and so she said Becky was calling and gave her number, with a brief reminder as to who she was, slightly disappointed at not making immediate contact. She had chosen an alias as a form of protection against the uncertainty of who he was, and a way to keep some distance between them.

The call back came that evening. Jamie was sitting on her bed, her knees tucked up and a text book open against her raised legs when her phone rang on the bedside table next to her. Still reading she absent-mindedly picked it up and put it to her ear.

"Hello," she said.

"Hi Becky, it's Steve."

For a moment, the name didn't register with Jamie, her mind still focussed on what she had been reading, but the penny suddenly dropped.

"Oh, hi," she said, "Thank you for ringing. I don't know if you remember me. I served your table the other day in the restaurant in Beauchamp Place. You gave me your business card. You said something about earning money modelling."

"Of course I remember you," Steve said, his voice soft and quiet. "Becky, right? How could I forget those eyes?"

Jamie giggled, flattered by the compliment. "Can we meet up to chat about it?" she said.

"Of course," he replied. "How about tomorrow after work? Say six o'clock, El Vino in Fleet Street? I have a meeting near there so will be in the area."

"That's fine," Jamie replied. "I have a lecture that finishes at five so I can easily make that."

"See you there then," Steve said. The phone went dead. He had obviously rung off. Jamie assumed she had caught him in the middle of a meeting or dinner and so he had no time to chat more. She put down her phone and returned to reading her book. After a couple of sentences she realised she had not taken in a word of what she had read. Her mind was already drifting towards the meeting with Steve the following evening and on what the modelling might entail. Giving up the unequal struggle to concentrate, she closed the book and went to the living room to join her flatmates in front of the television.

Jamie arrived at El Vino slightly early so she killed time by exploring the area. Cutting down through Old Mitre Court, she strolled past The Clachan Pub and on into King's Bench Walk, where the quiet backwaters of the Inner Temple and its unexpected gardens opened up to her. She sensed the gentlemanly and enduring traditions of the law, manifest in the unchanging uniform of the barristers as they walked calmly through the hushed streets between the tall buildings, some with gowns billowing behind them and wearing their wigs, many with bundles of ribbon-wrapped papers under their arms. Jamie wondered at the weight of responsibility those innocent looking documents brought to the barristers as they prepared arguments and pleadings that dictated the fortunes, or otherwise, of those they represented before the seats of justice. Did they find it a heavy burden that denied them sleep at night, or were they trained and inured enough to detach from the outcome, wherever that led? The added tension of the death penalty no longer existed and she shivered as she imagined her own feelings of responsibility and guilt if she had been accountable for a client's appointment with a modern-day Pierrepoint. Her carefully chosen clothes, which she had picked to show off her slim figure, now seemed out of place, perhaps frivolous in an environment that reached back to a different time. The gowned and bewigged barristers hurrying through the calm of the cloistered buildings seemed unashamedly unchanging, defiantly holding on to their heritage in the face of a modern world that hustled and bustled about them outside their sanctuary. Jamie suddenly felt self-conscious, strangely out of place, a role reversal where, outside that sheltered world, its citizens would be the anomalies, not her. She hurried on down towards the river which flowed on its relentless way through the city, a part of a more familiar world she understood.

Reaching the Embankment at the bottom of the gardens she glanced at her watch and saw it was nearly six o'clock so quickly turned to retrace her steps up the gradual incline to Fleet Street. Tentatively pushing open the door to the wine bar she stepped into its gloomy interior. The dark panelled walls accentuated the sombre atmosphere as the bar's almost exclusively male clientele stood against the bar, or sat at tables in the more open areas. Jamie strained her eyes in the poor light before picking out Steve. He was seated on a green leather-backed bench at a table at the back of the bar, tucked in a small alcove. She pushed her way through the chattering throng to reach the table, aware he had not seen her come in as he was reading the evening paper.

"Hi," she said, standing nervously in front of the table.

"Well hello Becky," Steve said as he folded the paper. "I didn't see you there, sorry. Have a seat." Steve indicated the seat on Jamie's side of the table that would place her directly in front of him. She pulled it out and sat down, placing her small brown handbag in her lap.

"What can I get you to drink?" Steve asked.

Jamie saw he had a half-finished glass of red wine in front of him and nodded at it.

"Oh, a red wine is fine, thank you," she said. "Shall I get it, and would you like another?"

"No, I'll do this," he said as he slid out of his seat and walked up to the bar.

Steve's absence gave Jamie the chance to calm herself. She had not been aware that she was nervous until she had reached the table to announce herself. Turning slightly in her seat and glancing over her shoulder, she saw him returning with two glasses which he held in one hand and a couple of bags of roasted peanuts in the other. He placed the glasses and packets on the table, slid easily back into his seat and smiled at her.

"So, tell me about it," he said, opening his peanuts and pouring some into his hand.

"It?" Jamie replied.

"Yes, you. Your life. What are you doing, or rather, what do you do? Apart from waitressing in bars that is, or is that what you do all the time?"

"No, I do that for some money," Jamie replied. "I'm a student. University. I do that sort of work to try to make ends meet, except it doesn't really do that. The cost of living in London is horrendous." She took a sip of her wine, carefully placing the glass back on the table in front of her. "The trouble is my course is pretty full-on so it's hard for me to fit in more hours. In any event, casual jobs are hard to come by after the financial crisis. To be honest with you, I'm struggling a bit financially at the moment and it's been getting to me as I'm pretty desperate. That's why I was interested in your question about modelling. It must pay better than waitressing or baby-sitting, surely?"

"Oh yes, yes it certainly does that," Steve said, smiling and raising his glass to his mouth. "Are you in financial difficulty now?" he asked.

"Yes," Jamie replied, blushing and fiddling with the strap on her handbag, embarrassed at the admission. She was not sure why she was opening up to this complete stranger but suddenly it was a relief to talk to someone. His smile was empathetic and he seemed genuinely concerned for her.

"So what about this modelling?" she asked.

"It's quite a mixed bag," Steve replied as he glanced away at the bar behind her. "There are some photoshoots for magazines, modelling clothes or make up, that sort of thing. And there are also evening jobs where executives need an attractive escort at business functions. Often these are guys from overseas whose wives have not been able to travel here with them and they need an attractive escort because their hosts and business connections like to go to dinner and theatres as couples."

"I'm not sure I'd want to do that," Jamie said.

"It's easy money," Steve replied. "And good money. How much do you make from an evening in the bar?"

"About twenty pounds I should think," Jamie replied.

"Twenty pounds?" Steve scoffed, waving his hand dismissively. "For the same time and less effort you can make a hundred and fifty in an evening," he said. "And you get a good meal thrown in, and sometimes a West End show. Anyway, what's the difference between being someone's companion for a dinner and serving at tables? You're going to be smiling and charming for either. The difference is the money, and with this way you're the one sitting down in the restaurant and being waited on for a change. You'd be crazy to miss out."

Jamie averted her gaze to her glass, picking it up to take another sip. She was lured by the temptation of the money, and more pressingly, of the knowledge of her debts and the corrosive stress they brought her. It was becoming all consuming, intruding into her thoughts and waking moments, even now. She was exhausted by the relentless tension.

"Why don't you think about it," Steve said, intuitively sensing the conflict of the appeal of accepting his suggestion and her reluctance to commit. "You've got my number so give me a call to let me know. In the meantime, this might help a bit, and there's no commitment. I don't like seeing young people struggling. I was there once and know what it's like." He pushed some folded notes across the table to Jamie.

"Oh, I couldn't take that," she said, pushing the notes back to him. "But thank you for the offer, it's very kind of you."

"Take it," Steve said, pushing the bundle back to her. "You can always pay me back one day if you'd rather treat it as a loan." He smiled gently at her.

"Are you sure?" Jamie asked, knowing the money would resolve the immediate problem she faced of how she was going to meet this month's rent, which had been due a few days before but which she still had not paid.

"Of course, take it," Steve replied.

"Thank you so much," Jamie said as she slipped the notes into her handbag, oblivious of the power of emotional debt. "I will pay you back, I promise," she added, noticing Steve glance at his watch. "And I'll call you as soon as I can. Thank you for the drink."

Jamie stood up and held her hand across the table. Steve took it and held it firmly as he gazed intently into her eyes.

"I look forward to hearing from you Becky. Have a nice evening."

Jamie turned and left the wine bar, slipping across the road and into Chancery Lane where she joined commuters rushing for home. Walking at a slower pace than the racing throng streaming past her, she had time to admire the magnificent and imposing buildings, the face of so much history and so many dramas played out in the nearby courts. Reaching the Underground she caught the escalator down to the platform for her journey back to the apartment.

Of course, the lure of the money had been irresistible and she had said yes. The first couple of months passed with a number of escorted dinners, but the photoshoots and modelling never materialised. She had asked Steve about them and each time he had made some excuse about the right person for the right job and he was looking for sessions for her, but they clearly came to nothing. Even now Jamie could not remember how the slide from platonic escorting to selling her body had happened, but she was acutely aware of her naivety. How could she not have seen what his intentions for her were from the outset? He must have thought her a complete fool.

After paying Steve his usual cut from the dinner escorts, she was only a little better off and still under severe pressure from her accumulated and mounting debt. She seemed to remember Steve had suggested she could earn a lot more if she was, in his words, 'kind to them,' a euphemism he didn't immediately elaborate on but in truth, didn't need to. She had resisted at first, of course, but the debts just kept getting worse and ultimately she somehow came to the conclusion she had no other option. Steve must have known that would happen.

Jamie cried after the first time, cried from the very depths of her soul with a bottomless grief. She left the hotel in tears, ashamed of herself and desperate to get home and scrub herself clean in the shower, to wash away the smell of the man, to rid herself of the image of him on top of her, his greasy combed-over hair and the drops of sweat that trickled down his nose and fell on her turned face. She still felt that same revulsion each time, not only of the men physically but also of them as people, to the extent her misandry seemed to extend to all men as she lumped them into a single category of predatory perverts. She sometimes mourned her lost innocence, but generally she refused to allow herself the luxury of regret, burying those thoughts deep within her, cutting off the indulgence of emotion and becoming numb. In time she felt nothing and became an emotional desert behind a facade of independence and self-reliance. The money her extra-curricular activities brought in was the difference between graduating with her degree, her ticket to freedom, and having to drop out. It was too late to turn back now with the finishing post in view, the race three-quarters run, so she clung to the thought that she would soon never have to shut her eyes and blank out what was being done to her body by yet another rutting stranger, closing her ears to his grunting pleasure.

The sound of the lift's arrival and its doors opening brought Jamie back to the present. The door opened and she stepped in, joining two businessmen who were chatting as they leaned against the back wall. The familiar feeling of their eyes undressing her as she turned her back on them and pressed the button for the ground floor filled her with contempt for them. She just knew they would glance at each other and wink an obscene look or gesture to each other, blind to their arrogance in thinking she'd be remotely interested in men old enough to be her father. She watched the descending numbers above her head, conscious of the uncomfortable silence that sits so uneasily on strangers gathered together in a lift. As the doors opened, her phone rang in her rucksack. Retrieving it quickly as she walked across the hotel lobby, she saw it was Steve calling her and for a moment she was tempted to ignore it, fearful and aware of why he was calling. It was sure to be one more trick for the night. Much as she detested the thought of it, the money would be useful, if not essential, and in any event, Steve would not take kindly to being ignored or refused. He knew her whereabouts that evening because he had arranged the job she had just completed, both its time and place. He would have spoken to the punter and know she had just left him so would know she was not home yet. Yet again she had overspent her meagre budget for the month because of the expensive course books she had unexpectedly had to buy.

"Yes," she said curtly.

"Where are you?" said Steve. He was not known for his charm. What little she had seen so long ago at their first meeting proved to be an act, a masquerade to lure her to comply with his wishes. Even those notes he had given her in the wine bar were a lure, a trap designed to earn a gratitude from her that would make it difficult for her to refuse him in the future when she was in his debt.

"I'm just leaving the hotel," she replied. "In Park Lane and on my way home." She had learned not to lie to Steve. The consequences were unpleasant.

"I've got one more for you," Steve said. "He's one of our regulars, a big payer. He's at the Ritz Hotel in Piccadilly. Room 310 and he's expecting you in half an hour. Don't be late. And by the way, he likes some special stuff so don't let me down. He's one of our best and tips well so this one's worth your while."

"What do you mean by special stuff?" Jamie asked.

"Not sure but I think a bit of restraint, you know, tying up stuff.

Spanking. Just the usual. Just do it, it's good money. He's just a bit kinky, not dangerous. None of the others have ever complained."

The phone cut off and Jamie wondered how anyone could become so callous, so inured to deviance that it could become common currency in their attitude to her. He had no interest in her or what she had to do to make the money he craved, no doubt to continue to feed his voracious drug habit. All Jamie wanted to do was go back to her apartment, to turn her back on the repulsive older men she used as a means to an end, to fund her education. Ignoring her instinct to go home, Jamie turned and reluctantly walked down Park Lane to Hyde Park Corner and followed the road round to start the walk up Piccadilly. A cool breeze moved the naked branches of the trees in Green Park on the other side of the underpass, but the trees' semaphoring was mute, the sounds of their signalling buried under the roar of the traffic. A newspaper billboard headlined a news story about a young girl in Pakistan who had recently been awarded the Nobel Peace Prize. She had survived being shot in the head for the simple act of resisting the country's misogynistic mores, and for having the temerity to insist on girls being educated.

'And I thought I had problems,' Jamie thought to herself. 'At least I haven't got a hole in my head.'

Jamie walked past the imposing buildings on her left, some housing the Gentlemen's Clubs, the bastions of probity and moral rectitude whose members she so often met in the course of what she told herself was her evening job. As she walked she thought of them in there at that moment, relaxed in their old leather armchairs, no doubt pontificating to anyone who would listen about the loose morals of a young generation who should each be flogged to remind them how lucky they are and to drive some decent values into them. Hypocrites all, she thought. As for their views on homosexuality, she just knew that to a man they would voice their disgust, unaware of how many of their own number lived a life hidden in that very closet.

Banishing them from her mind, she turned her thinking to the headline about the injured young girl's award, which set her mind down a path of thoughts she rarely visited or followed, a dark cul-de-sac where the eddies of her thoughts trapped her into a spiral of despair. Unable to resist the pull of the vortex of memories, she pondered on how she had reached this point in her life. It was so far removed from the privilege of her outwardly respectable middle-class upbringing, with its obligatory years of banishment and exile at the age of eight into living at school under the care of the primly austere nuns to whom her parents had subcontracted not just her education but it seemed her entire upbringing. Being sent to boarding school so young had felt to her to be a complete rejection, an abandonment and banishment that reinforced her belief that she was not really wanted, a disappointing irritant that could be hidden by institutionalising it.

Despite the nuns' patently unqualified and inadequate best endeavours, Jamie had passed sufficient exams at grades that were acceptable to all the Universities she had chosen. Looking back she felt she had obtained her passes in spite of her schooling rather than because of it, although no doubt the teachers there would claim all the credit. She had chosen the London offer principally because it was far enough away from the family home in Oxford for her to have to leave the dreaming spires of her childhood and live away. The perceived magic of London was also a big attraction to a provincially sheltered girl. She remembered the excitement within her as she read the acceptance letters, a memory in stark contrast with the later conversation with her father about her choice.

The family home was an old red-bricked Georgian house that had once been a vicarage. Jamie and her older brother Charles were both born there and had known no other home. Its large sash windows allowed the rooms to be bathed in the light that streamed across the south facing lawn. Situated just by a village about ten miles out of Oxford, where her father was a successful lawyer and pillar of the business community, the house allowed uninterrupted views across rolling fields in which Jamie used to watch tractors methodically working autumnal furrows into the land, or harvesting the crops. Roe deer frequented the fields in the early mornings and late evenings, and she liked to watch them whilst she hid from them in the hedgerow. She especially loved it when the young fawns first appeared in the early summer, their dappled and spotted coats in contrast to the uniform colour of their mothers. She grew into the habit of getting up at dawn in those months and watching for their first cautious outings in the fields with their mothers, often ghosts in the low mist hanging over the land. They were the harbingers of hope, of new life, each new heartbeat drumming a steady optimism that Nature's relentless cycles would continue.

In her child's mind the fields were vast, the vista endless, rendering the distant tractors that laboured in them to the size of insects. She would often sit at the edge of the field where it bordered the house's garden, her back against the stone wall boundary and with the family dog nestled under her arm. She was always mesmerised by the metronomic motion of the tractors as they passed to and fro in front of her, moving ever closer as they turned at the end of each leg of their relentless journey. Often each tractor would tow behind it a fluttering stream of bunting sea gulls and other birds, dancing like wind-blown flags as they dipped and soared in search of insects and seeds that had been disturbed. When close, the tractors towered over her as they roared past, the farmer often giving her a friendly smile and a wave. He had stopped once and asked her if she would like a ride. She clambered up into the cramped cab and sat beside him as they powered their way around a full circuit of the field, cutting the long grass for the haymaking as they went. Her dog ran beside them the whole way, his tongue lolling and flapping alongside his mouth in the heat of the late summer afternoon. Every now and again he barked up at her and she responded with a cheery wave to him, which seemed to re-energise him because each time she did, he picked up the pace and raced ahead before falling back to run alongside. He was so intent on watching her, he missed the rabbits that came flying out of the long grass as they escaped the blades of the hay cutter.

Jamie marvelled at how uncomplicated and unconditional a dog's love is. So unlike its poor relation, human love, a love that so often comes with conditions, warranties and retribution, but so often with almost inevitable breaches of trust. Her own experience of a coldly undemonstrative and authoritarian father had bred into her a cynicism about the concept of love. She now wondered whether the emotion we call love is merely an aspiration that competes in an unequal struggle against the innate selfishness and self-absorption of humankind. She had come to the conclusion we are all born utterly selfish. It is society that forces us to think of others before ourselves. Some never quite get the message or, more heinously, choose to ignore it.

With her father's exalted position in the community, and as a Churchwarden in the beautiful Norman church in the village, came an arrogance and pomposity she had at first found embarrassing in her early teens, but ultimately hateful. If anyone were to ask her adult self what her memory of him was, she would have to say 'a disappointment.' Whilst there was no doubt he had provided materially in her earlier years, he had never given her what she craved, the love and tactile affection that comes with deep caring. Instead she had always interpreted his cold indifference as disappointment in her, no matter her endeavours and achievements that she had hoped would at the very least be acknowledged if they were not going to be applauded with pride. Even her name was a constant reminder that she was not the son she knew he had really wanted. Shortly before her tenth birthday she had wandered into his study at home holding a piece of homework she wanted to show him, a short essay the class had been set to write in their half-term holiday and which she felt she had written well. He was sitting at his desk, working on some papers, his open briefcase on the floor next to him, from where it disgorged more documents onto the carpet.

"I've nearly finished my homework," she said to his back while she pushed the essay onto the desk next to his elbow. "I need some help with it."

"I'm busy, Jamie," he said without looking at her, picking up another paper and beginning to read it.

"It'll only take a minute," Jamie said, pushing the paper further onto the desk.

With an over-acted sigh of impatience, her father took the essay and quickly read it. Jamie could see his lips moving slightly as he scanned it, too quickly to take it in fully. Finishing it he handed it back to her without looking at her.

"Receive is spelled 'ei' not 'ie'," he said as he leaned back over his work.

Jamie turned and left the room, quietly shutting the door behind her, crushed, disheartened and disconsolate, at a loss as to what to do to please him. The tears started to flow as she climbed the stairs to hide in her bedroom. Sitting on her bed, her knees tucked under her chin, her thoughts drifted back to a conversation she had had with him a few weeks before. She had been teased about her name at school that day, a group of girls saying Jamie was a boy's name. She felt humiliated and ashamed, a dagger to the heart of her burgeoning femininity and sense of self-worth, which was fragile at the best of times. She broached the subject with her parents in the kitchen that evening.

"Why did you call me Jamie?" she asked. "Everyone teases me that it's a boy's name."

"I thought you were going to be a boy and had chosen the name James," her father replied. "It never occurred to me you might be a girl. What's the point in having a girl when she'll go and get married and change her name so my name doesn't carry on? Even her children will have a different name and so be no part of me and my family. It was a nuisance because your mother had bought baby clothes for a boy. I'd told her to get rid of Charles' clothes because after he was born I didn't want another baby, so you were a mistake. A big mistake. When you appeared I decided I liked the name so I thought we'd keep it, but obviously had to change it slightly."

To this day Jamie felt she was a living memorial to the much-mourned boy who was never to be. She was the embodiment of disappointment to her father, who seemed to make no secret of the fact he had no second son to watch playing rugby, to play really competitive tennis with and with whom to share his misogynistic views in the village pub. She once heard him on the telephone saying to someone he had never really wanted her. And yet she still strove to win him over, for him to notice her, perhaps one day to love her.

When she received her university acceptance letter she had excitedly gone to see her parents to share her achievement with them. They were sitting by an open log fire in the drawing room, a glass of wine by each of them reflecting the flames that danced in the fireplace.

'They've accepted me in London," she blurted out.

"Oh, that's nice," her mother said taking a sip of wine.

Her father said nothing and continued to read the newspaper. Jamie walked around them and sat in an armchair to the side of the blazing hearth.

"It's amazing," she said. "I'm so excited. There's an introductory week this month that I shall go to so I can organise my halls and other stuff, and then in October I go up for fresher's week."

"So how are you going to pay for it?" her father said, at last putting down the paper and turning his head to look at her.

Jamie's heart stopped beating and she felt the blood drain from her face. She felt slightly faint, disembodied at the shock of his question.

"What do you mean?" she said.

"I would have thought it fairly obvious," he replied. "How are you going to pay for University because I'm not? I've already paid for your education, and for what you laughingly call your results, which were not exactly a great return on the money I spent. I see no reason to carry on wasting money on you, and particularly not for the course you have chosen. We've done our bit so if you want to go to university and waste three years, you can do it with your money, not mine. I've told you before, I want you to study the law. Now that's a real career, not this frolic in the park you insist on pursuing. Our job is done. You're an adult now so you're on your own. Time to stand on your own feet, not to stand there with your hand out."

"But how will I manage?" Jamie said tearfully. 'You paid for Charles."

"Well, that's your problem, not mine," her father replied. "Charles did a proper degree, not some airy-fairy art subject that has no value in the real world. It'll be a good lesson for you. Not everything's handed to us on a plate in life and we'll see how much you really want this. When you fail and drop out you can get a real job in something that's worthwhile, make some money and get an education from the university of life instead."

"But…"

"I don't want to discuss it," her father interrupted. He picked up his paper and continued reading as he took another sip of wine.

The room fell silent. Jamie glanced at her mother who looked uncomfortable but just shrugged her shoulders in a gesture that said, 'You know your father,' whilst averting her eyes to study the flames in the fire. Jamie wasn't sure if it was an expression of resignation, or an indication of agreement with her father. Either way, there was clearly going to be no profit in discussing it with either of them. Her mother was so dominated and controlled by her bullying husband she had long ago lost any remnants of her own personality. From the clothes she wore to the lipstick she bought and the friends she was allowed, everything in her life had to have her husband's prior approval if her life was not to be made insufferable. Worn down, her self-esteem in tatters, her focus in life was to please the man she had married, despite the obvious futility of trying to placate the obdurately and deliberately unpleasable.

In the face of the stubborn silence that had descended on the room, Jamie returned to her bedroom, sobbing quietly, her dreams in shreds. Lying down slowly on her bed, she curled into a small ball of pain, frustration and humiliation, her arms tightly crossed over her chest. She was not aware of falling asleep and woke with a start in the early hours. She was still lying on top of her bed, the cold of the night air bringing her to consciousness. She quickly undressed and put on warming pyjamas, turning on her electric blanket before jumping into the bed where she slept fitfully until the early morning light brightened her bedroom.

As she slowly surfaced, the memory of the previous evening's conversation flooded back into her mind and her eyes immediately flooded with tears again. She could hear her parents moving about the house, the smell of toast and fresh coffee filtering up to her. Their breakfast was clearly under way and she decided to stay in bed in her room until her father had gone to work rather than go down and face him. As she lay back on her soft pillow, she wondered when and how love could turn to fear.

Jamie was suddenly ashamed to face the stark truth of her real feelings about her father. She could not remember the last time she had felt that hot rush of love, of emotion. When was she last excited at the prospect of seeing him at the end of his working day, or him coming home from one of his many business trips? When did she start hoping it would be her mother and not her father who would collect her from school at the end of term, or for a weekend at home? When did she start praying it wouldn't be him stepping out of the car in the school drive? She had listened to her school friends speak of their easy relationships with their fun fathers, of trips to shops they had taken with them, of country walks filled with fascination and discovery, of a love she found incomprehensible and yet one she so yearned for. These were alien concepts to her, and the dawning thought that what she had experienced through being parented was the aberration and was not normal was chilling. In that moment, she decided she would take his advice. One way or another she would stand on her own feet, not only to get back at him and to show him she could, but more importantly, for herself. University was going to be for her, not him, and she determined to do whatever it took to fulfil that ambition. The decision was liberating and in that single moment she knew he had lost her forever. Or so she thought.

"Where did all that come from?" Jamie muttered aloud to herself. She had been so lost in her thoughts and memories she had not noticed she had completed the walk from Hyde Park Corner and was now standing opposite the colonnaded entrance to the hotel. Seeing a break in the traffic she trotted over the road and walked around the corner into Arlington Street where she went up the steps and through the front doors, striding confidently forward towards the lifts, bypassing the Reception and Concierge desks. As usual for her work, and as always insisted on by Steve, she was smartly dressed, her jeans clean and pressed, her blouse crisp and white, and she knew she did not look out of place in the opulence of the hotel. She fitted in as part of the elite and was therefore unlikely to attract attention, a modern business woman at home in her environment.

Taking the lift to the third floor, she stepped out into the corridor with a sense of déjà vu. How many times had she done this? Shutting her mind to the thought and what lay ahead for her, she followed the arrowed directions to room 310 where she knocked on the door, noticing it was not quite closed.

"Who is it?" a muffled voice called out from the room.

"Becky," Jamie said, pushing the door open a little further and using the working name she had given herself when she had first contacted Steve to say she would like to do the modelling work. She was glad she had decided on a degree of anonymity, even then, and that was before she had known the truth about Steve and what he was offering. The name somehow separated that person from the real her.

"OK," the man replied. "Just push the door, it's open."

Jamie pushed the door open further and stepped into the darkened vestibule that led into the room. The lights in the bedroom had been dimmed and she could just see the end of the bed with a pair of bare feet on it. The man was obviously lying on his back on the bed. Shutting the door behind her she stepped forward past the bathroom into the room. The man was completely naked, lying on his back on the bed with one hand manacled to the bedhead, the other at his crutch grasping his erection. He turned to look at her as she appeared.

"Dad…" Jamie gasped.

# CHAPTER 2

## PORTLAND, OREGON, DECEMBER 2019

"Love. What is love? What do people mean by it? I mean, do they even understand it?"

Mackenzie rested her gesticulating hands in her lap and looked around expectantly at her three companions. Her long legs crossed at the ankles, she sat upright in her seat and flicked her long blonde hair out of her eyes with a slight toss of her slim face. Usually elegant and composed, she seemed uncharacteristically unsettled and emotionally dishevelled, her forehead wrinkled by a worried frown.

Jamie reached forward and picked up her coffee from the wide, low table in front of her. Its surface seemed to have been made out of old tea chests, framed off in regular shaped rectangles that gave it a comforting shabbiness. No one was going to panic about a spilled drink on it. She sank back into the comfortable, ramshackle green sofa that backed onto the large picture window of the hotel. The light from the unseasonably clear sky poured in over her shoulder, brightening the high-ceilinged seating area of the Stumptown café in the Ace Hotel. Its dark, wood panelled walls absorbed and muted the light, softening its tones and harsher edges. She closed her eyes and listened to her friends' conversation. The girls met as regularly as their busy working lives allowed, and when they did it was always just before mid-day, ahead of the lunch crowds. Compacted lives left little time to keep in touch and one evening some months ago, over

26

numerous glasses of wine, they had resolved to make time for a regular daytime gathering to keep their friendship alive. Meeting in bars in the evenings was all very well, but those gatherings brought a different dynamic, with boyfriends involved in conversations, or men on the hunt intent on predating the many women frequenting the bars in the city.

"Is that a statement or a question?" asked Stephanie.

"A question, of course because I have absolutely no idea anymore," Mackenzie replied.

"Well, that's because of Greg," said Mia. "I'm sure you knew what it meant when you first started out with him. Don't you remember how all loved up you guys were?"

"So how come that all changed?" Mackenzie said. "How come he suddenly turns it off and wants out?"

"To love is to be hurt," said Jamie, opening her eyes and looking at her friends. "It's to have your heart broken, as sure as night follows day. I think love's a myth in the long term. At first it's just great but it never lasts. Someone always gets let down. Hurt. I find it's better to get it in first. Don't let them get too close and push them out before they leave, which they always do. Do unto others before they do it to you, that's what I say. You should be feeling angry, not upset."

"Wow, so not cynical then," said Mia.

"I don't know," said Mackenzie. "I agree. That's pretty much how I feel at the moment."

"Hardly surprising," said Mia. "Greg only walked out a week ago. Just give it time, you'll be fine and in any case, he may regret his decision and ask to come back."

"Don't weaken if he does," said Jamie. "Tell him to stick it. You deserve better; if there is such a thing. Men are just a commodity and you should keep control in any relationship. I speak from bitter experience." She drained the rest of her coffee, put the large cup back in the saucer and patted her hands on her knees. "I have to go. We're putting together an exhibition. Post Modern Abstraction which pretty much means anything goes. You should all come along when it opens next week. I'll get you all passes to the private viewing. There'll be wine."

"I'm definitely in for that," said Stephanie.

"Me too," said Mackenzie, "I could do with a night out, now that I'm alone."

"Well, hardly alone," Stephanie said quickly.

Jumping up and kissing each lightly on the cheek, Jamie went out into the street through the old doors of the hotel, leaving her friends to go around in the circles she knew the conversation would take them through. Their words and advice would make no difference to how Mackenzie viewed what she would consider to be her predicament. She would take Greg back in a heartbeat, terrified of being rejected and isolated, still under the shadow of his dominant character. Jamie stood for a moment under the large permanent awning that reached out across to the edge of the pavement on Harvey Milk Street. She wondered how a street came to be named that, but then she always did when they met at the hotel, one of their more regular haunts. What on earth was Harvey milking to warrant naming a street after his activities, or perhaps hobby. Turning, she pulled up the collar of her coat against the cold and set off on the ten-minute walk to the Portland Art Museum where she had worked since arriving from London.

That had been two years ago, and now her formative years in England seemed to belong to another life, another time. Her degree had been the pinnacle of her ambition then, but of course an ambition achieved is an ambition that's about to be replaced, supplanted by a loftier dream, or an ever-greater desire in humankind's fruitless quest for total fulfilment. Ambition is a ladder with a seemingly endless number of rungs, a relentless drive upwards to a top that does not exist because there is no end to it from our desire for more, other than in the grave. In our minds, it is a one-way ladder, ever upwards with an accompanying fear of taking backward steps down it. In that, we so easily forget where we came from, and how easily we can slip back to that starting point when fortune deserts us.

Jamie had graduated alone, estranged from her father and mother, and walked out of the graduation ceremony elated but somehow empty. A by-product and essential part of the pleasure of achievement is the joy of sharing that moment with loved ones and friends. She returned her mortar board and gown to the rental shop and left the Queen Elizabeth II Centre which had hosted the graduation ceremony. All her friends and contemporaries were busy outside the Centre with their families, proud parents taking photographs of their offspring, when they could interrupt their children's excited collective hugs with friends. She had never felt more alone in the face of such an accumulation of pride in achievement. Walking across Parliament Square, Jamie passed under the soaring Queen Elizabeth Tower, from which Big Ben chimed the hours, before turning onto the Embankment, following the silent flow of the Thames on its endless journey to the sea. She slalomed through the meandering tourists, the runners, the hurrying business people, all rushing about in their busy lives. Lost in thought as she strode out, she felt she was starting the process of drawing a line under her past. The future glowed bright and a fierce urgency to grasp it gripped her. She determined to bury the dark parts of her life in a vault within her, a secure place whose contents would never see the light of day again. Each step took her away from pain and nearer to a happier place. Optimism is a powerful force in the moment, no matter how misguided in its outcome, and the sense of it lifted her spirits.

When she reached the Millennium Bridge she crossed it and walked over to the Tate Modern. Housed in Gilbert Scott's stark and austere cathedral of power, his monument and architectural paean to the future of energy, Jamie thanked the day it had been rescued from its grave, the mausoleum to its history. It had been saved by the inspired decision to convert it to a centre for modern art, an amalgam of its mixed heritage and history, and its modern persona. Scott could not have been aware that his inspiration would have a lifespan of less than forty years before its massive turbines were silenced. For a while its only occupants were a pair of peregrine falcons nesting high on its chimney, their urban cliff face providing a vantage over the city, and security from predators.

The gallery had been a sanctuary for Jamie over her years at university, and in particular the last turbulent months. It had become a place in which to lose herself, to shed the reality of her world for a brief while. She loved the feeling of space in its vast old turbine hall, its roof towering high above. Like an enormous womb, it nurtured and sheltered her as she walked through the galleries and exhibits, safe and alone, beyond reach of grasping hands and Steve's controlling habits. Now she instinctively relaxed into the comfort of its familiar space, feeding off its maternal nurturing of her soul. She peered over the edge of the barrier to gaze down into the depths of the engine floor far below before meandering up through the galleries laid out on the building's different levels. As she walked, her thoughts turned to her future. Her priority was to be financially independent. She had been completely independent of her parents for three years but now she had to cut her ties with Steve as well. She had never given him her address so he had no idea where she lived, but he did have her phone number and she was conscious there was a message on her voicemail from him to which she had no intention of replying. For Jamie her graduation was a holistic and all-encompassing parting, a graduation both from academia and from her past life. She wanted a new start, the freedom to leave the dark and the nightmares behind. She had done what she had hated but felt she had been forced to do, debasing herself and burying emotion in order to survive. Now she wanted to draw a line under the horrors of that existence. Her first priority was to get a new phone with a new number, to disappear and seek succour and peace in anonymity.

Leaving the gallery Jamie crossed back over the bridge, the timeless river scudding beneath her on its relentless journey. She walked up to St Paul's, perched on Ludgate Hill, its iconic dome London's own Golgotha. She walked past the cathedral's imposing flank and on to Cheapside, going into the first phone retailer she could find. In the sterility of the shop, she shed her old skin, thankful she'd had the foresight to save some money over the last year to build a substantial cushion against this day, and the immediate future that would follow. With an overwhelming sense of liberation, like a prisoner released from a long sentence, she left the shop and headed back to her flat, intoxicated by a sense of freedom, a new phone and a new number representing her new life. Becoming invisible to her old life was exhilarating.

After quickly getting a full-time job in a pub near her flat, Jamie spent the next weeks scouring newspapers, magazines and recruitment agents whilst also calling the few contacts she had made in the course of her studies. The new world is one that is increasingly driven and controlled by algorithms, and their tentacles were such that when she went into the internet to make yet another search, an advertisement popped up on her screen for a job in Oregon. Not entirely sure where Oregon was, Jamie looked it up on a map and was immediately attracted to it for the incongruous reason it was about as far away from her past life as she could get whilst still remaining in a similar culture and speaking the same language. Like planets aligning, Jamie's qualifications and degree course lined up to match the criteria set by the Portland Art Museum, which was seeking applicants for a newly created position in the recently renovated Masonic Temple. Renamed the Mark Building, it was designed to house a substantial new collection of 20th century modern and contemporary art. The job being advertised came with the promise of a work visa for a successful foreign applicant, which addressed the first obstacle that came to Jamie's mind. Emboldened by the sheer novelty of the idea, and the chance to start again with no history other than the one she wanted to create for herself, Jamie applied, and was surprised to be short-listed for an interview.

With the energy of a zealot, she had immediately bought a plane ticket. A week later, staring down through the plane window at a white and barren Greenland and then the wilderness of northern Canada far below, she contemplated the enormity of what lay before her. She did not yet dare imagine herself into a new life in America, just as someone buying a lottery ticket might not dare to dream of the untold riches winning would bring, but it was very hard not to do that. Our fecund imaginations so easily create a cornucopia of alternative realities that can lift us out of an actuality we wish to escape, but Jamie did not have the courage to go to a place in her mind where she had already got the job and was established in a new world. The fear of the disappointment if that did not happen kept her feet on the ground and helped to manage her expectations. Too many uncertainties lay in her path, not least of which was whether she would be offered the job, no matter how she might dream she had been. To focus on anything other than the interview ahead was to indulge in fantasy, a luxury she had long denied herself. Too much hurt and disappointment lay in the uncharted and murkily opaque waters of hope to risk venturing into them.

Jamie leaned forward to pull a small bottle of water out of the pocket on the back of the seat in front of her, and as she did so the sleeves of her shirt and sweater rode up her arm, revealing the scars on her wrist and lower forearm, the not quite parallel lines of release and calming relief. They were the self-made openings she had created to allow the blood to flow to purge her unbearable feelings of rejection, of the loss of her innocence and love. There was a numbness within her and her self-harming was an unexpected antidote to her emotional vacuum. With its accompanying pain, she could at least feel something to balance the emotional void, the intense discomfort replacing the utter deadness. Perversely that pain brought a peace and calmness to her. A part of her was aware that harming herself as she did was not normal behaviour but she justified it to herself by telling herself the cuts were relatively shallow and could be worse. On a couple of occasions she had gone onto on-line forums and read other people's stories of the damage they were doing to themselves. One girl talked about putting a hot iron to her face until she could smell her skin burning, so to Jamie a few small cuts that would soon heal couldn't be a big deal, could they?

Seeing the scars didn't bring the same calming relief and quietude the actual act of cutting herself did. Instead she felt a self-conscious embarrassment. She glanced quickly at the passenger in the seat next to her to see if she had noticed, and was relieved to see the woman's eyes were fast closed as she slept. Jamie quickly pulled down her sleeves to hide her shame. She couldn't quite remember when she had started self-harming or what had triggered the thought to do it, but she did remember the escape from her chaotic feelings it brought every time she had done it. It's ability to combat the tsunami of her tortured emotions as they threatened to overwhelm her made it become her go-to remedy, an addiction to a ritual, an opioid in a blade.

After a stop at Seattle, where she entered America for the first time, her plane change was easy to negotiate and gave her time to stretch her legs for a couple of hours before the next leg of her journey. Jamie finally landed in Portland where she indulged in the luxury of catching a taxi to an inexpensive single bedroom apartment she had found online. It was in the north eastern quadrant of the city. Knowing no one there, and on a limited budget, she welcomed the security of a temporary base, just as she welcomed the prospect of the ten or so days of acclimatisation she had decided to have before her interview. A bad sleeper at the best of times, she knew the eight-hour time difference would play havoc with her circadian rhythm, resulting in long periods of unwelcome consciousness in the nights. Habit told her those empty hours would give her too much unoccupied time in which to think, so she had deliberately flown out earlier than she might need just for a meeting. Inexperienced at the art of interviews, the waiting became increasingly stressful. She felt like a near bankrupt gambler, foolishly optimistic at a roulette table, putting her last chips on red, banking all on one final spin of the wheel. A win would mean a ticket to deliverance from her past with a new future to build for herself. The consequences of not getting the job were too dystopian to contemplate and she tried to banish the thoughts of failure from her mind.

Fall was over and home owners in the district were busy clearing the last of the fallen leaves from the sidewalks and putting away their outdoor furniture in their garages in preparation for the winter rains and snow. Jamie went for long daily walks near her apartment, as well as trips on the bus to downtown as she quickly learned to call it, going there to learn its layout and the shopping opportunities she might find in anticipation of the day she had a salary that might support the luxury of spending money on anything that wasn't an essential need. These were outings of discovery, particularly as she explored the largely residential area around Laurelhurst Park. With its soaring Douglas Firs and giant sequoias interspersed with a variety of deciduous species, the Park was the culmination of Emanuel Mische's plan when he designed it in 1910. Did he know what his vision would be in his mind's eye? Jamie used to wonder that same thing at home when she ever visited a stately home that had been landscaped by someone like Capability Brown. They created their designs knowing they would never see them in their maturity, but did they somehow know exactly what future visitors down the centuries would see when they walked in those artfully laid out gardens and spacious parklands?

In the afternoons Jamie would return from her explorations in the city the other side of the river and sit in the dappled shade on the bank of Firewood Lake at the eastern end of the park, or in some of the many other parks in the neighbourhood. From there she watched mothers bringing their young children to feed the ducks before leaving the seemingly endlessly famished birds and walking around the end of the lake to cross the road behind her to join in the games and play in a small playground, adding their joyful voices to the shrieks of other children already there. Each morning she exercised by running along the wide pathways that bisected the Park's shaded lawns. Cheerful joggers waved and greeted her as she passed them, bringing into sharp focus the contrast of the natural open friendliness of Americans with the insularity and natural reserve of the British.

On some mornings she ran along the sidewalks for her daily exercise, enabling longer journeys through her neighbourhood. She was struck by how Portland seemed to be more of a large town than a city. Very few tall buildings dominated the skyline and the city centre had a homely feel to it with its areas where artisanal shops and cafés lined narrow streets. As she walked and browsed amongst them, she could feel her old life gradually sloughing off her.

'I could do this,' she said quietly to herself as she sat in a café one morning, nursing a coffee in an armchair by the window, daydreaming as she watched people passing by on the sidewalk outside. Some strolled slowly whilst holding hands or arm in arm, peering into shop windows as they browsed, whilst others rushed headlong into their day, oblivious of a calmer life about them as they chased the elusive corporate dream.

"Do what?" a voice said at her shoulder. She turned as a man slipped into the armchair next to hers and put his coffee and croissant on the table between them. Tall and lean, he was wearing a duck egg blue linen shirt that was fashionably crumpled, and which he had partnered with a dark blue sleeveless cashmere sweater. He leant back in the chair and settled his clear blue eyes on her, pushing his fingers through his carefully tousled, sun-bleached hair. His long legs in immaculate blue jeans were stretched out, his ankles crossed, his bare feet in brown penny loafers. He was a study in relaxed confidence, his tanned face holding a broad smile that revealed his perfect teeth.

"I'm sorry?" Jamie said, flustered by the intensity of his gaze.

"You said 'I could do this'," he said, leaning forward and breaking off a piece of croissant before dipping it into his coffee. "I was wondering what your 'this' might be."

"Oh, I didn't realise I'd said it out loud," Jamie said.

"Well, you did," he said with a half-smile, a raised eyebrow signalling a question mark of amusement.

Jamie studied him for a moment, trying to weigh him up. Good looking with a winning smile but perhaps slightly too pleased with himself. His self-confidence portrayed a sense of entitlement, and perhaps an expectation or plain assumption that he was of course attractive to her, as a male peacock must feel he is when he fans his tail feathers before the girls. He was right, she was, and that slightly derailed her emotions and thoughts.

"Oh, I don't know," she said, "just sit here and chill. I come here most mornings to just enjoy a moment and have some time out, and the coffee's good. I could easily live life in this city is what I meant I suppose."

"You're not from around here are you?" he said. "English?"

"Yes. Yes, I am," she said. "English, that is, so no, you're right, I'm not from around here. Oh dear, I made a mess of that. The simple answer is I'm British." She blushed at her confusion.

Jamie was taken aback by his direct intrusion into her privacy and solitude. She turned to look out of the window again, hoping to signal her wish to be left alone. Apart from friendly waves and greetings on her morning runs, she had not yet encountered the innate friendliness of Americans when they come together, where everyone met is an instant conversation companion, no matter they have never met before, nor will again. She would come to realise that social boundaries in America were more porous than the walls of impenetrable reservation that are the hallmark of the British.

"I arrived the other day," she added to fill the silence, immediately regretting the additional information about herself. She was hoping he'd let her retreat back to her thoughts and solitude.

"London?" he asked. "I was in London two years ago," he continued before she could answer. "I did a semester at university there. You Brits sure know how to party. Not sure how much work I got done but who cares. I had a great time, a ball. That's one great city you have there. I want to go back one day. Work there perhaps. What do you do there?"

"Oh, I was at art college in London, but I've come here for an interview for a job." Why the admission of what she was doing in the city? Why did she not just give the impression she was on a short holiday? His direct gaze was disconcerting and throwing her equilibrium, to the point she knew she was gabbling, filling the empty voids in their conversation that were unsettling her, as silence does for so many when presented with gaps in conversation. We in the western world find that silence disturbing and so we speak to fill it, often giving more information than we intend.

"An interview?" he said. "What are you interviewing for? What's the job?"

"It's at the Museum. The Art Museum around the corner from here. I doubt I'll get it so I shall probably be on my way home in a couple of days."

She hoped the likelihood of her imminent departure would be enough to douse his curiosity, and was relieved to see him lean forward to pick up his phone when it buzzed to announce an incoming message. He quickly glanced at it and stood up.

"OK, I have to go. A meeting. You know how it is. Hey, it was nice to talk to you. Perhaps we'll meet again sometime."

As he reached the door to the street he turned and said, "I didn't get your name."

"Jamie," she replied.

"OK Jamie, good luck with the interview. Have a nice day."

He was gone, as suddenly as he had arrived. Jamie relaxed back into her chair, the tension flowing out of her. What was it about the brief encounter that had caused such anxiety within her? As she calmed down she realised it was not only that she found him attractive, but also her fear of her past catching up with her and resurfacing, exhuming the memories she was busy burying behind her in another life, another place. Him saying he had been in London had shocked her. Blood had drained from her face and a cold sweat of fear broke out. Luckily, he hadn't seemed to notice. What if he recognised her, if their paths had somehow crossed? As she calmed down, Jamie realised the chances of them having met were nil. He had never been one of her 'clients,' so how would he ever know what she had done to pay for her education. She realised she didn't even know his name. It was as though he had been playing with her, teasing her, in control of her emotions and amused by her fluster.

Jamie picked up her coffee cup and sat back in the armchair, trying to concentrate her mind on the interview she was to have in two days' time. It was not really something she could prepare for in detail, and so she focussed on the generalities of why she would want to leave home and come to America to work. They were bound to ask her what it was about the job that had attracted her and why she would want to leave home. She could hardly admit she had seen it as the opportunity to escape her history, so she had to create a viable and credible alternative response. What was her story going to be for them when they inevitably asked?

The encounter with the stranger had triggered the still shallowly buried memories of home. She had left England without telling anyone other than her brother, either that she was going, or where. She knew the rest of the family would have no idea whether she was even alive and, whilst she had little care about her parents, she wondered whether that was fair to Charles in that she had never told him her whole story. Shame had sealed her mouth, and in not telling him she could in a perverse way pretend it wasn't happening, no matter how ostrich like that might be. The shock of seeing her father on the bed in that hotel room was too catatonic for her to be able to express her feelings. She had told her mother, assuming she might hear anyway, but there had been little reaction from her. Any words she could conjure up for anyone else would be completely inadequate in describing the cascade of horror that poured over and through her, how that emotional storm had shaken the very bedrock of her life and its meaning. And so she had let Charles assume that she wanted to lead her own life away from home, whilst recognising that their father had probably driven her away. It was not Charles with whom she had a problem and they had always been close growing up, perhaps because of a shared endeavour to survive in the face of what had for her become the enemy. He had ever been protective of her, and once he had left university and started work and had become guiltily aware that the support he had been given was denied to her, had occasionally sent her money to help her. She missed him and knew she owed him a full explanation of what had happened. One day she would tell him and would just have to hope that he wouldn't judge her when she told him. At the moment her courage failed her and she felt that was too big a gamble, and not one she was prepared to take. At one point he had asked her why she had cut herself off from their parents and she had just replied that she didn't want to talk about it. Now, in that moment in the café, she felt acutely the distance that separated them. She felt very alone and isolated, knowing the contradiction in that this was exactly what she had wanted in making the decision to leave. As is so often the case with our hopes, wishes and dreams, the reality of achieving them is generally a very different proposition.

Opening her laptop, Jamie logged into the café's internet and settled down to write an email to Charles to let him know she was fine and finding a new life. She asked him not to let their parents know she had been in touch. As she sent the note to him, she felt relief that one slender thread with home was still intact, suddenly conscious that perhaps it was going to be harder than she had at first realised to walk away from everything she had ever known.

Rising at dawn two days later, Jamie started her preparations for her interview later that morning. After showering she made herself a coffee and sat with it by the open window listening to the early birdsong. Shutting her eyes and hearing Nature's crepuscular cacophony took her back to her childhood, to the sounds of the countryside around home. She yearned for the plaintive call of a tawny owl in the near distance, the raucous awakening of the parliament of rooks that roosted in the spinney on the other side of the big field. Ever an early riser, she had always relished the solitude of the dawn with its pastel skies in the summer months and the dark of the pre-dawn through the autumn and winter. The morning's background murmur of the early commuter traffic making its way towards the river before crossing for downtown didn't detract from the sense of embracing a wilderness, a place where the world

41

belonged to her and her alone as those around her slept on into their own versions of dawn. Today she had lain awake in the early hours, unable to sleep with the tension of anticipation. The haunting cry of a freight train's horn in the semi-distance in the night soothed her nerves. America beckoned, the land of opportunity, always moving, always travelling, always striving but never truly changing.

Putting her empty coffee mug in the sink in the small galley kitchen, Jamie addressed the conundrum of what to wear. Not wishing to appear either too formal or too casual, she sat on the fence by choosing a white blouse, tied with a bow at the neck, a knee length skirt and sensibly comfortable court shoes. Feminine and understated flounce without being clerical she felt. Shrugging at her reflection in the mirror in acceptance that her decision had been made and would have to do, she picked up her purse and left the apartment to walk to the bus stop for the ride into the city. As she stood waiting, the morning sun bathed her face and she closed her eyes and lifted her face to its warmth, allowing it to provide the calming push to the opposing pull of her anxiety about the meeting ahead, her appointment with her destiny.

The bus arrived with a hiss of doors and a sigh as it lowered itself to the pavement. Jamie stepped onto the entrance platform and found a seat by a window on what would be the predominantly sunny side all the way to her destination. As the bus crossed the river she gazed south at the city's skyline and towards where the Art Museum was situated. Dark clouds in the distance heralded rain and a wet day ahead. The streets were busy with commuter traffic whilst the foot soldiers of commerce and business hurried along sidewalks, a phalanx of coffee carrying worker ants out foraging for their monthly salaries. The bus stopped near to the Art Museum and, because she was early, she walked across the road into a small park opposite it. There were sculptures in the park and she filled the empty minutes wandering amongst them, losing herself in the talent that had created them. The shrill cry of the alarm she had set on her phone disrupted her reverie and reminded her the moment had arrived, the moment that could change her life. Crossing back over the road she told herself that whilst she might feel she had everything to lose, in fact she had nothing to lose since if this door closed, there would surely be another somewhere. For the moment, this door was the easiest to push open, and the only one.

# CHAPTER 3

# FRANK

"A flat white please, Rebecca," Jamie said to the girl behind the counter, reading the barista's name on her name tag. "Oh, and one of those almond croissants too, please."

"Sure," the girl replied, "I'll bring them right over. Are you British or something?"

"Yes, yes I am," Jamie replied.

"Cool," Rebecca said. "I just love your accent. I could listen to you all day. You keep coming in and I have wanted to ask you."

Jamie laughed. "If I had a dollar for every time I'm asked to 'Say something' in the stores here I'd be rich."

"I guess," Rebecca said. "It must annoy you but you British sound so sophisticated to us. We feel a bit Wyoming rhinestone in comparison."

Jamie smiled and turned to walk over to what seemed to be becoming 'her armchair' by the window. She had continued to habituate the café, creating somewhere familiar where she could start to lay down roots and belong to a community.

Rebecca delivered Jamie's coffee and croissant, breaking her reverie as she gazed out of the window with unseeing eyes.

"Thank you," she said.

"You're welcome," Rebecca said, "I'll just bring you some water."

Jamie pulled her laptop out of her battered and stained backpack, and opened her emails, settling back into the comfort of the seat to compose an email to her brother. Earlier that week and after agonising for days, she had finally decided to tell Charles why she had to leave so suddenly and so completely. She had needed him to know her recent history, the reasons behind her urgent need to leave everything behind, why she could not stay and to explain her wish for a new start. She had called him on FaceTime and poured her heart out to him in the sanctity of a sibling confessional. It had been a painful but cathartic moment to share her secret, to pin so much hope in trust. In doing so she had worried about being the catalyst for conflict between Charles and their parents but on balance she decided he needed to understand why she had left with such apparent finality. She owed him that. She had said to Charles it hadn't been her who had chosen their father's extra-marital excursions as a hobby, but she felt it had been his fault she had been forced down the path she had taken.

"God, why didn't you tell me?" Charles had said, shocked to the core as the blood drained from his face at the full implications of what his sister had done. "I could have helped you."

"I was terrified you'd reject me," Jamie said. "That you'd lose all respect for me. I still feel that and I cannot tell you how I've had to pluck up courage to make this call. I knew you'd never have the money to help me at that time, and I didn't want to give up on my degree. I never thought I'd be capable of doing something like that, ever, but I didn't know what else to do. I felt I had no other choice. Believe me, I would have done it differently if I could have."

Charles buried his face in his hands. She could see his shoulders shaking and that he was moving his head slowly in a silent keening. Was it a mistake to tell him? Had she lost him?

"I'd never reject you," he said, tears on his cheeks. "Who am I to judge. It must have been awful. It's so much to take in, but nowhere near what you've had to deal with. Thank you for telling me. A lot of things become much clearer now."

Charles bit his lower lip, an old habit from his youth whenever he was stressed. Jamie's tears trickled down her cheeks at the familiarity of his reaction, and in relief he was still talking to her. He had always been her safe place to go, the ever-watchful protector she knew her father had never been. She felt suddenly overwhelmed with love for him, and relief that he did not seem to be judging her.

"It was at first," she said, "but I stopped thinking about it and just became numb inside. It became no different to fitting a tampon."

"Too much information," Charles said as they both burst into laughter. "Far, far too much."

"I know, but ridiculing all those pathetic men in my thoughts made it bearable and helped me detach. God, some of them! But I don't want to think about it."

"What a bastard. Dad I mean. Bloody misogynist, he could easily have helped you. Just because you didn't want to do law. More of his bloody controlling."

"I don't want this to come between you and them. It was more to do with me being a girl I think. I always felt he wished I was a boy, that I was a disappointment to him. In fact he told me so. You were his favourite but funnily enough I never felt jealous about that. No idea why not."

"He's always controlled Mum so you were part of that. It's his way and always has been. There have never been any soft edges to him, anything any of us could grasp and say we loved that about him. There's only ever been one agenda, and that's his and he's always been at the centre of that."

They talked more on line, about their shared experiences growing up, amazed at the differences they had taken out of their childhoods, their different perspectives as well as the similarities. As they spoke and some of the stresses of her experiences surfaced, Jamie felt the familiar urge to find the privacy of the bathroom and the healing balm of the razor blade on her arm, the pain to replace the far greater pain of her utter emptiness that was invisible to the world. She fought the thoughts but knew she would not be able resist them when she had finished the call with Charles. Perhaps she would have wine instead, another sanctuary she had found in the last couple of years. Alcohol too had become a sedative for her, another addiction that she denied to herself existed. She could not imagine life now without it to act as her crutch, and sometimes just to get her through the day. Her drinking had started after the jobs, as she called them, in London. She'd get back to the apartment and share a glass of wine with the other girls, but this soon became inadequate and she'd make excuses to get things from her room where she would drink quickly from bottles she kept hidden in her wardrobe, before returning to rejoin the conversation. When the others started to drift off to bed, she'd go to her room, shut the door and often have more to erase the memory. Sometimes she'd drink a bottle or more in a night as she sat on her bed. Then came the first time she drank a glass before going out to one of Steve's jobs, and soon that became her habit. Two glasses before and a bottle and more after. Now a day could not pass without more wine in it than was good for her.

When she had told Charles of her plan to go to America he had asked if he could take her to the airport and see her off. "I mean, I want to make sure you actually leave the country," he said, laughing and nudging her.

"Yes please," Jamie said, "although I'm bound to cry so you'd better bring tissues with you."

And so he had picked her up from her small flat in London, watching her as she put her key on the kitchen table with a note to her flatmates, then picking up her bags and carrying them out to his car. On the drive to Heathrow he reached across and held her hand. She squeezed it hard and covered it with her other hand as she turned to look away out of the window, a large tear rolling down her cheek. The reality of impending separation filled the car with silence and unspoken loss.

"I care about you," Charles said, suddenly filling the void and breaking into Jamie's thoughts. "I shall miss you and will want to come to see you."

"Thank you," she whispered.

"Not a problem," he said. "It's not exactly far if you don't mind sitting in a plane for ten hours."

"No, I meant for being you. For looking after me as you always have."

Charles glanced across at her face, freed his hand and lifted it to her face, wiping away her tear with his thumb. She leaned her cheek against his open hand and dripped another tear onto it.

"You'll be okay," he said. "Just get that job. And keep in touch. I shall hound you."

Jamie smiled and turned to him. "I'd like that," she said.

She had been right. Their parting had been painful. She checked in and watched her bag start its own journey as it joined the others flying past on the moving belt behind the check-in desk. Turning she walked back to where Charles was standing and put her arms around his neck and hugged as she'd never hugged before. Is there ever a greater sadness than that of parting? They stood like that for what felt like eternity compressed into a minute, and then parted and whispered their goodbyes. They turned and walked away from each other. As she scanned her boarding card to go through the gates into the security check area, Jamie turned and saw Charles was standing by the revolving entrance doors to the Departures Hall, silhouetted by the light coming in from behind him. He lifted his hand and gave a discreet wave then turned once more and was gone.

'Hi there,' she typed, turning her attention back to the email she had started. 'I'm sitting in this café I have been coming to a lot. You'd love it. Delicious coffee, artisanal bread and pastries, deep armchairs and a fireplace with a log fire burning in it. I can't wait to show it to you when you eventually come here. I had my interview for the job a couple of days ago.'

"Well, hi there. Jamie, right? Mind if I join you again?"

She looked up, startled. The same man who had sat with her a few days ago was standing looking down on her, a cup of coffee in his hand, a broad smile on his tanned face and in his eyes. He was wearing a light pink shirt that she noticed was linen again. Linen Man she thought to herself. Pale coloured chinos replaced the jeans but the penny loafers stayed. Jamie noticed he actually had a penny wedged in each one. This was someone who spent time in the sun, and perhaps in front of the mirror. Jamie wondered whether he was a surfer or just a sunbather. Her instincts told her he wasn't going to be the sort of man to lie around on a beach or a sun lounger. There was a vitality and energy about him, an easy charm that beguiled her, stirring an unexpected interest in him within her.

"Of course," Jamie replied, shutting her laptop and waving him to the sofa opposite her on the other side of the wide, low coffee table. There was a seat next to her but she instinctively felt the need to keep a space between them, to resist or at least control her attraction to him.

Putting his coffee on the table, he ignored her gesture and sat down in the seat by her side. He leant back into it, crossing his legs and gently bouncing his free foot, exuding a suppressed energy in need of an outlet.

"So, how is it with you?" he asked. "You were having a job interview, right? How did that go, or have you not had it yet?"

Jamie was taken aback by the directness of his question. How had he remembered that? She was still immersed in and imbued with British reserve. Once more she realised it was going to take time for her to get used to how openly friendly America and its people were, how uninhibited in speaking to complete strangers. It still felt uncomfortable to her, an invasion of her privacy, and that would take time to shake off, but despite her reticence she felt compelled to reply.

"Yes, I was," she half answered.

"So, has it happened?" he asked.

"Yes, a couple of days ago," Jamie said, involuntarily adding, "I got the job." She realised she must have been coming across as coldly distant when he was only offering a friendly hand.

"Cool," he said. "I suppose that means you'll be around for a while then. Not going back to London?"

"No, I'm here to stay, I hope," she said, at last smiling. "There's a probationary period I have to work, but I always expected that. Six months. I hope I pass that because I like it here. Well, so far I do. It's not what I expected of an American city. We all think of New York or Chicago where everything's tall and new and so intensely hectic and busy, but here's so different."

He seemed to have remembered so much from their last meeting, which she found strangely unsettling. She had a sense, not of an intrusion by him, but of a need in herself to keep him at arm's length. At the same time she had a curiosity about him. She found him attractive and was drawn to him, and that scared her a bit. She hadn't come all this way for relationships. Well, not yet. Perhaps she was still bruised from being abused, as she felt she had been by those anonymous men who had funded her through university and been her meal ticket. But there was a contradictory inconsistency about her thoughts, which were so in contrast to her actions. In her heart she knew she had to accept responsibility for what she had done. She knew the person she truly held responsible for that, her father, would never accept blame, even now with the ruination of her relationship with him, if that was what they had actually ever had. In retrospect, she realised he had been an emotional absentee in her life, a void that even now left an ache of longing within her. She now knew his love and affection were a figment of her imagination, an illusory will-o'-the-wisp, the *ignis fatuus* she had grown up chasing. The true father she yearned for was a doomed and delusional dream which had metamorphosed into a nightmare, daily crowding her thoughts. The futility of the years of wasted investment in hope she now realised had left her emotionally bankrupt and on the precipice of an abyss of embarrassment at her own foolish hopes. At what point does reality trump hope and truth filter through the curtains we draw across our eyes to blind us to the facts before us?

"I'm sorry, I don't know your name," Jamie said, breaking into her thoughts, which had created the silence that had developed as her mind had drifted to her past. She glanced around the café as though looking for someone to rescue her from her unaccountable awkwardness.

"Frank," he replied. Jamie noticed parenthetic creases at each corner of his mouth as he smiled, dimples that gave him a boyish charm. "Can I get you another coffee?" he said.

"Yes, thank you. That would be great," Jamie replied, grateful for the distraction. She watched his easy stride to the counter, his relaxed and confident exchange with the barista, but she turned her head to look out of the window as he brought the cups back, feigning a lack of the intense interest she felt.

"So," he said as he sat down and put the cups on the table between them. "Tell me about you. What are your plans while here? Tell me about your life. What's your story?"

"Oh dear," Jamie said, "where do I begin?"

"Well, my father always said the start of a story is a good place to kick off from. Were you born in London? Have you always lived there? They'll do for a starter for you."

"No, I grew up in Oxfordshire, which is where I was born," she replied. "It was quite a small village without a decent primary or secondary school near, so I was sent away to school, a boarding school. It's a sort of tradition for people like us, but no one asked me if that's what I wanted. I would much rather have stayed at home, even though that wasn't perfect. I moved to London after I left school. So where do you come from? Apart from America that is," she added with a giggle. "Did you grow up here, in Portland?" she said, eager to move the conversation away from herself whilst interested to know more about this Frank.

"No, California," he replied. "I'm originally from San Francisco but moved up here a couple of years ago for work. San Francisco is changing, getting too crowded for my liking so I was looking to move away."

As they talked, gently probing each other's lives and past history in the eternal fandango of discovery that leads to joy and heartbreak in equal measures, Jamie relaxed into the conversation, welcoming the contact and human connection. She realised she was lonely and had been increasingly so since she had arrived in the city but had rationalised it by reminding herself she had only just arrived in the country so what did she expect. That would surely change once she settled in, especially now that she had got the job.

"Hey," Frank said looking at his watch, "I have to go. I've got a meeting. This has been cool. Give me your number and maybe we can hang out and I can show you some of the town."

The way he asked for her number and the confidence in his request left her no option to withhold it without looking rude by slamming a door in the face of a proffered friendship and kindness. She wondered whether she had somehow been manoeuvred into a no choice response as she read out her number to him. She had yet to commit her new number to memory, particularly since she had had no opportunity to give it to anyone other than the Art Museum and her brother.

Frank stood up and offered her an open hand to high-five and then strode to the door, opening it to allow a couple in before exiting and walking out into the Friday morning sunshine where he disappeared down the street. Now he was gone she missed his company, his effortless and casual charm that somehow seemed to beguile her, to make her want more time with him. His pale blue eyes were cold, seemingly slightly detached as they held her gaze when they were speaking, almost emotionless and in stark contrast to his relaxed easy smile. It reminded her of the way her father used to look at her, which had always unsettled her, but Frank's smile was something her father had never bestowed on her.

Opening her laptop again she returned to the embryonic email to Charles, rereading the opening words of her interrupted message as she marshalled her thoughts to concentrate on the gossamer connection reaching east across the continent and ocean to home. Where was home now? In some ways she felt stateless. Was this going to be the new 'home' for her? Parents of young children will talk about going home when visiting their own parents, the grandparents, so do we ever truly cut that umbilical cord to the nest in which our journey of life started? Jamie felt very physically distant from Charles and was suffused in a sudden desire to be held in his fraternal hug, that ever-constant sanctuary that shut out reality for her. It had so often been the only escape she could find from the swirling vortex of her confused and conflicting thoughts. It was still painful to her that her instinct was to reach for her brother and not her father when she wanted to satisfy the ubiquitous need of humanity for physical contact. Touch and physical contact is one of the essential ingredients that bonds and binds us, and floods our system with the oxytocin that triggers our urge to hug and to hold. Even now, no matter how she might deny it, hope refused to die in her, hope for a rapprochement between them that would give her the guide and benchmark in her life that she had always craved. She realised rapprochement implied the reinstatement of a former connection, but that had never existed in their relationship. Theirs had been like two one-way streets lying parallel to each other and never touching, the traffic flow from her on her street being desire, but coming the other way from him on his, only ever rejection.

Fraternal love was wonderful but it could never replace the paternal version. Somehow she had to learn to extinguish the faint embers of hope and optimism that still glowed in her heart.

Jamie's fingers flew over the keyboard as she told Charles her news and how she had got the job. She started to write about her conversation and meetings with Frank but stopped and on reflection deleted the sentence. There was nothing to say of interest about it. He was just another guy who had stopped to chat. There was no agenda if you chose to ignore the request for her phone number, and his comment about showing her some of the city was no more than an innocent offer of kindness to a visitor to the city and country. She didn't expect to hear from him so no point in setting a hare running.

Clicking on the send icon, she closed the lid and left the café to catch the bus back to Laurelhurst Park near her little apartment. It was a sunny morning and she had the weekend ahead of her to prepare for starting work on Monday, so after she got off the bus she strolled through the shaded paths of the park until she reached the pond where she found a spot in the warm sunshine and sat down on the grass. On the other side of the water a grandfather was walking with his young granddaughter. Next to him the little girl skipped and frolicked as she issued an uninterruptible stream of scribble talk filled with stories and instructions that carried across the water to Jamie. How could something so little produce so much energy? A bonsai nuclear power station of enthusiasm and vivacity, an unquenchable sponge of inquisitiveness and wonder. When they neared the lake, she rushed to the water's edge clutching a paper bag from which she was pulling bits of bread as she ran. She immediately started throwing them towards the water and to the ducks paddling around in it, without any hope of reaching them. Her grandfather smiled as he watched her run, allowing her the freedom to take a risk as she approached the shallowly shelving edge of the pond. Seeing the snowstorm of breadcrumbs landing on the ground around her, the ducks charged out of the lake towards her, surrounding the now panicking girl who shrieked as she tried to run away from them, heading towards the water as she looked back over her shoulder. The ducks were pecking at her shoes and the bag in her hand as they chased the crying bonsai Pied Piper. The paper split and the bag sprayed its contents around her feet where the ducks flapped and fought each other in their eagerness to get to the feast. Jamie couldn't suppress a snort of laughter as the little girl tripped over one of the marauding ducks and fell face first into the water. Her wails of shock drowned the noise of the ducks flapping around in the water about her, and the laughter of a few children playing nearby in the park. The grandfather calmly pulled the girl out of the water and then picked her up and held her to him. Water cascaded down his shirt and trousers from her wet dress as he held her tight, her face buried into his neck as she cried out her shock and fright. He had one hand gently on the back of her head as he rocked her and turned to walk away, presumably preparing the apology he was going to need for his granddaughter's mother.

Jamie was struck by the obvious bond between the two distant generations, divided by so many years but so close in trust and love, and she envied the little girl that. She was not yet a parent herself, let alone a grandparent, but she was reminded of her own relationship with her grandfather, her mother's father. He had been a constant in her life when she was young, an ocean of calm consistency, and a source of unconditional love and fun who had been snatched away too soon when he so suddenly died. No one had known about his heart, how it's insidious incremental niggles as he had called them had finally collaborated in a sudden and catastrophic failure that closed the final chapter on his life's story, leaving Jamie with no more than fading memories of a protective embrace, a gentle smile and an untapped wisdom. She knew she had been the beneficiary of an all-encompassing and forgiving love, a love and true affection that enveloped her in a shielding carapace of security, her soft landing when she fell. Seeing the grandfather the other side of the water pick the little girl up and hold her was a déjà vu moment for Jamie, a key to the door behind which so many of her memories were locked. Somehow, despite an underlying sense of loss, the memory of her grandfather was a comforting one, calming her as she smiled to herself. She remembered his laugh and total disregard for convention, or embarrassment at the ridiculous games she had made him play. Strangely the small tear in the corner of her eye was not so much a sign of sadness and loss but more of a happiness at his memory and her good fortune at having known him. Her abiding regret was that she had never said goodbye to him. That opportunity was snatched away by the suddenness of his death and that was the first thought that came into her mind when she was told of his death, a profound and visceral pain that took her breath away. That stolen chance to bid him farewell and tell him she loved him cut deep into her heart and left a hurt she knew would never quite heal. She worried whether he ever knew she loved him, and just how much. Had she told him, really told him how much he meant to her? It was too late now and she knew her regret was a waste because it was one of the things she could not change in her life, nor his.

Jamie got up and walked back through the park towards her apartment. As she passed under one of the tall Douglas firs that dominated the park, an unaccustomed tone from her phone signalled an incoming message. She wondered who it could be from since very few people had the number. Assuming it was from the Art Museum with instructions about her first day, she pulled the phone out of the back pocket of her jeans.

'Hi, coffee was cool. Meet me at the café tomorrow at 10.30 and I'll show you around. F.'

Jamie stared at the message for a couple of seconds, trying to work out who 'F' was before it dawned on her it could only be Frank. Her mind had still been in her childhood and with her grandfather as she walked. Transported there by the intimate scene of the man with his granddaughter she had been watching, she had felt slightly voyeuristic with her uninvited glimpse into the intimacy of their relationship, but the pleasure of the moment and the memories it evoked in her mitigated and she felt excused the intrusion. Her immediate reaction to the message from Frank was of mild irritation at its peremptory tone, the implicit assumption that she had no choice other than to agree, but this was mollified by the need for some companionship. She had been feeling increasingly isolated and Frank's invitation represented an opportunity to spend time with someone, and perhaps to open a door to a wider community through his friends and acquaintances. She texted back her agreement and confirmation as she walked home. In any event, what else was she going to do alone with her Saturday?

Jamie's apartment was in a quiet, tree-lined street where so often the dominant noise seemed to come from the bounce of basketballs as teenagers and younger children challenged each other's skills in the road. Basketball nets stood proudly tall outside many houses and impromptu games often started, seemingly of their own volition when kids came out onto the streets. Skateboarders occasionally sailed and pushed themselves down the empty street. The small living room was furnished with a sofa and a couple of armchairs. Two chairs and a table to eat at were tucked into a corner of the room, the table covered with shopping bags and a couple of books. Jamie had bought herself a houseplant and put it in the middle of the table, feeling it would give her something to care for, and perhaps even to talk to. The kitchen was a galley with all the essentials she needed. Her sparse collection of clothes seemed lost in the cupboard in the bedroom, which was dominated by a double bed. Fortunately, the apartment had been let fully furnished and the first things she had bought on moving in was bedding. For the time being they were all she needed until she had an income with which to buy more than the mere essentials of life.

On Saturday morning she stood in front of her anorexic cupboard trying to decide what to wear. Despite convincing herself this was just a platonic date for a morning, as always she vacillated, this time between extreme casual and non-invitational and the alternative of something with a sense of allure but which did not hint at desperation. Backing both horses as she so often did, she chose a simple blouse that would show just a hint of décolletage and be the feminine ingredient to her ensemble, balanced by a pair of loose-fitting boyish jeans that would dilute any sense of fashion flirting. Relationships are often founded on the quicksand of a mixture of lust and misunderstanding, and she didn't want to give off the wrong signals. For the same reason she deliberately decided not to wear perfume, hoping to remain as neutral and neutered as possible. A thin gold chain around her slender neck completed the understated image she wished to project. She stood in front of the mirror assessing the impression she might make, slightly lifting her head and shaking it to free her hair and to allow it to fall attractively around her face, the subconscious contradiction to her careful preparations to be sexually invisible. Satisfied that she didn't look like an over-eager, love-starved and voracious vampire, she closed the apartment door behind her and headed out into the street to catch the downtown bus.

Arriving early at the café, Jamie settled into a comfortable seat, a coffee on the table in front of her, and relaxed to wait as she watched the procession of people passing in and out through the open door. They moved like the tide ebbing and flowing on a beach in a state of perpetual motion. Clearly caffeine provided the jump leads of Saturday morning and life in the city, kick starting people's day after a Friday night of end of week excesses. A young couple stood close together by the counter as they waited for their coffee to be prepared. He wore the uniform of the country's ubiquitous blue jeans and had a furled umbrella hooked into one of the back pockets, a casual embellishment to an image of urban cool. The fingers of both his hands were hooked over the front of the waistline of the girl's matching jeans and he pulled her unresisting waist towards him. Eyes locked together, they were young lovers in the early bloom of heart fluttering discovery of each other, oblivious to the life that continued about them. There was something powerfully erotic about their absorption with each other, alone in their shrunken world that had closed down to that one intensely intimate moment. We each have a range and variety of comfort zones that subconsciously govern the space we need from people, dependant on who they are and their connection to us. For *inamorati* worldwide there is no degree of separation needed, more there is a dislike of physical separation. Instead a universal and irresistible need to touch and be touched underpins our close bonds and ties, our form of mutual grooming that is happily free of the removal of the ticks and parasites of the animal world.

The café door opened again and Frank strode in confidently, glancing around as he looked for Jamie. On seeing her he smiled broadly and came over and sat next to her on the couch.

"Hi there," he said, throwing an arm along the back of the seat so his hand was inches from her shoulder. He crossed one leg over the other, his body turned inclusively towards her.

"Another coffee before we go?" he said, nodding to her cup.

"Why not," she said.

Frank stood up and reached into his back pocket for his billfold, patting it and then the other.

"Oh hell, I left my wallet at home," he said. "Could you lend me ten dollars. I'll pay you back next time I see you. Really sorry. Embarrassing." He shrugged and smiled, looking like a small boy caught with his hand in the cookie jar.

"Of course," Jamie said as she pulled her wallet from her purse. She opened it and pulled out a twenty-dollar bill. "That's the smallest I've got I'm afraid," she said, handing it to him.

"Thanks, no problem," he said, taking the proffered note and heading to the counter to place their order. Jamie watched him as he waited for the coffees to be made, noting the easy charm and manner in which he talked to others in the queue and how they quickly warmed to him, mirroring his stance in a positive affirmation of his social aplomb.

"So, are you ready for a bit of a tour?" he said, sitting down again and placing their coffees down.

"I am," Jamie replied. "I'm intrigued. Where are we going? What's on the agenda today?"

"Ah, a surprise, a mystery tour, and then I thought we'd hang out. Lunch and then perhaps dinner tonight?"

"Let's do the lunch but tonight I want to do some research for the job. Monday's my first day and I want to try and be ahead of the game," Jamie said.

This was partially true in that she did want to do some preparation, but her main driver was a feeling that things were being rushed along a bit fast and she didn't want to end up with questions hanging in the air over what happened after dinner. The 'your place or mine' conversation for the etchings show and tell. She wasn't ready to show Frank the particular etchings she assumed he would want to see. Why did men feel that paying for dinner gave them the right to expect a free pass to a woman's bed? Could they not see that was just another form of prostitution? If you accused them of that they would of course deny it, but surely payment in kind in the form of a meal is no different to payment in cash. Jamie felt the attitude was tantamount to a form of *droit de seigneur*, a modern version of a gross sense of entitlement and ownership over women. She never looked upon herself as a feminist, certainly not an evangelising fundamentalist who would proselytise her misandry to anyone who would listen, but she did feel outrage at any display of entitlement or assumption of ownership over her or her body. She was no longer for sale. That part of her past was buried very deep and she'd hidden the shovel to avoid any temptation to exhume it, retaining only the lessons she had learned about male behaviour and expectations. Perhaps it was her recent past that made her more sensitive to the issue and to the perception by so many men that all women were driven by a need for a physical relationship, particularly with them. In her experience most of them had no understanding of the different drivers behind most women's sexual behaviour and desires, and what influenced their attraction to men, which so often had absolutely nothing to do with their pectorals.

Finishing their coffee, they left the café and walked around the corner to where Frank had parked his car, a rather beaten up and slightly ageing, nondescript saloon. It's appearance surprised Jamie as it struck an overt discord with the way Frank dressed and presented himself. He obviously picked up something in her expression as he opened the passenger door for her, a charming gesture that was a subtle nod to a more genteel world, and one she would more expect from her parents' generation.

"I apologise about the car. I usually keep the Porsche out of sight so people don't get the wrong impression. My family is very wealthy and that brings privileges with it, but I don't want people to assume anything by that or to feel they can take advantage of me, or befriend me for the wrong reasons. It has no bearing on who or what I am and so I like to blend and downplay my background. I have had too many false friends in the past."

"The car's fine," Jamie said, climbing in and reaching for the seatbelt at her shoulder.

"Okay," Frank said as he slid into the driver's seat, "do you like roses? Silly question I suppose. What girl doesn't like roses?"

"Yes, I love them," Jamie said, "although I'm not sure it's just confined to women. Why do you ask?"

"Well, that's where we're going," Frank said as he indicated and slid the car out into the traffic. "One of the hidden gems here is the rose garden in Washington Park, which is pretty much right in the city. I think it's called the International Rose Test Garden or something like that, and it's where they experiment with new varieties. They have a display of hundreds of different plants. It's a beautiful day and whilst the roses won't be in bloom it seems a good place to start because you can also get views of some of the city from up there. It will be a great site from which you can check out downtown and some of the districts. We can come back in the summer months when the blooms are out. It's really beautiful then."

"Wow, sounds great," Jamie said as they filtered into the fast-moving traffic on a freeway that ran through that part of the city. She picked up the subtle hint that Frank was already making the assumption that their nascent relationship had the potential for longevity and a future. Entering a forested area they climbed a long hill and eventually turned off to continue climbing on a small road. Going further up into the forest, Jamie could see the area was quite dense with trees and undergrowth. Reaching some form of summit to the hill, the road flattened and they came out of the trees into the open and to a car park. Jamie could see ordered flower beds on terraces to her left down the hill, each bed filled with rose bushes of every size and shape. Frank parked the car and they walked across to a set of steps that took them down to where the rose beds were laid out. They wandered along paths, taking in names of different plants and species until they arrived at a terrace from which they could look out over the city below. Frank pointed out the different districts and some of the more distinctive buildings. Bridges crossed the river at various points and on the other side she was able to see the residential north east. Tall green water tanks stood proud of the rooftops at various points.

"The river you can see down there is the Williamette," Frank said. "It flows into the much bigger Columbia which is the other side of that hill. Can you see a plane taking off over there? That's the airport and the Columbia's just the other side of that."

"It's amazing up here," Jamie said. "You're right, I can get a real feel of the layout now. Thank you."

"You're welcome," Frank said.

As she stared out at the view, Jamie's mind drifted back in time to her father's pride in his own rose garden. Each morning in the summer she would go out to one of the flower beds to pick him a rose for his buttonhole, careful to find an unopened bloom, a tight bud she knew he would like. The ritual was another of her never-ending attempts to please him, to make him love her, a fruitless quest to sate the desire within her to have his approval. She had made the mistake once of cutting one that was too open for his liking.

"Stupid child, can't you see what's wrong with this?" he'd said coldly, impatiently throwing the flower in the trash basket by his desk. "Tighter, not so open. Go and get another. Quickly or I'll be late."

Never once had he said thank you, not only for her morning floristry but for any of the multitude of little things she did to please him. At times he made her weed the rose beds without ever acknowledging her work, other than to point out anything she might have missed. Appreciation and gratitude were reserved for Charles who seemingly could do no wrong. Academically gifted, he sailed through his education, at the top of every subject and equally talented on any sports field. For her an abiding memory was coming home at the end of a term at school having earned A's in all her subjects except French, which languished behind with a humble B grade. She had hurried to him with her report when he had come home from work and shown it to him as he came through the front door, smiling proudly as she handed it to him.

"No A stars?" he said, glancing at it. "And what's this B? Just not good enough. So disappointing. I'm obviously wasting my money at that place." He'd dropped the report on a table in the hall next to the car keys, from which it slipped to the floor, and walked into the house and up the broad stairs to his bedroom to change out of his suit for the evening.

Jamie stood in the hallway, transfixed by self-doubt and

overwhelming inadequacy. Yet again the inevitable tears poured down her face, more tears of frustration, of disappointment in herself, another layer in the confection of low self-esteem she was gestating within her mind. He'd called her report disappointing, and that was how she now felt she was to him, a disappointment. As always, she resolved to try harder, to be worthy of his love and affection. She loved him and she was mystified by why he could not see that, or reciprocate with a love of his own. It wasn't her fault she had not been born a boy. Tomboy was the nearest she could get to his ideal. Very occasionally, with a glance and what could be construed as a half-smile, he would hold out a fragile piñata filled with hope and dreams for her to tilt at, but each time it turned into an empty fantasy, a Quixotic quest with her hopes dashed on the rocks of an unrequited love. What is life without hope, a life sustaining force without which there can be no purpose? Jamie often felt religions and their reliance on an unquestioning belief were built on a foundation of hope that translates into faith, faith that there is a supreme being presiding over an afterlife, a heaven that truly exists, without there being a scrap of empirical evidence to support the theory. To her this belief was delusional and illogical, a dream that was destined to be illusory. And yet she could not see the ironic parallel in her own life where a similar hope still burned in her that one day her father would at least acknowledge her, appreciate he had a daughter he was proud of and loved, despite her lifelong experience that this had never been the case, or would ever be any different. Her powerless attempts to change him, or to influence his feelings, left deep wounds in her that never truly healed. Instead they festered in her thoughts, deep in an abyss of longing.

"Hey there, where did you go?" Frank said, startling Jamie as he broke into her dystopian daydream.

"Oh, I'm sorry. These amazing plants just brought back memories. My father loved to grow roses in the garden at home. I used to help him with them and it just made me think of home. Seems a long way away at the moment."

"Homesick?" he said.

"No, not really," Jamie said, knowing that wasn't quite the truth and an inadequate explanation of how she really felt. "This is such a wonderful place," she said, waving an arm to encompass the gardens and to change the subject. "How come it ended up in sleepy old Portland?"

"I think it started in the early nineteen hundreds," Frank said. "I looked it up last year. There was a Portland Rose Society late in the century before that, and at one stage many of the streets of the city were bordered with roses. Miles of them apparently, which is why it's called the City of Roses. They test them up here, which I suppose means they create new types. A sort of rose stud farm I suppose. There's a Japanese Garden in the Park as well. It was put in just after the war, which is pretty amazing considering Pearl Harbour and how irritating the government here found that little episode. I read somewhere the two governments were trying to build bridges between our countries and quite a few Japanese gardens were built in the US. Fortunately one of them was in the park right here. I love being there. It's so peaceful."

"Let's go there," Jamie said.

"What, now?" Frank said, glancing at his watch.

Jamie noticed the glance. "Well, no, it doesn't have to be now," she said. "Another time's fine. I'd love to see it though."

"Great," Frank said. "That's a date. We'll do it next time out."

They walked through the gardens for what was left of the morning and then drove back into the city, parked the car in 23rd Avenue a few yards away from a small burger bar called Little Big Burger, which left little doubt about what they had on offer to eat. Getting out of the car Jamie followed Frank into the small and very simply furnished bar where they ordered their meals and sat down at an empty table to wait for them to be ready. And that was where Jamie ate her first truffle fries.

"God, these are good," she said. "I've never seen these anywhere in London. I'd never stop eating them if I found somewhere selling them there. It would be a waistline disaster."

"Yeah, that's why I suggested you try them. They're pretty cool and I like the burgers here too, the best in town I reckon. The joint doesn't look much but it's very popular."

When they had finished their meal, Frank glanced at his watch again, picked up the bill, glanced at it and said, "Split the check?"

"Of course," Jamie said, hiding her surprise. "I'm an independent girl so it suits me." Whilst unexpected and a little disappointing, his suggestion that they share the cost of the meal played to her desire to keep a little distance between them until she knew him better. His paying would have created an emotional debt but this way she owed him for nothing other than a couple of hours of his time.

"OK, that's twenty each including the tip," Frank said. He took her proffered note and went up to the counter where he paid, dropping the check on the counter as he turned for the door. Jamie got up and followed him to go out to the street. As she passed the counter, she glanced down at their bill, which still lay face up by the till. It came to twenty-five dollars. Even with the tip it could not have reached forty dollars and she was left feeling she had been duped by a cheap trick, but not understanding why or exactly how. Deciding to say nothing for the time because despite her statement of independence she felt embarrassed to say anything because he had been so kind to her all morning, and by taking so much time out for her. She joined Frank on the sidewalk where he was looking at his phone as he waited for her.

"I've got to go," he said. "A work thing has come up and I need to go to the office to deal with it. Are you OK to get back yourself?"

"Yes, yes I'll be fine," Jamie said. 'I'll find a bus stop. There must be one near here somewhere. Thanks for showing me the rose gardens. I enjoyed the morning."

"Yeah, they're great aren't they," Frank said, pulling his car keys out of his pocket as he suddenly leaned forward and kissed her lightly on the cheek, a hand placed firmly on her upper arm. "I'll show you more next time, and we'll definitely go and do the Japanese Gardens. Very Zen."

Letting his hand drop from her arm, brushing her hip lightly as it fell to his side, he turned with a cheery wave and walked off down the street to where his car was parked. Jamie turned and walked the other way up the slight hill, deep in thought. She glanced back once, just as Frank was getting into his car. He too looked up the street to where she was and waved again when he saw her turn. She waved back and then disappeared around the corner at the top of the street into Johnson Street without having any real idea where she was in this part of the city. She saw the street dropped down a hill towards the river and, knowing she had to catch a bus that would take her over it, she followed the street down until she spotted a bus arriving at a nearby stop, the very one she needed. She ran to it and hopped on, as usual finding a window seat from which to look out onto the life going on outside. The bus stopped at lights further down the street and while it waited for them to turn green, Jamie watched a homeless man on the other side of the street. He was dressed in filthy, tattered clothes and had matted hair and a long, tangled beard. He was shouting and swearing at his image in a shop window, leaning against the glass with one hand whilst urinating on the sidewalk and over his ragged trainers and soiled trousers. Numerous shopping bags filled with newspapers and what seemed detritus sat on the sidewalk around him, the universal luggage and paraphernalia of the destitute. Jamie had heard there was a big drug and alcohol problem in the State, and particularly in Portland, by some accounts making Oregon one of the worst States in the country for illegal drug use. This brought with it the inevitable epidemic of crime that is the inseparable conjoined twin of substance abuse. She had overheard a conversation on one of her earlier bus rides into the city where a couple of elderly passengers were complaining to each other about a homeless encampment on the Springwater Corridor in the east side of the city. A popular biking trail, she discovered it had been adopted by many homeless people who had created a form of shantytown along a stretch of the trail, bringing trail users into conflict with the homeless people living in the tented city. She had read that some five hundred residents who lived there in about two hundred tents and that it was probably the largest such encampment in the country.

Jamie felt the crime, drug and vagrant problem in the city and State was almost counter intuitive for such a laid back, liberal minded place and population. The last thing she would have expected to find. But then perhaps it was that very liberalism and easy-going attitude that created an environment that attracted the disadvantaged, many of whom were being harassed and hounded in other cities such as San Francisco and Los Angeles. It seemed it was widely known the police in the city weren't enforcing clearance of the encampment, nor the many other itinerant homeless who existed without even the shelter of a tent. That very lackadaisical liberalism seemed to Jamie to have been the magnet that attracted the great forgotten, those who had lost their place in the world. They were the universally unwanted and unaccepted, the Dalits of American society. The public demanded that the police should move them, but the police had no policy governing how they should deal with the situation and so largely ignored it, only responding to known incidences of crime. In any event, moving them on without a clear end objective as to where they would settle would merely shift the problem to another location through a form of State enforced nimbyism. It would be a refined form of the Partition in India that so divided a nation, and left so much unresolved, so much hate and the ever-lasting potential for conflict. Jamie had some sympathy with those in the homeless communities who committed crimes when there was no other means of survival. How could anyone judge them if they had never experienced the vacuum of hopelessness? Would we not all steal and commit crime to feed and clothe ourselves and our families when there was no other way? The whole system of acceptable society conspired against them, even in trying to get a job or help, which was impossible without a permanent address, something that was beyond the reach of so many. Even the rental market's increasing cost had driven a significant number of people to take to their cars as their homes, in doing so creating a roadside sub-culture and community. Prosecution and the election winning and much-loved solution of incarceration were no way of unravelling an intractable Gordian knot, especially when mental illness was so inevitable and prevalent amongst the desperate. Imprisonment and other more lenient sanctions merely attempted to bury or hide the outcome from the gaze of a nose holding public. It did nothing to deal with the cause, so the cycle continued with inevitably more prison beds having to be provided to house the criminals, which is how the public described them all. In truth they were victims in their own right, casualties of an indifferent or negligent and often abusive upbringing. They were subject to circumstances and a society that is focussed on a dream of a utopian world, a life without imperfection or blemish, the sort of life daily paraded on the lie that is social media.

Jamie knew that if her feelings were made public, she would stand accused of being a tree-hugging libertarian, a snowflake who gave no credence to the plight or justifiable outrage of the targets of the criminal actions of some of the city's homeless. To her both sides were victims, each in their own way and with their own perception of victimhood. She felt she was far removed from that person and was more aligned to those who believed sanctions, whilst at times necessary, should somehow be restorative for those whose circumstances, and often accompanying mental illness, collaborated in an outcome over which they had no choice or control. Incarcerating them could only ever end in recidivism and the hopeless spiralling vortex of State provided, secure accommodation. Devoid of civilising amenities or effective help, imprisonment had no hope or even aim to cure people, its sole purpose being to hide the unspeakable from the disdainful eyes of the public. It instead created an inescapable whirlpool that trapped the bottom feeders of humanity in a well of despair, satisfying the lust for revenge in the wider community which is where the votes lay.

Jamie realised she was staring out of the window of the bus with unseeing eyes as it swung out onto the Freemont Bridge over the Willamette River that bisects the city, separating the downtown area from the predominantly residential east side she had only that morning been looking down on from the terrace at the rose gardens. Shaking her head slightly and taking a deep breath, she withdrew from her daydream and emerged into the daylight of consciousness. She turned her thoughts to reflecting on the morning, trying to fathom Frank. Fun and good company, his charm was beguiling and alluring. He seemed to make her feel good about herself and she felt she was the centre of his attention when they were together, that he understood her. Witty and knowledgeable, his conversation was never dull and there were no uncomfortable silences. He somehow made Jamie feel as though she had known him for years, that she was important to him and that in some way they connected. And yet there were contradictions in some of his behaviour that confused her. It now dawned on her that she had effectively paid both for their morning coffees and for their inexpensive lunch as well. The sleight of hand over the bill she imagined he assumed would never be revealed was increasingly bizarre the more she thought about it. Yet his kindness in devoting a morning of his time to introduce her to the city and giving her some companionship when she knew nobody and faced a lonely weekend made her feel uncomfortable about mentioning the mistake over the incidents. The episode was in stark contrast to his generous gift of a morning of his time given to a complete stranger, so surely it was a mistake and he would pay her back when they next met, if they did as he had suggested they might? She felt it would appear churlish and mean spirited to say anything, so she convinced herself it was just a mistake, a convenient solution and escape from the awkwardness she felt. Anyway, even if it wasn't, why should he have to pay any more than her or for her when he didn't know her? She wanted to see more of him for the fun it might bring, but perhaps she would be a bit more careful over anything that involved payment for any entertainment.

Settling back into her seat as the bus came off the bridge and swung round past a large hospital on its way to the stop at Laurelhurst Park, her thoughts turned to Monday and her first day of work. She had some homework to do before the night was out.

Jamie woke up to the sight of a dark sky framed in the window in her bedroom. She could just make out wisps of cloud that spread across it like spun sugar, waiting to be tinged pink by the sun that would rise to shake off the night. She lay in her bed for a while, watching the stars flickering in the blackness of space as the first rosé threads in the clouds deepened in richness with the gathering strength of the light. Looking at her watch she realised she had woken up an hour earlier than her alarm. Perhaps the effect of the time zones she had crossed on her journey to her new life were still impacting on her sleep patterns. Picking up her phone from the small bedside table, she saw a message had come in from Charles, arriving after she had gone to bed, having been sent from his early morning start to set off to continue his quest to be 'something in the City.' He had embraced the Mammon Worship Church, which Jamie hoped would not change the essential kindness of the brother she knew. His new church was more secular than the one the biblical scribbler Matthew must have had in mind when the original publisher of the Bible asked him for some additional pithy comments to plump out his overall contribution to the best seller he was planning. Jamie remembered the subject of yet another boring sermon given by the village vicar which she'd had to sit through on one of the family's enforced Sunday visits to the weekly service with her father, allowing the opportunity for her father to strut his peacock feathers and superficial image as a pillar of society. The vicar was preaching to his preponderantly affluent congregation and she recalled something about Matthew telling his future readers that no one can serve two masters, and you certainly cannot serve both God and money. This seemed to her to be somewhat at odds with the hypocritical irony of collection plates being passed around the congregation as he descended from the pulpit.

In Charles' case, God had definitely come a distant second in the Worship Cup, that race which is the motivational force of a modern and more worldly society. It drives a sense of self over others in the millennial generation, to which Jamie had been a latecomer, having been born in the period's autumn years. At university she had occasionally attended debates arranged by the Philosophical Society. One lecture had been about modern society and the self. One of the university's senior lecturers had posited his belief that it was the 1980s decade that had brought with it the sea change in social attitudes so at variance from the previous definition of normal, which assumed a more collaborative society. Some said it was the inevitable result of Thatcherism, but the lecturer's opinion was it had been a pan-global development, an osmotic process that could not be associated with or blamed on one person. The movement away from putting community before self, and the slow evolution of a more secular, perhaps more selfish and self-centred society, fostered a belief in the value of materialism over the less tangible values that formed the bedrock of religious belief and preaching. People felt disinclined to await their reward in a nebulous heaven when it could be had today by wielding a credit card and the making of money, a modern interpretation of the saying that a bird in the hand today is worth two in a hoped-for bush after death.

Jamie was touched that, despite his focus on work and career and the time pressures that brought him, Charles had remembered this big day in her life and had also taken the time to contact her. That she was in someone's thoughts back home was a comfort to her and soothed her anxieties about the day ahead. Getting out of bed she showered and changed before making coffee and settling in the armchair to savour it, her knees tucked up to her chin, both hands wrapped around the warm mug. She closed her eyes and emptied her mind of extraneous thoughts in a brief moment of meditation before taking a deep breath and setting off for the bus stop.

Alighting from the bus near the Museum, Jamie walked the remaining yards to the front door of the Mark Building. For the first time she noticed the four words carved in the broad lintel above it: Temperance, Prudence, Fortitude and Justice. She immediately decided that once her salary started to be paid and she could enjoy its benefits, she would ignore the first of these laudable exhortations. A little intemperance was going to go a long way in the months ahead. She was still drinking at least a bottle of wine each evening to suffocate the images and memories that crowded her thoughts in the quiet of the solitude of her dark hours, but with her limited funds, that was at the expense of other essentials such as proper meals. The large brass doors of the building were open and she walked through them and made her way to the offices she had been told to go to in her letter of appointment. When the lift doors opened she stepped out into a large open plan office with the ubiquitous layout of serried ranks of desks, each in its own small self-contained booth, the stables of a form of corporate intensive farming that epitomises modern working practices in offices.

"Hi, you look kinda lost. Can I help you?" A tall, blonde girl stood up in one of the booths near the lift and smiled at her.

"Yes, thank you," Jamie said, grateful to have someone to speak to who might relieve her sense of being that wallflower at the party who knows no one and feels invisible. "I'm here to see John Mitchell. He's expecting me I think. Do you know where I can find him?"

"Sure," the girl said. "Follow me, I'll take you to him."

Jamie fell into step beside the girl as they set off for a couple of closed offices at the far end of the large, low-ceilinged room. The low hum of conversations, phone calls, tapped keyboards and busy printers, each disgorging words on paper that would often not be read, created a comforting background that she found calming.

"I'm Jamie by the way," she said. "Jamie Wilson. I'm starting work here today, so it's my first time in."

"Well 'Hi,'" the girl said. "I'm Cath and y'all welcome here. I was expecting you. It's always crazy busy, but we don't bite so just ask if you need help."

"Thank you, that's kind," Jamie said.

"Y'all speak funny," Cath said. "Where are you from?"

"London," Jamie said.

"Oh gee, London England?"

"Yes," Jamie said. "That's the one."

"I could listen to you speak all day," Cath said.

"You're not the first to say that," Jamie said, laughing. "If I had a dollar for every time I heard it said I'd be quite well off. Someone once said we are two nations divided by a common language and I suppose that's true. It's more in our pronunciation really I suppose, as well as the differences in vocabulary of course. I asked for a croissant in a bakery shop a couple of mornings ago and the girl who served me had no idea what I was saying. I had to point to one before I could make her understand what I wanted. As for basil and oregano, no chance with them." Jamie's nerves were making her chatter to fill any possible silence.

"I suppose going to the store must be interesting for you," Cath said with a laugh as they reached the closed door of one of the offices. Through the glass in the door Jamie saw a tall man standing by the window, looking out onto the street below. He was on the phone, his other hand behind his back with his fingers tucked into the waistband of his blue jeans. His long hair, tinged with strands of grey, was in a ponytail and the sleeves of his pale pink button-down shirt were rolled up to mid-forearm. Clearly this was John Mitchell and not a man obsessed by formality. Cath opened the door without knocking and ushered Jamie in as the man turned and smiled at her. He pointed to the chair in front of his desk, mouthing to her to take it, and then gave Cath a little wave. Jamie sat down and Cath tapped her on the shoulder.

"Come see me later when you're finished," she whispered before withdrawing, leaving the door open.

Jamie looked around the office as she waited for the conversation she was trying not to hear to come to an end. Modern and bright, the walls were adorned with posters of art, some famous pieces and others works she had never seen. A small table pushed against the wall boasted a coffee machine, a pile of coffee capsules heaped in a basket next to it and some mugs turned upside down. The desk was glass topped and spread out on it were art brochures and catalogues, some with coloured tabs noting pages that had been earmarked. A framed photograph of an attractive woman with two young children was on one side of the desk by the telephone, and in front of it a cup with what looked like a cappuccino in it sat on a small coaster.

"OK Paul, I gotta go now," the man said, closing down the conversation. "Get back to me when you can and when you're ready to talk about which pieces we are going to be able to have. I'd like as much time as possible to plan things at this end and to get the brochure to the printers. Okay, yeah. Ciao my friend."

Turning off his phone he turned around and held out his hand to Jamie.

"Hi, good morning. Sorry about that, I had to get that moving. Jamie I assume?"

"Yes," Jamie said. "John Mitchell?"

"Yeah, sorry. Everyone calls me Mitch. Welcome and thanks for being on time. What have you seen so far?"

"Oh, nothing yet. I just came straight up here. Martha told me to do that after my interview the other day."

"OK, great, I'll organise a walk round for you so you can get the hang of the layout. Cath can do that. You're going to be working with her and her team anyway. She's been here some years now and she knows all the exhibitions we have running at the moment and the whole story of how we run things here. We've grown some over the years. First I suggest you get down to HR and do all the paperwork. They love their paperwork. I don't, which no doubt they'll tell you. When you're done there, come back here and we'll chat before you go exploring. HR are the floor below. I'll see you again when you're finished with them. Knowing them it could take some time. They always have lots of forms to fill so I'm not their favourite person. I don't do forms."

He smiled as he finished and walked around the desk to usher Jamie through the door. She walked back to the lift but chose the stairs next to it to descend a floor on her way to spend what turned out to be the next hour or so in the HR department. As Mitch had said, there was a lot of paperwork, interspersed with instructions about her employment and citizen rights and the behaviour standards expected of all staff to ensure there was no discrimination of any minority group. Possible contentious issues that could be thought of as offensive or offending sensibilities were explained, leaving Jamie with no illusion that a sense of humour about most aspects of life was not looked on as a useful skill or trait. Finally she was given practical details about local eateries and cafés which she found the most helpful part of the conversation. Where to eat seemed to be the only matter HR thought to be a subject where someone's feelings might not be offended or hurt. It all played to a gallery of a movement that pandered to the agenda of a society where every subject was a potential hand grenade, primed to upset the faint of heart and the minds of those seemingly too sensitive for the world and therefore in dire need of protection from it. As Jamie absorbed the myriad of instructions that formed the Museum's bible of political correctness, the lyrics of Don McLean's song came to her mind:

*"But I could have told you, Vincent*
*This world was never meant for one*
*As beautiful as you"*

There seemed to be a lot of beautiful and extremely delicate Vincents around, their ranks swelling each month as more libertarian groups emerged like worms at the first rains. Each was more critical than the ones before, confronting anyone with thoughts or beliefs that did not conform to theirs. Jamie felt that in their acts and attacks on beliefs and even thoughts that contradict their ultra-liberal views, they forget their own preachings and set out to curb freedom of choice and thought for others in an act of supreme hypocrisy. They condemn anyone holding an alternative view to the trash can of shame for having the temerity to have an opinion that disagreed with their own. So much for their form of liberty which, in their definition, was a one-way street, but she felt that was an irony that is lost on them. Social media has become weaponised, she thought, and with its advantage of anonymity, it is a coward's paradise, a platform from which to attack and demean those who have the audacity to express what they consider to be deviant opinions. Jamie wasn't grateful for much about her upbringing, but she was thankful to have been gifted a more robust emotional constitution, one that did not succumb to a fit of the vapours at every innocent remark or view that didn't agree with her own outlook. Taking offence had become a badge of pride it seemed.

"Okay, you're good to go," said Charlotte, who had been patiently reciting by rote what appeared to be some form of employee's operating manual for the Museum. "I'll get your bank details set up for payroll as soon as you have opened a bank account. We'll sort out your Social Security number under our special visa arrangement and let you have that when we have it. You've got your pass to the building so I think that's all for today. Any questions or help, you know where we are here. We're here for you." She stood up and extended a hand.

"Thank you for everything," Jamie said, accepting the proffered greeting and noting Charlotte's firm handshake. She wasn't necessarily convinced that HR was there for her exclusively, nor indeed for any of the employees at the Museum. She assumed they would more generally have the employer's interests as their primary focus, their main job being to prevent the Museum from being sued. 'I must try to be less cynical,' she thought as she left the room and headed back upstairs to start work at last. The rest of the morning passed quickly and was spent with Cath, who showed her around the building, introduced her to colleagues and departments and took her on a tour of the Museum's various galleries before returning to their starting point and showing Jamie the desk and cubicle she would be using.

"We have two big exhibitions planned for October," Cath said.

"Hockney and a new venture for us of Japanese children's clothing. Well, kimonos rather than western clothes to be exact. It's a bit of a departure from what we normally do and Mitch said you'll be helping with that which is great because there's a heck of a lot to do, so let's get started and I'll introduce you to the team on that project."

And so, Jamie's new life began. On a clear, blue, bright day, projects already littered across her new desk, she felt she no longer had a care in the world, that she had now truly shed her past and it was forgotten, happily replaced by a present that excited her and filled her with an urgent eagerness to embrace every opportunity that came her way. Delusional of course because no matter how we detach ourselves from the past, it still retains a connection, a slender thread that is invisible to our conscious mind. In intangible ways it shapes us and is part of the nurture that partners with the wiring of nature's motherboard we are each born with, the melding of the two that make each of us unique. The past exists forever in our preconscious mind and can be unexpectedly exhumed and deposited into our conscious state at any time by a panoply of sensory triggers, whether that be a scent, a sound, a face or a moment. We have no control over those sensory triggers to things we thought we had forgotten. The future and its surprises lay ahead of Jamie as she revelled in the innocence of her present.

The first week in work was a blur of memorising new names, exploring the galleries in the museum and making external connections with suppliers. Most interestingly, Jamie loved her contact with custodians of art collections around the country. The culture of philanthropy amongst the wealthy with private collections meant the museum had a veritable cornucopia of options of exhibitions it could curate and display. With her entry into the world of work came the benefit of the green shoots of a new social life which meant some of her after work hours were spent in local bars with some of her new colleagues, all of whom seemed eager to show her the fun side of Portland night life. With friendly and welcoming co-workers, Jamie quickly felt accepted as she shed her outsider status to become one of the team. She felt a growing sense of belonging in a city that seemed to be an amalgam of local, homegrown Portlanders and an increasing population of émigrés seeking a quieter, more liberal life. Many previous honeypots of America had become victims of their own success, becoming overcrowded and with increasing levels of crime and their own homeless and disaffected cohorts.

At the end of her first week Jamie joined a group of colleagues at a bar where they gathered around a table, each there for no better reason than to welcome the coming weekend. Most of the group seemed intent on filling the next two days with hiking and exploring the natural beauty of the State that lay on their doorstep. She had quickly come to realise everybody she met seemed to have a passion for the wilderness, or at least the open spaces of the countryside on the city's doorstep. She had no knowledge of the rest of the country and so had yet to discover its breathtaking beauty, but listening to her new friends talking about it and about their weekend plans, she looked forward to when she could afford a car and start her own journey of discovery.

The conversation around the table turned to the coming election. Donald Trump had just been elected by the Republican Party as their candidate for the Presidential race to come to the astonishment of many in the public and the media and to the apparent horror of the GOP old guard, the traditionalists with no interest in changing a status quo that suited their self-seeking agendas that placed their interests ahead of the country's. The Democrats were crowing at what they perceived to be a gift that came with the keys to the White House, which was now sure to be theirs for the next four years. The contest had been bitter, and made very personal by Trump, who disdained any form of convention, and seemed to lack any self-awareness, or the remotest sense of empathy with the feelings of others. Because of his unconventionality and worrying rhetoric on issues such as immigration and relationship with the world, the consensus amongst the group enjoying their drinks was of optimism that Hillary Clinton would win.

"What are her chances d'you think?" Jamie said.

"Trump hasn't got a chance," Cath said. "Oregon will vote for Hillary. The State has voted Democrat in every election since 1988 and that's not going to change. No one's going to take Trump seriously. Even the Republican Party don't want him and if he wins he'll be a complete lame duck because both houses and both Parties will block everything he tries to do, just to get rid of him."

"It's amazing how engaged all of you are in politics here," Jamie said, "and how open you are about who you vote for and which Party you support. Back home, apart from the fanatics and those fully engaged in the art of politics, we tend to keep these things to ourselves. Our voter turnout is pretty low most of the time. Around sixty percent I think so obviously there's quite a bit of apathy."

"It's about the same here," Jay said. Jay worked in the Museum's IT department and was often an integral part of its exhibitions so Jamie had been working closely with him on the two she was involved with. She had quickly come to admire his non-conformist approach to life and his work. He kept his dark hair tied in a pony tail and had grown it so it hung down to his shoulders. His grey eyes behind his John Lennon glasses fixed on whoever he was conversing with an unwavering and uncomfortable intensity.

"We should follow the Australians and make it compulsory to vote here," Jay added. "I think it's a duty but I imagine there'll be those who say it's a constitutional right not to, and to force it would erode our rights, our freedom of choice." He sat back in his chair, satisfied he'd made his position clear and feeling no need to add to it, or embellish it.

As she returned his unblinking gaze, Jamie felt her phone vibrate in her pocket signalling an incoming message.

'Hi, what are you doing this weekend? I can show you around more if you want. It would be great to see you again. F X X.'

Frank had crossed Jamie's mind a few times in the week and she found she was surprised to realise she was missing both his company and a male presence in her life, so this unexpected contact was welcome. She very much wanted to develop a life outside work, one she could enjoy in a parallel existence, an encrypted life that was private to her alone. Frank's continuing interest in her was flattering. His natural charm was compelling, and she found his clean-cut all-American boy looks very attractive. She had been a bit disquieted by the payments for lunch and coffee when they had spent the morning together, but had justified this to herself by remembering he had left his wallet behind that day and therefore what had happened was quite understandable.

'Great,' she texted back. 'Where do you want to meet, and what time?'

'How about I pick you up from your place? Ten or 10.30 – whichever suits you,' he replied.

She texted back her address and suggested 10.30 before putting her phone back in her pocket and rejoining the conversation, which was still focussed on the likely outcome of the election and the prospect of life under a Trump Presidency.

"So, what do you think about it Jamie?" Cath said. "What's the view back in England?"

"I'm not sure I'm qualified to comment," Jamie said, "and in any event I'm not sure I want to get involved in another country's politics. In England, I can tell you we've watched the televised debates with a little surprise. It's not meant to be a clue as to what everyone back home thinks but I read the other day apparently some Professor in a university here said that we shouldn't question anyone wanting to vote for Trump, but should instead question an education system that produces people who think that's the right thing to do. That's a much wider issue and opens up a can of worms, the contents of which I most definitely am not in a position to debate. I say that especially given the state of our own education system in some parts of Britain, particularly the poorer parts of inner-city populations. Our politicians keep interfering, changing the curriculum, then changing it again when a new Government takes over. Like everyone in any form of governmental or regulatory power, they only feel effective if they are changing things, without any regard as to whether change is really needed. I don't know if it's the same here?"

"Of course it is," Jay said. "If you give someone a job regulating something, they're out of a job as soon as they've regulated it, so they look around for something else to regulate. That's how the State expands its influence and control."

"Our only equivalent at the moment is us leaving Europe I think," Jamie said. "What we call Brexit. I don't know whether any of you know about it or have been following what's been going on?"

"I've sure heard a little about it," Steve drawled.

Everything about Steve screamed Texas, from where he had drifted up to Oregon in search of cooler climes. His fair skin and red hair were not suited to more southern temperatures and the sun, but while he had left the climate behind, he had imported his home State's culture. His jeans, adorned with a belt buckle the size of a bull bar on a truck, were tucked into cowboy boots. He was habitually hiding under a Stetson hat, chewing gum and walking with a slightly rolling gait on gently bowed legs. An uninterrupted choice of check shirts completed the stereotype of the urbanised cowboy he presented to the world, but the rustic and slightly agricultural image he adopted belied the sharp mind and extensive knowledge of art that lay behind the slightly sleepy, freckled face.

"Yes, what's that Brexit thing about?" Helen asked.

"It's about the UK leaving Europe," Jamie said, going on to explain the country's entry into the Common Market some time after the War, and the growing dissatisfaction of a significant proportion of the population about membership. She talked about the mounting opposition to it by certain elements of the voting public which ended up with the country having a referendum where the nation was given a voice and an opportunity to express an opinion at the ballot box.

"Unexpectedly for the Government, which totally misread the public's mood, the outcome was a slim majority to leave and so they have no option now other than to come out of the Union. The Government was completely caught out, which just shows how arrogant they are," Jamie said. "They and a lot of people expected the result to be a walk in the park for those who wanted to stay in the European Federation, because that is what it has become. Modern America pretty much started out as a federation, but Europe was and still is, despite the Union, a collection of very different countries, different cultures and economies that have been forced together, often against the people's will. Different languages as well, creating their own sort of Tower of Babel outcome. Some politicians and much of the population have become increasingly disgruntled about laws being made in Brussels, and the collective seemingly being run by non-elected regulators. Exactly the people you were talking about Jay, bureaucrats who subtly expanded their power base to create an entity that was never the intention when the Common Market was created after the War. One of our politicians in particular, who is a Member of the European Parliament, put his finger on the zeitgeist of the nation, the disaffected and disgruntled, and pushed that one point, especially immigration. That's what people latched onto, completely ignoring peace in Europe for many decades after two devastating wars that became global. Of course, being an island I think we have always felt something apart from mainland Europe, different somehow, which didn't help the cause of those who voted to stay in."

"Wow, that's quite the speech," Steve said.

"I know, I'm sorry. I have no idea where all that came from."

"No, it's interesting because that's Trump. Exactly the same. A lot of people here seem to be thinking the politicians and established political system have repeatedly messed up and frankly, where's the harm in letting another guy have a go, an outsider who doesn't owe anything to a particular Party. Then there's the fact he's a businessman and a deal maker so he'd come to the job with experience in negotiating and running big business, unaffected by politics and the Washington machine or status quo. Hard to argue with that. Weirdly he's also focussed on immigration, unfair trade deals and building that stupid wall and keeping people out. No wonder he likes your guy, Forage?

"Farage," Jamie said, laughing. "Nigel Farage. He's really what we call a one trick pony, someone who only has one policy. In his case it's always been to get us out of Europe. He may only have been giving his followers one option but he's a very effective speaker. He's never said how he would make the country manage if he won, which he has now. He's just taken to the hills in fright and appeared here to help Trump with speeches. Many feel he's run away from his obligations. He's probably having that 'oh shit, what do we do now' moment because I really don't think he or his team thought they'd win. I think they asked the wrong question in the referendum. They should have asked whether we wanted to stop creeping federalism and go back to the old Common Market, which was basically a common trading platform, not do we want to leave Europe completely."

"So what's wrong with federalism?" Jay said. "It works fine here."

"Well, as I said, you pretty much started with federalism as far as I can see. I never studied American history but it seems to me you've never known any different, or at least not for a very long time. You adopted it early in the country's development whereas we had it forced on us, but through stealth. Slowly and insidiously so no one noticed what was happening. We are all different countries, some of whom hate each other at a grass roots level. Many of us think federalism doesn't work in the long run, well, only if it's a true union, and I don't think Europe has ever been that. Not a union of equals anyway, so the smaller and poorer countries have never had an equal voice or choice at the table. They're just there to make up the numbers and pay into the central budget. Some of them like Slovenia and Hungary have conveniently forgotten just how much they've had out of it as they hint at coming out too. And look at what happened in Russia. It finished as a federal state in 1991. We have it in the UK with Scotland wanting to break away and be independent. The Greek Empire, the Romans and the British Empire, and others before. They all eventually failed. It's probably treasonous to say it but I can almost imagine California saying enough, we're sick of supporting the country. I read somewhere they represent about fifteen percent of the US economy. That's huge and they probably think they could go it alone."

"Pretty radical," Jay said. "I think they'd be crazy to break away and anyway, the rest of the country wouldn't allow it."

"The thing you've got going for you here is everyone's devotion to the country, to your flag. It's amazing," Jamie said. "You are so united in that, and Trump has picked that up with his make America great again slogan. We don't feel any allegiance to Europe, or the European flag, and I shouldn't think anyone in the rest of Europe does either when their own interests are threatened. Especially the French. For the people it's a business arrangement but not for the bureaucrats in Brussels, or the European Parliament's politicians. For them it's a gravy train, a job preservation project. Their own jobs that is. Pigs at the trough with their enormous expenses. Are you aware they move the Parliament between Brussels and Strasbourg every month? It would be like moving the Washington government to New York and back every month. It costs about one hundred and twenty million dollars a year to do it and they can't stop it because they all have to agree to do that and the French won't agree to it. So much for a Union. It's a Union until one country's self-interest comes up. Madness, so no wonder people have had enough."

"Talking about enough, I need to go," Cath said, standing up and gathering her things, which became the signal for the others to do the same, bringing the evening to a close. In the general melee of farewells and 'have a good weekends', Cath turned to Jamie.

"What are you doing over the weekend?" she said.

"Well, until a short while ago, nothing," Jamie replied, "but I got a message a few moments ago from some guy I met in the café I've been going to. He asked if I want to spend some of the day with him tomorrow. He took me up to the rose gardens last weekend and asked me if I'd like him to show me more of the city so I said yes. I've no idea where we'll go. We're not dating or anything, so it's nice of him to spend the time on me."

"OK, that's cool," Cath said. "Does that mean you're free Sunday?"

"Yes," Jamie said.

"Great because I'm having a few friends over for a barbecue so y'all welcome to come along," Cath said.

"Oh wow, that would be amazing," Jamie said. "Thank you, yes, I'd love to be there."

Cath gave Jamie her address and suggested she arrive at about mid-day and then they said their farewells and parted. Jamie had called an Uber which was waiting for her outside the bar so she quickly hopped in and settled back into the seat. The driver pulled away from the curb and, glancing in his rear-view mirror said,

"Hi, how you doing? Late night uh."

"I'm fine, thank you," Jamie said as she gazed out of the window at people walking along the sidewalks on their way home, some hand in hand. Young lovers, lost in their impenetrable bubble of desire, oblivious to the world about them. As the driver waited at red lights on an intersection, she saw one young couple waiting for the walk sign. Arms around each other, Jamie saw him drop his hand off the girl's hip and let it linger on her bottom before dropping it further to squeeze her hard, low between her buttocks. Their eyes were interlocked, her head upturned so her long blonde hair fell down her back. The girl giggled at his act of intense, erotic intimacy that from anyone else would be an unspeakable invasion of privacy, what otherwise would be an assault. Instead it was an intrusion she rewarded with a kiss on his lips, one of welcome acceptance. How elastic our comfort zones are, Jamie thought, malleable and pliant, instinctively accommodating every nuanced relationship or connection we have.

The car moved forward and Jamie turned her head to see the couple step off the pavement to cross the street, aware she had yet to experience a relationship of such intensity. The few boyfriends left behind in the wake of her journey had all been transitory, in many cases no more than a meal ticket and a short-lived connection so she didn't get too involved with them. If she was honest with herself, perhaps they were no more than a better option than no companionship, that loneliness that ached the heart and demoralised the spirit. She had an instinctive aversion to letting anyone get close to her, especially not after the catatonic shock she had suffered on discovering her father's serial philandering. It had left her hating men at a deep level, swearing to herself she would never trust one, no matter what. She had never understood the concept of being alone in a crowd before, but now realised that was where she was in her life. Now she thought perhaps she wanted more. She wanted to be needed, to be wanted, to be loved, just like that girl at the lights. She hoped for the nirvana the girl had found in her boyfriend's arms, but to do that she would have to start to trust, to let someone in, and that was going to be difficult as distrust was now part of her DNA and her soul. Perhaps she might find that ability to trust with Frank, without the distraction and discomforting deceit of a secret life being carried on in the twilight of shame, a life she had reluctantly adopted as a sordid necessity to sustain her very existence as she planned her escape into the freedom of adulthood.

"Oh, I'm sorry," Jamie said to the driver. "How rude you must think I am. I was lost in thought. I'm good, thank you. I was having drinks with some workmates. Friday night's party night, eh?"

"Sure is," the driver said. "I love Friday nights. I get to make money. Y'all not from round here are you? East Coast?"

"No. I'm from England," Jamie said, amused she might be considered to be from the east coast and an American. Had she started to pick up an accent already? We can be chameleons, adopting an accent, a style, a vocabulary that helps us to blend, to fit in and not be the dandelion in the pristine rose bed.

"Hey, a long way from home then. How you doing here? You like it?"

"Yes, it's all so new," Jamie replied, "but yes, I am enjoying it and I think I can be happy here."

Jamie wondered if Portland Uber drivers were like taxi drivers in London, always ready to share their opinion with their passengers, opinions that knew no territorial limits on subject, or veracity of fact. This driver seemed more interested in just chatting and exploring rather than using his seat as a soap box from which to opine his beliefs and views on every aspect of life. He told her he had migrated to Oregon from Iowa, getting away from a toxic marriage and narrow-minded, small-town parochialism that had been suffocating throughout his formative years and into young adulthood, as any outpost of Peyton Place can be.

Jamie said goodbye to the driver as she got out of the car at her apartment block and watched his red lights disappear down the tree lined street before opening the door and climbing the stairs to her little sanctuary. Locking its door behind her, she kicked off her shoes and poured herself another glass of wine, the one that morphed into a bottle and which she hoped would silence her dreams.

The early dawn promised another bright, sunny day. Jamie woke with a headache. She reached into the drawer by her bed and took a couple of tablets before getting up to make a mug of tea. Climbing back into bed with it, she turned on her laptop to catch up with the news at home. For those who thought the Brexit referendum result would be the end of the debate and the start of a new place on the doorstep of Europe but not in it, the continuing denial of the result of a legitimate democratic vote lost by those who had voted to remain in the Union was disturbing to her. She could not understand what part of democracy those people didn't understand, particularly the politicians who owed their positions in Parliament to that very process. Their denial hinted at a fascist, autocratic mentality, born out of a sense of entitlement that separated them from mainstream and majority thinking. She shuddered to think what they would have done if they had a majority in Parliament as a group. Jamie felt outright majorities in Parliament almost inevitably led to autocracy, where anything could be pushed through into law at will. She was not particularly political but she did feel democracy as it exists is deeply flawed and open to corruption. Party mandates at elections promise and offer the earth, but once a substantial majority is achieved, the Government has free rein to enforce whatever agenda it chooses, steamrolling over any objection and any objective debate, with no obligation to implement their election promises. More locally, with Donald Trump possibly about to take over the role from President Obama, she felt America faced a seismic shift in its own policies and governance, and particularly with its relationships with the rest of the world, where it appeared only America's interests would prevail.

She skimmed more headlines and then sent another email to Charles before taking a shower and heading out for breakfast at Proud Mary, an Australian inspired café in the nearby Alberta Arts

District. She had read about it when researching her area of Portland and had started going there to enjoy it's exotic menus and delicious coffee. Relaxed and friendly, the artisanal café was the perfect fit for the area, with its art and craft shops and laid-back atmosphere, where no shops seemed to open before eleven in the morning. They reflected a work life balance that brought with it a near perfect equilibrium. The café was, as ever, alive and buzzing and by the time she left to go back to the apartment, a queue had developed in the street outside.

Back at her apartment, Jamie settled down to read her book as she sat next to the open window, enjoying the warm sunshine bathing her face. The deep throated rumble of what sounded like an expensive car pulling up outside the building broke her concentration. Standing up she saw a Porsche manoeuvring into the curb. Bright red, with a distinctive waved white stripe down its side, the car pulsated its power. The driver's door opened and Frank climbed out into the road and looked up at the building. Seeing Jamie in the window he smiled broadly and waved, then beckoned her to come down. Grabbing her handbag and a light jacket, she locked the apartment door behind her and skipped down the stairs and out onto the pavement.

"Hi there, morning," Frank said stepping around the car and onto the pavement. He opened the passenger door of the car and as Jamie reached it, he leant forward and kissed her lightly on the cheek. She instinctively pulled back, but it was quickly and effortlessly done, making it feel a natural greeting and an attempt to break down any invisible barrier with a confident step into her comfort zone. Jamie felt uncomfortable with the familiarity and the presumption it implied, but said nothing and got into the car. Frank closed the door as she settled herself into the contoured seat and walked around the front of the car to climb into the driver's side.

"So, how you doing?" he said as he started the engine and began pulling out into the road. She noticed he only started putting on his seat belt as they were moving, a seemingly ubiquitous habit amongst men, who are clearly genetically programmed to do things in the wrong order.

"I'm fine," she replied. "Really good in fact, and looking forward to getting out for the day. I must say, this is quite the car, isn't it?"

"Yeah, it pulls like crazy," he said. Jamie wasn't sure whether he meant its acceleration capabilities or as a babe magnet. She decided not to ask him to elaborate. "I don't know anyone who lives in this part of town so it's okay to bring it here." Jamie remembered his comment about his wealthy background and his wish for that not to influence people's opinion of him.

"So where to today?" Jamie said.

"Okay, I thought we'd start with the Japanese Gardens I mentioned the last time we were out, and then we'll head out of town to an island where we can have a picnic on a beach. Sauvie Island. I've brought some food and drink for us. Does that sound good? Do you have to be back for any time, a date or something?"

"No, that sounds great," Jamie replied. "I've got all day today and have nothing on this evening. Just a quiet night in. I've heard about the island from people at work so it'll be good to see it."

"That's great," Frank said, "Let's go have some fun."

Jamie recognised the latter part of the drive to Washington Park as they retraced the roads they had taken to the rose gardens. The Japanese Gardens were in fact a collection of different, theme-based areas but each was the oasis of calm she had expected and hoped them to be. She particularly loved the Sand and Stone Garden, which the guide leaflet said was to express the beauty of blank space. The intricate lines in the sand formed static ripples around the strategically placed rocks and stones, a moment frozen in time. They seemed to represent water after a rock had been thrown into a pond, wavelets and ripples spreading silently to the edges but never reaching it. She and Frank sat on a bench and settled back into the intense tranquillity for a few moments.

"This is just the right place to meditate," Jamie said, realising she had whispered the words, afraid to disturb the quiet which even the birds, normally so loud with their calls, seemed to respect. She leaned into him as she spoke softly, breathing in the cleanliness of his scent as she did.

"I come up here by myself sometimes," Frank replied quietly, "just to think and be alone. I sometimes see one or two people doing Tai Chi up here. I've always meant to learn but I've never found the time."

"Well, that itself means you need to," Jamie said, looking into his eyes as he turned his head to her, their faces close. "You should put that on your New Year wish list. Do you do that here, make a resolution at New Year that you have no intention or chance of keeping?"

Frank laughed quietly. "Yes," he said. "I don't think I've ever kept one. I think this next one I'll make a resolution that I'll keep next year's resolution, and then just repeat that every New Year. That way I shall never fail to keep it."

"Genius," Jamie said. "I'll do the same."

Frank looked at his watch. "Hey, let's get a coffee or something on our way out and head out to the island. It's out of town and a little bit of a way."

Getting up they headed for the exit, dropping into the Umami Café where Jamie studied the menu and ordered a Mecha tea whilst Frank ordered a mango juice. The café was light and airy with tables and a long bar with a large glass roof above it. They perched on tall bar stools to have their drinks before heading back to the car. When Frank asked the waitress behind the bar for the check, Jamie glanced at it and put down a bill to cover half.

"Thanks," Frank said, picking it up and adding a bill from his billfold.

"So what's this island we're going to?" Jamie said when they were back in the car and leaving the car park.

"It's north of town," Frank said, "on the Columbia River. Sauvie Island. It's quite big with farms and stuff but luckily not yet developed with large scale housing. Some of the farms there started growing weed after it was made legal last year. We can use it for personal use here. You may have noticed some people are beginning to set up shops to sell it in town."

"Yes, I've seen them and it's really weird for me to see that. Mind you, they've been doing that for years in Amsterdam so I shouldn't really be that surprised by it."

"There are petting farms there as well," Frank added, "and some of them put on hoedowns in the summer evenings. We should go to some. They're a lot of fun. There are beaches on the river and they're always pretty empty so I thought it would be a good place for you to see and to spend some time by the water."

"Sounds amazing," Jamie said, "especially having it so close to the city."

When they were about twenty minutes out of the city, Frank turned off the highway onto a bridge that took them over a small river onto the island. They drove on through open farmland, passing widespread farmsteads. As Frank had said, some had commercialised widely, with children's entertainment areas, petting farms and mazes.

Most had large, converted barns that sold the farm's produce to the public. After driving through the rural scenery for about fifteen minutes they came to a country store Frank pulled in and parked in front of it. Behind the building Jamie could see a lightly wooded area with parking sites for recreational vehicles. Some were occupied and the vehicles and trailers were hooked up to electrical points. Chairs and tables were set out for meals and camping kit, bicycles and toys were strewn around. Children were running about playing and laughing together as adults sat in some of the chairs, beers in hand, or stood at picnic tables preparing food in the fresh air.

"What happens at Reeder Country Store?" Jamie said, reading the sign outside the low wooden building.

"We have to buy a permit for the beach. It's private," Frank said. "Come in if you want. You can see a good old country store, just as they used to be."

The store inside was cluttered with a wide range of goods. A grizzled elderly man was behind the counter. His unkempt grey beard straggled down to his chest, covering the collar of his threadbare checked shirt. The antediluvian denim dungarees he was wearing were clean but frayed at the edges. A battered, sweat-stained Stetson completed the unashamedly hillbilly ensemble. He stood with his arms straight out in front of him as he leant wearily with his hands on the counter. Jamie noticed the age spots on his meaty hands and his dirt ingrained fingernails. These were hands that had worked hard over a long life. She wandered up and down the aisles as Frank addressed the old man.

"A permit for the beach please, Sir."

The storekeeper didn't reply, perhaps intent on conserving his diminishing reserves of energy as he slowly started to prepare the ticket. Jamie picked up items on the shelves, turning them to look at prices and ingredients, comparing the prices with those in town and also back at home. Since first arriving she had been surprised to find how expensive food was. She had quickly realised she was going to have to nurture the money she had brought with her if she was going to be able to stay solvent until her salary started to be paid. Her first salary payment had not yet arrived so there had been little room for the luxuries of life for her since her arrival, apart from the wine she bought which she felt fell into the category of an essential.

"Ten dollars," the man said in a rasping voice, coughing into a handkerchief he pulled from the bib pocket.

"Here you go," Frank said, handing over two five-dollar bills. "Thank you, Sir."

The storekeeper tipped his hat with his forefinger and nodded. "Y'all welcome," he said, his gravelled voice giving a hint of decades of tobacco addiction. Perhaps that explained his rattling cough Jamie thought, one the medical world might describe as 'productive.'

Frank took the ticket and nodded to Jamie, inclining his head to the door as he opened it. She followed him out to the car and they set off, soon turning into woodlands and onto a single-track road that ended in a clearing where a solitary car was parked next to the start of a sandy path that led into the trees. They got out of the car and Frank opened the trunk and took out a soft cooler bag and a rug.

"Lunch," he said, holding the bag up and pointing towards the trees. "It's this way."

They set off along the narrow track which wound its way through the shaded woods until it suddenly opened up onto a long, deserted and grey-sanded beach by the broad calm river. The beach was littered with shells, and it's higher slopes that climbed steeply up to the wooded shoreline were in places a tangle of fallen trees. Far in the distance they could see a family playing on the edge of the water so turning, they set off to walk the other way, eventually finding a spot in the shade of an overhanging tree in which to lay out the rug. As Frank put out the picnic on the sand next to the rug, Jamie kicked off her shoes and went down to paddle in the cold water. She stood in it half way up her calves, digging her toes into the soft sand and lifting her face to the sun. She shut her eyes and lost herself in the quiet. She became aware of a presence next to her and opening her eyes, saw Frank with a glass of chilled white wine in each hand, one extended to her. She smiled and took the glass, lifting it to him.

"Cheers," she said. "Thank you, this is amazing. So lovely."

"Another place I often come to," he said. "Mainly for the peace. It's always empty like this."

"I can see why you'd want to be here," Jamie said.

They stood close together in companionable silence, sipping their drinks. A low rumble started to grow from down the river. Jamie could see a large tug coming into view in the middle where the fast stream ran, and as it drew nearer she could see it was towing two long barges, each low in the water under the weight of their cargo. Small ripples lapped against her legs after the short convoy had passed. Turning, they returned to the rug and sat down to refill their glasses and start their simple meal. Jamie sat with her knees tucked up to her chest and, hearing a shrill cry in the air above, looked up to see a large bird drift over their heads and out across the water. She watched as it floated on an invisible updraft of air before it suddenly twisted and turned its body, diving towards the river. At the last moment it tucked its wings back and plunged into the water with its legs extended below it. It emerged moments later with its wings spread out on the water's surface and, shaking its head, it started flapping its large wings and lifted off, revealing the fish it held in its talons. Climbing above them, it seemed to stop in mid-air as it shook its body and wings to dry them, shaking off droplets of water before it then flew on up into a nearby tree where it settled on a branch and started tearing at the fish's flesh.

"Wow, did you see that?" Jamie said. "Amazing. I wonder what sort of bird that is?"

"It's an osprey," Frank said. "There are a lot of them here. I was hoping we'd see one. They often build their nests on top of big posts and signs on the river, like that one over there." He pointed at an untidy pile of sticks and twigs perched on a trio of inward leaning posts that were joined at the top to form a slender pyramid. Another osprey was standing on it and seemed to be feeding something in the nest, looking up when the bird in the tree behind started its high-pitched call. The cry was almost effeminate for such a proficient and fearsome predator. The bird in the tree suddenly leant forward and took off, clutching its now slightly ragged catch, and flew over to the nest to join what Jamie assumed was its partner.

"They're so beautiful," she said, leaning back on her elbows. Frank had stopped drinking, she assumed because he was driving, but she had finished her third glass of wine and, feeling mellowed by it, poured another before she lay back on the rug and closed her eyes as their conversation floated between them.

"It must be very different living here to where you grew up in San Francisco," she said.

"Yeah, it sure is," Frank replied. "Less crowded for a start."

"Were you happy back there? Was it hard to leave and come up north?"

"No, I wasn't happy. My father was an alcoholic who beat my mom, and also beat the crap out of me. He sexually abused me too so no, happy isn't what I think of when I think back to home. Those years were hard and I couldn't wait to escape it all. I was pretty much brought up by nannies and the staff. Poor little rich kid, eh? So the answer to your question is it was a breeze coming here. The first time I was happy in years. I had to leave my poor Mom of course, which was tough, but she told me I should go and she'd be fine. She said she was used to it because it was the only life she knew, and in many ways she felt it would be easier with me not there. She had the staff to help her. I'm not sure why I'm telling you all this. Normally I keep it to myself."

"That's terrible," Jamie said, feeling a surge of protective empathy with him. "I was unhappy growing up too. My Dad didn't want me and he never stopped telling me that. He didn't beat me or anything and there was no abuse. I almost wish he had because at least it would have shown him having some emotion, but he just treated me as though I didn't exist. I suppose I just feel I was completely abandoned. Rejected. He completely dominated my mother, and because of that she was terrified of upsetting him, so she always had to choose him over me. It was almost as though he was jealous of me and of any attention she gave to me, so she only ever gave a little and that was when she had to. She was always slightly distant and I suppose I learned not to go to either of them for anything. I definitely learned not to trust them."

"Sorry to hear that," Frank said, topping her glass up again before lying back next to her on the rug, his hands folded behind his head. "Did you ever think about running away?"

"No, I don't think I did. At least, I don't remember wanting to, but I do remember when I started comparing my home life with what my friends at school described as theirs. That was when I was older. Until then I thought what I had was normal."

"Well, the trouble is we have nothing to compare it with at first so of course we're going to think it's normal. It sounds pretty bad for you. Funny, we have something we share that no one else would understand. I mean in how we were treated when we were young. I totally get how you must be feeling and how shit your life must have been." Frank reached across and stroked her hair.

Even years later Jamie could never remember how it was they came to be kissing on that sunny afternoon, on that remote beach by the river, nor why she had opened up to Frank about her childhood. It was unlike her on every level and against all her instincts. Perhaps it was all the wine she had drunk that had dismantled her defences, or maybe the warm sunshine and peace of the isolation they were enjoying. Maybe it was less complicated and she had just responded to being ready to take the first tentative steps towards building a relationship that might assuage the loneliness and social exclusion her secret life had created. Guilt and fear of discovery had long dogged her every step and haunted her dreams. Most probably the key had been Frank opening up to her about his childhood and its harshness. Only the hardest of hearts could fail to sympathise with the story of his childhood, and the unhappiness it must have brought him. It somehow appealed to a hidden nurturing and protective part of her that she had not realised might exist. Whatever it was, it was completely against her nature, which had become one of maintaining a distance between herself and other people, to avoid any close emotional connection with them lest they reject her, or let her down should she need them. Trusting anyone wasn't even an option. Better to be self-sufficient and independent, for therein lay the path to not being disappointed.

As the sun began to set they packed up the rug and picnic basket and walked down the beach to the car. On the drive back to the city, Frank suggested they have dinner together in a Thai restaurant he knew on NE Killingsworth. He said there was a cocktail bar nearby they could go to before their meal, and also after if they wanted to do both. Jamie immediately agreed that would be fun. She didn't want to spend another evening by herself. When they arrived at the restaurant, Frank parked the car and they went to the cocktail bar he had talked bout. There Jamie perused a long list of cocktails, some of which she had never heard of, and then spent a happy hour or so trying out a couple. As the evening progressed and became fuelled by more alcohol, the reality of what she had missed out on for so long threatened to overwhelm her. At one point she excused herself to go to the bathroom to compose herself, tempted by the urge cut an arm to release the pain of the images of past solitude in her mind. Not having a knife or her favourite razor with her, she scratched one arm with a fingernail until a few droplets of blood appeared in the raw skin. Relief flooded through her as she watched the little red beads form, tiny rubies of release. She washed her arm and rolled her sleeve back down before making her way back to the table, aware she was walking unsteadily. Frank was settling the tab as she sat down.

"A drink to finish off the evening?" he said.

"Yes, I'd like that," Jamie said.

Frank put an arm around Jamie's shoulder as they walked back to the bar they had used before their meal. More used to keeping an emotional and physical distance from people, the unexpected touch of him against her confused her. Her instinct was to pull away, to get back behind the barrier she had so long ago built around her, but a smaller part enjoyed the warmth of his touch. Opening the door for her when they reached the bar, Frank ushered her to a stool at the tall bar and sat down in the one next to it, waving at the bartender who made his way over to take their orders. A football game was playing on two large television screens high on the wall above the shelves of liquor bottles and glasses, and the predominantly male customers were watching it while they talked and drank, occasionally shouting instructions to an unhearing team. After a couple of cocktails Jamie said she was tired and would like to go home.

"I'll call an Uber," Frank said. "I've had too much to drink so I'll leave the car here and come back and collect it in the morning."

"Do you want to come up?" Jamie said when they reached her apartment, her defences completely dismantled by alcohol.

"Yeah, that would be great," Frank said, opening the door and getting out before helping her out of the car.

On Monday morning, Jamie caught the bus into work slightly late, nursing the hangover from two days of over-indulgence that had made her oversleep. She had grabbed a coffee to wash down a couple of paracetamol tablets and then walked slowly to the stop, running the last few yards to catch the bus as it arrived, an effort she soon regretted. Sitting in a seat at the back, she gazed out of the window at the passing houses as she reflected on her busy weekend. Frank had left after a late breakfast on Sunday saying he had some work he had to do. After tidying up and completing other chores, Jamie left the apartment and caught the waiting Uber to Cath's house where she spent the rest of the day, meeting new people, drinking too much and eating whilst luxuriating in the unaccustomed companionship. It had been wonderful and so unusually conventional, which she realised was not how her life had been for a long time. Only one or two of the other guests there worked at the Museum and so she had the opportunity of mixing with people from a much broader spectrum of

Portland society. She was still the outsider but as such she was a novelty and many of those she wasn't introduced to sought her out to question her about her background and her story, eager to hear how she had come to end up in Portland, and to choose it as her destination. There seemed to be a universal affection for Britain and some mentioned ancestors who had come to America from there. It was as though they were trying to reach back in time to make a connection with earlier times, conscious of being citizens of a country with a relatively short history, one that in the modern view started with the landing of the first colonisers. This of course ignored the earlier history of the indigenous people who were ultimately pushed to one side and eventually relegated to a life on prescribed reservations, where their own history had been destroyed and any hope they might have in their hearts for an acceptable future died.

As her mind drifted over the weekend and the novelty and excitement of discovering new people and wider connections, which she hoped were the first tendrils of a new social network, she saw a large car sales showroom and lot on the other side of the street. It was filled with new and used cars. Parked in the front row and facing the street was a bright red Porsche with a distinctive waved white stripe down its side. There was a large card on the dashboard announcing the price it was selling for. A banner hung between two poles at the entrance to the lot:

FREE TEST DRIVE A CAR FOR THE WEEKEND

TRY IT AND YOU'LL LOVE IT

EASY TERMS

And so it began.

# CHAPTER 4

## MEXICO, DECEMBER 2017

J amie followed Frank down the aisle of the plane and walked out onto the steps into the heat of the late morning. Puerto Vallarta airport gleamed white in the Central American sunshine. The temperature contrast between the heat beating up from the tarmac and the snowy cold of Portland they had left behind four hours before was a shock, even though Jamie had expected it. It seemed to have been a long, dull winter and she was longing for the healing balm of sun on her skin, the smell of suntan lotion and the feel of hot sand between her toes. A few chilled mojitos in the evenings would round off the perfect days she hoped stretched ahead of them. It had been a few weeks back that she and Frank had sat in her apartment where he now lived with her. As they relaxed in companionable silence, coffees in hand and books on their laps on a wet Sunday morning, the rain beat against the glass as the last leaves of the fall swirled in the air, never quite settling, the wind teasing the ground with them, whipping them back up as they tried to float down to land. The sight of the small maelstrom outside reminded her of the glass balls filled with a figure and fake snow she used to see at the fairground when it paid its annual visit to the village green at home. They were displayed as prizes at some of the stalls and she used to love shaking them and seeing the little white specks swirling around before slowly settling to the bottom.

"Look at that weather," Jamie said, closing her book. "What wouldn't I give for some sun." Thanksgiving was four days away and she was going to be celebrating it by herself. It didn't really matter to her since it was not a festival she was used to observing, but because the whole of America gathered for a few days, each with their family, she faced four empty days by herself. Frank was spending the holiday with his elderly and reclusive parents, who she had still not met. Despite his frequent trips to see them in California, he had not yet taken her with him. She had asked him a couple of times if she could but each time he had said they were not very well, both with incipient Alzheimer's. He said they often seemed to struggle remembering who he was, and strangers in their house frightened them. Fortunately, because of their wealth, they had a small retinue of carers and staff who enabled them to stay in their home rather than have to go into care, and that meant Frank was free to continue his life in Oregon. He said that, being an only child, their care programme rested on his shoulders and he needed to protect and shelter them, despite how his father had treated him. He explained that his primary motivation was to check his mother was alright. He told Jamie they would both be fearful of meeting a stranger and he did not want them to have to deal with that.

"This is Portland for you," Frank said. "If you think this is bad, you should try Seattle."

"I've heard," Jamie said. "But wouldn't you want to escape this, just for a few days? Get some sun."

"Yeah, that could be good. We could go south for Christmas. I know a small place in Mexico, opposite Baja. I've been there before to surf. A lot of West Coasters go there in the winter, some even to work for a couple of months. Let me look into it." Frank returned to his book as Jamie mused and daydreamed herself onto a sunny beach, almost feeling the heat and sand on her skin.

And so plans were made over the following days, a small Airbnb apartment booked in a coastal fishing village called Sayulita, flights to Puerto Vallarta arranged. For Jamie it was the light at the end of a wintry, frozen tunnel and it lifted her spirits immediately. She had become so downhearted and dispirited she had begun to wonder whether she needed to get a sun lamp, or join the ubiquitous rush to tablets to lift her Vitamin D levels. Now, the universal panacea of hope made that thought redundant and brought a spring back to her step as she counted the days to getting on the plane with the gift of something to look forward to.

Thanks to pre-arranged visas and tourist papers, their passage through Immigration and Customs was easy and they walked out into the Arrivals Hall, looking around for the taxi driver they had pre-booked. He was standing by the exit doors, a scruffy paper in his hands with Frank's name written on it, so they went over to introduce themselves. Jamie thought he looked the epitome of a member of a Mexican drug cartel, employed at the more energetically vigorous, enforcement end of their activities. Short and swarthy with a luxuriant moustache that would probably require its own Passport if he ever travelled abroad, he stood with his tattooed and muscular arms slightly akimbo, the stance of someone used to being dominant. She assumed the only travel abroad he did was to the US, and that on narcotic delivery runs, using routes that bypassed any need for interaction with immigration authorities or a Passport. Frank signalled to him and the man nodded as he turned on his heel and beckoned them to follow him.

"You want currency?" he said. "I have a friend. Good rates."

"No, we're good," Frank said. "Sorted before we left. We'll pick it up when we get there."

The brief interchange seemed to have used up the driver's entire vocabulary of English as he remained silent for the remainder of the journey. Leaving Puerto Vallarta the road followed the coastline north before cutting across a large peninsula to the bay overlooked by the small town of Sayulita. Their Airbnb was close by the Sayulita Plaza in the centre, and from it they looked down on Calle Marlin, a semi pedestrianised street that ran down to the main beach. It was late afternoon by the time they had unpacked. Jamie was aware that the clothes she had brought with her would not really have been her choice of what to take, but Frank was very particular about how she dressed, even to the point of increasingly insisting on overseeing what she bought. He also dictated what make up she could and couldn't wear, especially if she was going out for an evening without him, when he would insist she wore no make-up at all and would tell her what clothes she should choose, which were always unflattering and uninviting. Not that it was a regular problem now as she rarely went out without him because he made it difficult every time she did, often sulking for a couple of days afterwards.

"I love you, and you're so beautiful, I don't want anyone else looking at you the way I do," he'd said. "I'm terrified of losing you. I want you to be with me all the time."

The first time it had happened, she'd felt flattered. Very much wanted and needed. "Don't be silly," she said, "that's not going to happen. Why would I want to mess up what we have by being stupid like that?" But she had complied, changing her skirt for something that was mid-calf rather than above the knee, and wiping off her minimalistic make-up. When it began to happen regularly, encompassing how she appeared when going to work or out shopping, she resisted and defied him by not complying, but the resultant awkward silence and cold shoulder meant it was not worth the energy and effort to fight him. And so she quietly acquiesced and fell in with his wishes. He very much liked a quiet life with her and said he didn't really like her friends. Soon after their relationship formed, Jamie had asked him to join her with her work friends, for that was what they had become, at a cocktail bar on one of their semi-regular Friday evening gatherings. He had gone with her and been very quiet during the evening and after as they went back to her apartment. She had said nothing but when this was repeated the next few times they were with her friends, she had brought it up with him.

"Are you okay? You're every quiet."

"That Cath at your work is so two-faced," he'd said to her. "I don't trust or like her, and she influences all the others. She's so friendly to their faces but behind their back she's something else. I heard her saying to one of them this evening what a dork she thinks that Jay is, and yet she was all over him like he was her best friend. She thought she was whispering but I heard."

"Are you sure?" Jamie said. "That doesn't sound like her at all. I've never noticed that. I really can't believe it. She's been amazing to me and really welcomed me to the job and the team there."

"Are you saying I'm lying?" said Frank, bristling.

"No, no I'm not saying that. It's just so odd. I don't understand because that's not the person I know."

"Well, that's because you're not looking for it, and you're too close to her so you can't see what's going on, what she does. I've watched her and she's playing you all. She's got some sort of agenda going on, that one. I'd be careful."

Slowly and insidiously it had become more difficult for Jamie to include Frank on those evenings, and also with any time spent with her other friends outside work. And yet, if she tried to be with them without him, he would stay back at the apartment and shun her when she got back. When she confronted him about it he again said it was because he loved her and he was trying to safeguard her from them. He told her she should see much less of them and that he should be enough for her.

"We can have just as much fun together without them," he said. "We don't need them, and I just don't trust what they're saying about you behind your back. Being a Brit, you'll never be a part of them. You'll only ever be an outsider. I'm just trying to protect you."

Gradually she found she became isolated from the friends she had made. She was torn between those newly discovered friendships and by feeling disloyal to Frank. She had found someone at last, a companion who loved her and wanted to care for her. It was a novel and exciting feeling, a new experience for her to be so needed, one she was reluctant to lose. The contradictions in her thoughts, and the fear of losing him, allowed her to normalise their relationship, to assume his Victorian sense of ownership of her was how couples behaved. Her perception was reinforced by the unconscious understanding and memory of how her father had controlled her mother throughout their marriage. A part of her still believed that was how all relationships were conducted and what she was experiencing was perfectly normal.

With everything tidied in the apartment, they set off down to the beach so Frank could book a surfboard for each day of their stay. The narrow, cobbled street was a blaze of colour, festooned with bunting hung across it. Laden stalls spilled out of shops and the street was lined with palm trees growing out of the wide sidewalks. The trees' leaves rustled above their heads in the light breeze as crowds of people, none of whom seemed to Jamie to be over thirty and many carrying surfboards, marched like ants to or from the beach which she could now see at the end of the street. Others meandered from side to side as they casually went in and out of the shops. Diners sat at tables outside small restaurants and bars with their drinks and meals, chatting and laughing in the cooling shade as the sun dropped below the buildings and headland. She followed Frank down the steps at the end of the street that led onto the beach where she immediately kicked off her espadrilles and dug her toes into the warm sand, feeling it cooling as she went deeper. As Frank went to talk to the surfboard hire team who were standing under a small canvas gazebo, Jamie walked on down the gently sloping beach to the water's edge and into the sea until the water reached above her knees. The sea was filled with surfers, catching their chosen waves or paddling out just one more time for that final run before the day's end.

The seven days they spent in the town brought the healing balm Jamie had hoped for, each day quickly falling into a familiar pattern where Frank surfed pretty much all day, stopping for a quick lunch with her before heading out into the waves again. Jamie filled her days reading the books she had downloaded onto her Kindle before they had left Portland, books she could never find time to get into when at home. On her way down in the mornings she would buy a fresh juice or smoothy from a trolley on one of the sidewalks, and then sip it slowly as she read. She had always loved reading and had spent a lot of her childhood with her nose buried in novels. They became a form of escape from her troubled thoughts about her relationship with her father, or rather lack of it, especially as she grew older. Now, on that beach so far from her roots buried in the English countryside, she devoured the words and when her eyes tired, she dropped the Kindle on her towel, put her head back and dozed or daydreamed. The Museum had been particularly busy recently and she had not been aware of quite how tired she was. For now and those few far too short days, the Museum and its stresses were many hundreds of miles away and not something she needed to think about.

The unaccustomed quiet moments in the sun gave her time to reflect on the year and a half that had passed since she had arrived in America. She now realised the enormity of the gamble she had taken in moving over, the whole enterprise dependent on the outcome of one interview, and an ocean of hope. It seemed lady luck had been with her and, after seemingly jumping off a cliff at night without a parachute whilst hoping for a soft landing, she now felt she had indeed landed on her feet with nothing broken. She had a job, a boyfriend and a future and could envisage the day she would apply for American citizenship in her adopted land. She loved the easy way of life and positive approach to everything in a more meritocratic society that didn't judge you by your accent or upbringing. The apparent lack of a class system of the British variety was refreshing and she welcomed the concept of being measured by what she did rather than where she came from or which school she had been to. Her fears of being alone were a distant memory. Frank had suggested he move into her apartment with her a couple of weeks after they started dating and, whilst she was instinctively concerned about the loss of her independence, she felt she owed him so much for the kindnesses he had shown her that she didn't have the courage to say no. When she combined that with her fear of losing him and being alone again, she quickly agreed to his suggestion. For the first couple of months they tried to juggle bills and household costs between them, with long discussions that were never quite arguments about who was to contribute what. Eventually Frank suggested they solve the problem with a joint credit card. He generously said that she need only ever pay the minimal amount the credit card company wanted each month, and he would cover the rest if she would pay for the rent on the apartment, which she was already doing. His logic for this was she could obviously already afford the rent and would be paying that whether he was there or not. That way, he said, she could feel she retained her independence and also be contributing meaningfully to their relationship rather than feeling she was a kept woman in the old-fashioned sense. Jamie buried any unease about the possible inequity in this arrangement under her held belief that their relationship sat at the pinnacle of what was important to her, so she agreed to it. More difficult for her to get over was the breaching of her defences. Whilst she seemed to have convinced herself she wanted a relationship, it was hard to abandon her instinct to keep an emotional distance from Frank in the face of his evident desire for more intimacy. This required her to trust, and trust was not something Jamie was used to giving, to anyone.

As her workload increased at the Museum and her confidence grew, Jamie was flattered that Frank took so much interest in what she did each day, always listening to her about planned exhibitions, questioning how the individual pieces of art were to be selected and the criteria behind those decisions and choices. He was clearly knowledgeable about art and always asked about the donors of the artwork and the patrons of the Museum. One evening soon after he moved in with her, Frank asked how her day had gone and she had excitedly told him about a wealthy philanthropist who was funding a new exhibition of works he was donating to the State, on condition they were displayed at the Portland Art Museum.

"We're going to have an opening night with VIP invitations going out to the great and good, especially in the city, and he's going to be there. It's wonderful and I can't wait to get it set up."

"Oh wow, that sounds great," Frank said, pouring more wine into her glass. "I'd love to be there. Any chance of you getting me a ticket for the evening?"

"Yes, sure. Sure, I think I can fix that for you," Jamie said, slightly hesitantly, unaware whether she had the authority to sanction it but wanting to make it happen for him, even though, for some reason, his request had made her feel slightly uncomfortable.

Frank frowned, which Jamie immediately interpreted as his disappointment in the slight hesitancy in her response, which she realised must have appeared to him to have lacked conviction.

"I'll get onto that straight away tomorrow," she said.

"Great," he replied. "It's your gig so I'm sure you can invite whoever you want. I'm already looking forward to it."

Torn between the two fears of telling him he could not be there and having to ask if he could be, Jamie wished she had not said anything about it, whilst aware it was too late as the cat was now out of the bag. The tension of her dichotomy gave her a sleepless night and a stressed journey to work in the morning. To confront the demon it had become in her mind as quickly as possible, she talked to Cath about it as soon as she saw her. A wave of relief washed over her when Cath said it would be no problem and that he'd always be welcome at their exhibitions and public relations events. Jamie immediately rang Frank to tell him.

"Hi there, I can't be long as I've got a meeting in a moment but I'm just calling to let you know I've spoken to Cath here and she says it's absolutely fine for you to come to that exhibition. In fact she said you're welcome to any I put on."

"Great, that's good," he said before quickly ending the call. He was clearly pleased but in a way that emphasised he had expected and would have accepted nothing less, which perhaps explained the lack of any thanks from him for what she had done.

From then on, Frank became a permanent fixture at all the exhibition opening nights Jamie put on at the Museum, and then soon at others she was not involved in as he pushed for more access to them. Whilst she was busy at those evenings, Jamie noticed Frank would only ever spend time with the wealthiest of the guests, particularly any benefactors who attended. She assumed that, because of his wealthy and privileged background, those were the people he was most comfortable mixing with, and with whom he had most in common. They were all always clearly charmed after their first conversations with him and this filtered back to Jamie from the Museum's management, which relieved her. She knew he often contacted some of those prosperous attendees after the events but he never divulged details of his ongoing talks with them, saying they were confidential and related to business matters that had to be kept under wraps because of their extreme confidentiality. He feared competitors could get to know of plans that were being discussed and laid, and might try to steal a march on them or worse, hijack their intellectual property or secrets, some of which would be of value to foreign governments.

Slowly over the first months with him, Jamie's life was subsumed into his, but it was a strangely solitary one. She asked Frank where his house was but instead of directly answering the question he generalised by saying it was in the south east of the city and he was having it completely renovated. The swimming pool was old and needed to be replaced, and he felt if he was spending that sort of money he might as well bring the house up to date with modern technology throughout. He described his plans for new bathrooms for each of the six-bedrooms, of walls coming down to create open, airy spaces and of a new state of the art kitchen. It meant the house was a building site and was going to be uninhabitable for over a year.

"I'd prefer you to see the finished article when it's all over rather than as it is at the moment," he said to her. "It looks as though a bomb's gone off in it and in any case, it's going to look completely different when it's done so there's no point in looking at what's there now."

Jamie thought it strange that Frank seemed to have very few friends but she put this down to the secret nature of his work which presumably meant he had to be careful who he mixed with. The very few she did meet if they hung out with them were all similarly financially independent, but none of them seemed to be particularly close to him. He obviously liked to move in the rarefied company of the entitled wealthy, and was very busy doing a job that gave him little time for socialising. He said he could not discuss what he did because it involved Government matters that he could not divulge. He said something about national security and that his technological and unique other skills took him to places such as the Pentagon and the White House.

"I'm only telling you this to explain why there are times I have to be away for days, or sometimes even weeks at a time. I can never tell you where I'm going though, so just don't ask."

From the way he bought new clothes and the latest technology in computers and watches, Jamie assumed his particular talents were very well rewarded. He still kept his Porsche under wraps he said because it suited his 'cover' to be seen as someone of lesser means. He said he had a special lock-up garage near his house in which to keep it.

The evenings in Sayulita were spent in some of the many bars and restaurants in the town, each spewing tables out onto the pavement. The small town was an easy amalgam of a traditional Mexican village and the community of foreign travellers who swelled the numbers. While members of the local community carried on their ordinary daily lives separate from the many seasonal tourists, the surfers and holidaymakers walked the streets, often bare footed, filling their days with trips to or from the beach, or around the town's shops. Interlopers and escapees from the colder neighbour to the north, they appeared to adopt the slower pace of life of the Mexicans. The sense of calm in the town very much reminded Jamie of the family's occasional summer holidays on Greek islands, where the same lack of urgency about anything meant *mañana* was too soon and time had no meaning so to hurry was to waste energy. There in Sayulita, surfboards were ubiquitous, almost fashion items. Retail therapy, hunger and thirst were the main connectors between the two disparate societies as the indigenous served the more moneyed outsiders who flooded the town, satisfying their many needs through their shops, restaurants and bars. Occasionally some of the tourists would stop and watch an episode of a Posada, the drawn-out Mexican celebration of the Christmas story, where long ago it is reputed two poor tourists with a donkey rental scoured a little village for somewhere to stay and give birth to the baby that would change and shape so much of the future world.

One late afternoon, as she made her way back to the apartment to shower, change and wait for Frank to come up off the beach, Jamie spotted one of the Posadas being enacted in front of the town's life-size Nativity scene in Sayulita Plaza. She joined the crowd which had stopped and gathered to watch. A large group paraded past, carrying candles and small torches as they tunelessly sang what Jamie assumed were hymns. A young girl walked at the head of the large group, carrying a small shrine balanced on a red and green painted wooden footstool. Two small dolls in elaborate clothes were on the stool, each wearing what looked like Stetsons, bringing something of the flavour of the wild west to the traditional Nativity scene. After ten years of education based on a heavy religious agenda, Jamie had left school a confirmed atheist, unable to grasp a fantasy afterlife and nebulous deity that had combined in people's minds to form the bedrock of Christianity. Of course the humanised object of faith and belief had to be a man and could not possibly be a woman. In Jamie's opinion, the existence of deity in any religion could never be more than a theory, in the same way quantum physics is awash with theories. Faith turns these theories into fact in the minds of those who style themselves as believers. Jamie could not help but think the whole story was the product of humankind's imagination, and perhaps men's rather than women's given how every religion she could think of was governed and ruled by men, with women being relegated to a supporting role, an outlook and ultimately a dogma that fed through to how the Christian churches had been controlled over centuries. She wondered to herself once whether a female Pope would be a Popess, a real poppet, and had giggled to herself at the irreverence of the thought. In time she came to the conclusion her own atheism was as illogical a stance as unquestioning faith since neither side of the argument knew the reality. She realised her own position was equally as tenuous as unquestioning belief, and so she converted to agnosticism as being the only honest stance she could take. Perhaps one day she would find out the truth behind the myth.

On Christmas Eve Jamie and Frank woke up to another cloudless Mexican sky. After a mug of coffee in bed, taken whilst gazing sleepily out of the window at the emerging day, they wandered down to a small restaurant on the Avenida Revolución where they sat at a table outside on the covered sidewalk for more coffee and delicious plates of fresh fruit and croissants. Electric golf buggies and old cars were busy in the street where the shops were beginning to open. Street vendors were setting up their stalls selling fresh vegetables and fruit and, now and again, junk snacks for tourists. Jamie was intrigued at how few tourist shops there were in the town, when she might have expected it to be awash with them. It was as though the locals refused to pander to the omnipresent desire of tourists and travellers to buy tat and pointless trinkets. Because she had buried her nose in her books every day, she decided she would like to spend her morning exploring the town rather than spending it on the beach.

"Shall we go for a walk around town?" she said. "I'd love to see more of it."

"The surf's really good this morning," Frank said. "I've just checked the internet and I don't want to miss it. We can see the town another time."

His response brooked no argument or debate, a *fait accompli*. Jamie turned her head and looked out at the scene with unseeing eyes that filled with tears, unnoticed by Frank who emptied his coffee mug and stood up.

"I'll see you later," he said. "Can you get the check?" It was apparent that wasn't a question. He strode off for the beach without a backward glance. Jamie sat back in her seat and waved an arm for the waiter.

"Un cafe mas por favor," she said. "Y la cuenta tambien. Gracias."

"No problem señora. I bring now."

As she waited for the coffee to arrive, Jamie reflected on the truth of the relationship, a truth she suddenly realised she had been busy burying under what had clearly been futile optimism. If she was honest with herself, she knew she had been unhappy for many weeks now, if not months. The relationship had osmotically leached into being completely one-sided, and it seemed to have happened without her noticing. There had been no one event, no particular day in which she had handed Frank complete control over every aspect of her life, but that was what seemed to have come about, and she had no understanding of how that had happened, or even why. How had she allowed it, especially given her propensity for independence? More disturbing was that she felt she had stepped back into her childhood, to a time when her father had treated her in exactly the same way, controlling every aspect of her life, dangling the carrot of hope in front of her emotions, always just out of her reach. Eerily, it dawned on her as she sat and sipped her coffee that Frank was a clone of him. She shivered at the thought. How could she have ended up in thrall to a mirror image of the man she had run away from, the man she still wished to build a relationship with? Despite everything he was still her father and the little flame of hope flickered in her heart. But Frank was not her father, and she felt sure she had never wanted him to be. Surely that was not what she had been looking for when she had first thought of him as a partner? She remembered reading somewhere that we are often at our most stressed when we are not in control of our lives or events. Perhaps that was one of the reasons she was so exhausted when they had arrived in Sayulita, and not just because she was busy at work. It was not too late to make changes and she needed to take back control of herself, but perhaps not today. She wanted to enjoy the rest of her time in the sun, so that was a battle that could wait until they got back home, but it was not a battle she was going to avoid.

Jamie's mind was too active to concentrate on a book so she shunned the beach and decided instead to complete her walk of discovery around the town by herself. Once off the main streets and away from the shops that were honeypots of attraction to the non-surfing tourists, she found the off-piste parts were quaint and somewhat dishevelled. They had the additional benefit of being quiet but sadly not as colourful without so many streams of bunting hanging across the streets. She found the solitude in the backwaters both calming and soothing. Here and there disembowelled piñatas hung from houses. Their seven spikes, representing the seven deadly sins, were bent and beaten, perhaps a metaphor for mankind's victory in beating sin, but this would probably be lost on the children attacking them from below as they shrieked with delight when the sweets inside finally cascaded out like a rain burst on their heads. Here and there elderly ladies sat in small groups on chairs or stools outside their houses, chatting together as they prepared vegetables for meals they would cook later. Jamie climbed a hill leading to the headland to the west of the town, and found a vantage point that gave her a panoramic view of the bay and the beach below. The surf was indeed very much up and the incoming waves were dotted with surfers weaving their way through the outgoing boards of their compatriots. She sat on a small bench and emptied her mind of the present, and turned instead to the future. In many ways she felt she had been in a state of mourning since leaving home. It was a mourning for the loss of what she had never had, the love of a father but also all she had known there, the land of her birth with all its ways and mores. No matter how she looked at her situation at home, it could only have been her fault that she was a disappointment to her father and she now realised the focus of everything she had done, and her plans for the future, had been to try to win his respect. Now, she just wished she could forget and escape from her memories, the ear worms that played repeatedly in her mind, torturing her quiet moments and exhausting her. How could she move on and leave that history behind and not have it intrude into her thoughts every day?

With a sigh, she got up and slowly made her way back down the hill into the town where she continued her tour of exploration before heading to the café she and Frank habitually used for their light lunch each day. She took a table on the sidewalk and ordered a glass of wine while she waited for him to arrive. After an hour, and a fourth glass, it was clear he was not going to make it so Jamie settled the check and made her way to a very modern looking clothing shop she had noticed near their apartment. Manyana was a shop quite unlike anything else in the town, and was clearly designed and curated for the wealthier tourists, many of whom rented one or more of the large, secluded villas that dotted the forest near the town. They each had spectacular views out over the ocean, and their occupants stood out when they came down to the town, just by the way they dressed. The clothes in Manyana were casual in their theme and expensive in their taste and price. Linen and fine cotton dominated the fabrics they were made from. Jamie would not normally have contemplated buying anything because of the cost, but on impulse, and perhaps in a fit of pique and rebellion at having been stood up at lunch, she selected a beautifully made shirt for herself. It shocked her to think that this was the first time for months she had bought clothes for herself that had not first had to have Frank's approval. Hugging the small packet to her chest, she took it back to the apartment and hid it in her case before walking back down to the beach with her book and a towel for the rest of the afternoon.

As usual, Jamie got back to the apartment before Frank. She showered and changed for the evening and then made herself a cup of tea which she drank in a small armchair by the full-length windows that opened onto a small balcony. She decided to say very little about the day and her concerns about their future together for fear of his reaction. That would end up ruining her Christmas Eve evening which she wanted to spend amongst the celebrating people who would be roaming the streets later. Talking to waiters in the restaurants they had eaten at, she had learned that Christmas Eve, or Noche Buena as they called it, was a big family event in Mexico. There would often be a final Posada and then people would have a family meal. The restaurants were going to be busy and Jamie was aware they might have to queue for a table. Jamie's reverie was broken by the door opening and Frank coming into the room.

"Hi," he said, throwing down his towel and kicking off his shoes.

"Hi," Jamie said. "Are you okay?"

"Yeah, fine, why?"

"Oh, it's just you didn't make lunch so I was a little concerned. You know, a banged head or something. I didn't get a message."

"No, I'm fine. Some of the guys on the beach suggested we go have lunch at a small strip joint they knew in the back end of town. It was great. One of the young strippers couldn't take her eyes off me. She thought I was hot and she obviously wanted me."

The shock of what Frank had just said, and the unashamed way he had said it without any self-awareness or embarrassment, must have shown on Jamie's face.

"You got a problem with that?" he said, defensively. "It's just a bit of fun and there's no harm in it. Perfectly normal for guys to go places like that so no need to look all self-righteous like that."

"That girl you thought wanted you? She's paid to make you think that Frank. That's her job. It's an act. She probably thinks you're pathetic, just another sad, dirty man ogling her body. And, what's more, that young girl is someone's daughter. Think about it. So yes, I do have a problem with it. Someone loved her, and probably still does.

I should think she was and is the most precious thing in their lives, a daughter to whom they gave life, not to have guys like you pay to see her take her clothes off and pretend to want you. Have you even thought about what happened in her life to make her strip for you? How desperate she must be to have to do that to make a living, to humiliate herself in front of you? Do you really feel she would choose to do that, and presumably more, if she had other options?"

Jamie felt enraged, and outraged on behalf of the girl, and indeed on behalf of all used women, as she herself had been. No matter that she had chosen that way of making money, in her mind it was the men who had taken advantage of her desperation, and of the fact she had no other choice, just as that girl in the strip club almost certainly had no other options in her desperation. To Jamie those men disgusted her and were dirty misogynists who treated her like a piece of meat at the supermarket, something to be bought and used for their own pleasure, without one thought about her and why she would choose to be there with them, to rent out her body. Did they really believe it was a career choice for young girls and women leaving school and home for the first time?

"You have no idea what you're talking about," Frank said. "They love it, being the centre of attention and seeing men wanting to hit on them. You can see they enjoy it from their faces, and I didn't hear any of them complaining about the tips. You need to grow up and get real about life, drop that frigidity you have. Have you thought that's why I might want to go to a strip joint? Perhaps you should take a good look at yourself."

He turned and went into the bathroom. So somehow it was her fault? How do men do that, she thought? How do they turn every issue around so it becomes the woman's fault? It had been the same with the punters back in London, some of whom would tell her their wives weren't interested in sex with them, or even trotting out the old cliché that their wives didn't understand them. Presumably, Adam blamed Eve for having planted an apple tree in the garden in the first place, thus setting a precedent for men forever after. Jamie heard the shower being turned on. She got up and took her mug to the sink, rinsed it and put it on the draining board to dry. She knew that Christmas Day was going to be the same for her, a day by herself, and surprised herself by feeling relieved at that.

Leaving the apartment later for dinner and the evening in the town, Jamie felt listless and depressed but Frank didn't seem to notice, or if he did he just chose to ignore her deflated mood. Either way, she felt as though she was watching the life and celebrations going on around her under the clear night sky as though she was viewing the scene on television, a detached voyeur looking into a life and existence she had no part in. She was glad when midnight passed and they went back to the apartment. She climbed into bed and immediately fell into the fitful sleep of the exhausted but troubled mind. Christmas Day came and went exactly as she had anticipated. Frank's gift to her of a small bottle of perfume did little to lift her spirits as she watched him unwrap her gift to him of the expensive cashmere sweater she had saved so hard for over a number of months. With its label stuck beneath it announcing it had been bought in a discount store that sold bankrupt stock, the perfume he gave her spoke volumes about how he took her for granted. His perfunctory thanks as he tossed her present to him onto his case by the cupboard without even trying it on seemed a hard-won counterfeit of gratitude. When he left for the beach and the day shortly afterwards, Jamie felt a bit ashamed that again she felt relieved that he had gone and that she could be alone and not have to worry about pleasing him. After clearing up the breakfast things she picked up her book and beach bag and went down to the sea for a long walk along the bay. She settled on her towel in a quiet spot far from the main throng, who were spread about on the sand like a colony of basking seals. She was going home early the next morning and she looked forward to getting back to Portland and being at work, where she knew her place in the order of life.

Flying into Portland Airport the plane circled Mount St Helens which stood proud over a white land. It had snowed again and Jamie was excited at the prospect of being back in a snow wrapped city. When she saw the volcano's crater and a bulging domed shape in its centre, she felt in awe of Nature's power. One side of the mountain was missing and the forces that could remove half of it in a moment were unimaginable to her. From her vantage point above it, the mountain looked terrifyingly close to the city, a time bomb the population ignored or were now blissfully unaware of. As the plane banked into a turn, the mountain slipped up out of her view, to be replaced by a pristine white landscape. Jamie spotted the runway in the distance as the plane began to level, a stark black scar against the snowy ground that disappeared from her view as the plane leaned once again into its final turn. The airport was quiet when they walked through it and they quickly made their way to the taxi rank and the ride home. Jamie watched the houses and stores, still with their Christmas decorations in the front yards and windows as Frank stared silently at his phone, presumably catching up on emails. Now and again his fingers flew over the screen as he replied to some of the messages. The rest of the time he swiped the surface to scroll through what he was looking at. For her part these were things she would do later. She felt tired after the journey and the days ahead looked bleak, with difficult conversations lurking in their shadows.

After drinking the best part of a bottle of wine, Jamie went to bed and woke in the morning with a headache and sore throat to find Frank had already left for the mysterious work that she still knew nothing about. She had learned at her cost not to ask or question him about exactly what he did with his days, or the many nights or weekends he was away. As she lay in the warm bed thinking of them as a couple together, she realised she really didn't know anything about him, only that which he had told her. Despite having been with him for some months now, her innate lack of trust of people had not dissipated and she had no benchmark against which to verify what he told her of his past, and indeed his present outside her life with him. The reality of him was invisible to her and, if they were going to move forward together, she not only had to take back control of her life and independence, but she also had to get to the heart of who he was. The bigger question for her was whether she wanted to be with him at all. The one-way emotional street of their partnership brought her no happiness or pleasure and surely she asked, it was not unreasonable for her to want that for herself.

Jamie felt hot and was sweating. She must have caught a cold on the flight and it seemed to be taking hold, but not enough that she didn't want to go in to work. She didn't relish the idea of a day at home by herself so got out of bed to shower in the hope that would help her feel better, but found she was still shaky, feeling both hot and cold. After drying herself and dressing, she put on an extra jumper, then threw a scarf around her neck and pulled on a dark blue woolly hat with a large white pom pom before setting off to catch the bus into the city. The morning passed with a mixture of work at her desk and meetings, interspersed with chats with colleagues and traded recollections of respective Christmas breaks. Jamie began to feel worse as the morning progressed and after lunch she excused herself to Cath and went home. Arriving back she unlocked the apartment door and was surprised to only have to turn her key once. She felt sure she had double locked it with two turns when she had left earlier. Perhaps not feeling well with whatever infection she had caught had muddled her mind. Shutting the door quietly behind her she took off her shoes as was her habit and put down her bag and then froze. She could hear quiet voices in the apartment. She heard a light laugh and realised she was not alone in it. Walking silently and cautiously down the corridor, she could see the bedroom door was ajar. Getting to the door and looking through the narrow gap, she could see the back of Frank's head on the pillow. As she slowly pushed the door open the girl he was talking to came into view as she also lay on her side facing him, the sheet pulled down to her waist and his arm casually over her. Jamie stood perfectly still and stared at the clichéd scene in front of her. The girl's attention was focused on Frank's face as she smiled at something he had just said and at first she did not see Jamie. Suddenly the girl glanced over Frank's shoulder and saw her. Her face blanched and she gasped in shock, grabbing the bedclothes to cover her naked breasts. Frank whipped round and stared calmly at Jamie.

"What the fuck's going on?" Jamie said quietly. She felt strangely calm despite her shock. "No, don't explain. Stupid question, it's bloody obvious. Get the fuck out of here. Now. Go, just go."

She was staring intently at Frank as she said this, infuriated at his smile in response. He swung his legs out of the bed and stood in front of her, stark naked, almost defiant. The girl stayed in the bed, wide-eyed and clutching the sheet as though fearful it might be pulled down off her nakedness. He picked up his clothes and slowly and wordlessly dressed. He pushed past her and she followed him down the corridor. He picked up his keys from the coffee table and when he got to the door, turned and looked at her, the hint of a shameless smile lifting the corners of his mouth.

"I'll clear my things out tomorrow," he said as he opened the door and stepped out of it and, Jamie thought, out of her life.

Jamie heard a slight noise behind her and turned to see the girl standing staring at her fearfully. She could now see the girl was young, about her own age and height. Slim and very pretty, almost elfin, her strawberry blonde hair was tied back in a ponytail, enhancing her fine jawline. Her large eyes watched Jamie hesitantly. She appeared almost like a frightened doe in front of a hunter's gun. Tight blue jeans hugged her legs and her white sneakers were stark against the dark carpet.

"So, who are you?" Jamie said.

"Well, I could ask you the same thing," she replied. "I'm Jo, Johnny's girlfriend."

"Johnny? You mean Frank." Jamie turned her shoulders and waved a hand at the door.

"Who's Frank?"

"Frank, him, the bloke you've just been shagging I assume," Jamie retorted. "In my bed. In my apartment."

"I don't know what you're talking about. That's Johnny, my boyfriend. This is his apartment. You must be his sister. He said you were living here while you look for a new place and that was why there were a woman's clothes in the closet."

Jamie took a deep breath and thought for a moment.

"Sit down," she said, pointing at one of the armchairs, and then more gently, "We need to talk."

The girl sat down tentatively, looking confused.

"Would you like a coffee?" Jamie said. "I think I could do with one."

"Yeah, that would be great," she replied.

The offer to make coffee was more designed for Jamie's benefit to give her time to collect her thoughts and to try to process what had just happened. This was something she had not seen coming and spoke volumes to her about how blind she had become, or allowed herself to be, about the reality of her relationship with Frank. Taking their mugs and a box of tissues with her, she sat down opposite the girl and put the coffees on the low table between them. Her temperature was not helping her confused thoughts as her mind tried to unravel the situation.

"Let me start," Jamie said. "It might help you, or us, work out what's been going on. I am not Frank's sister, he's an only child. He and I have been dating for nearly a year and a half and this is my apartment, not his. He moved in last year. That's it. Your turn." As she was saying this, Jamie started to feel the anger rise within her. How could she have been so stupid? How could she not have seen the truth in front of her?

"Well, I'm Jo," the girl said. "Johnny's got two sisters he says, and he and I have been dating for about eight months. I moved here from New York a couple of years ago and we met up at the beginning of this year. I was waitressing in the restaurant where I work and he came in for lunch and I served him. We got to talking and he came back to eat a few times, always alone, and then he asked me if I wanted to go on a date. I'm training to be a journalist and he said he could help me with his connections in the media world. I suppose it just went from there, you know, one thing led to another."

"Have you been to this apartment before?"

"Yes, a number of times. Always after my lunchtime shift, and he's always had to go back to work after we've, you know, finished. I've never stayed over. That always happens at my apartment where he comes to me from time to time, for weekends or a couple of nights. I live in the south east of the city. You say this is your place, not his?"

"Yes, I've never been to his house. He told me it's being completely renovated and is just a construction site at the moment so there's been no point in him taking me there. What's more important for both of us at the moment is who is he? He's Frank to me and Johnny to you, so what's his real name? Are there others apart from just you and me? This is getting a bit creepy."

"I have no idea," Jo said. "And I don't know where to start. I have his cell number but I don't know where he lives if it isn't here. What are we going to do?"

"I don't know," Jamie said. "I think the first thing we do is give each other our cell numbers. It's not you I blame or am angry with, it's him. What a complete shit. Bastard."

"Yeah, it looks as though we've both been had," Jo said.

"In more ways than one, but at last we know now before this goes any further. It makes me so angry to know what he's done to us both. Are there others?"

Jamie and Jo swapped phone numbers and chatted for a while, exchanging details from their respective relationships with Frank, which had so many similarities. After a while Jo looked at her watch and said she had to go and do a few chores before her evening shift started. She started crying quietly. Jamie went over and sat next to her, putting an arm around her shoulders.

"This is a shock for both of us," she said, "so let's do it together. You're not going to be alone in this. Let's not let the little shit win."

Jo wiped her eyes on her sleeve and sniffed. "You're right, and thanks. It's just I'm just so confused. What the hell is happening to me? To us? How are we going to sort this out?"

"By taking back control, for a start," Jamie said. "No more having someone else running our lives. Did he try to run your life for you?"

"All the time. Everything. The clothes I wore, the people I could see. It felt good to be wanted so much by someone I suppose."

"Yeah, well, perhaps it's a lesson for both of us. Look, we'll keep in touch. I'm going to try to track him down and face him with it all. Find out what's been going on. I'll let you know when I've got news. Just call if you need help or want to talk. We're not the enemies here."

Jo got up, picked up her bag and opened the door to go. She turned and looked at Jamie.

"Thanks for being okay about me, and I'm really sorry. I'd never have done this if I'd known about you. I feel such an intruder into your apartment and life. I'm not into sharing. That's not my way and I have principles. I hope you'll learn and understand that one day."

"Me neither," Jamie said. "It's going to be okay, we'll get through this. Just keep in touch and don't let him worm his way back into your life."

Jo closed the door behind her. Jamie looked around the silent room, searching for clues of Frank's presence. The book he was reading was open and face down on the arm of a chair. She picked it up and tore out half the pages, throwing them in the trash bin. Going to the bedroom she pulled out his case and threw the remnants of the book into it, along with every possession of his she could find, taking a pair of scissors to his jeans and shirts before she did, a vicarious assault on him whilst relishing a simple way of venting her anger. She stripped the bed and angrily pushed the sheets and pillow cases into the washing machine. When the machine started its washing cycle she called a locksmith she found on the internet and asked him to come over urgently to change the lock on her front door. She explained it was an emergency because she lived alone and was afraid a man stalking her would try to get in with a key he had stolen from her purse. He arrived within an hour and when he had finished she felt more secure. She put Frank's bulging case containing his shredded clothes in the entrance lobby downstairs and went back up to the apartment to start the process of expunging every memory of him from her mind. Of course memories are like any kind of matter and can never be destroyed. They can only ever be turned into something else, as fire turns matter into carbon and our every breath and exhalation turns oxygen into carbon dioxide. We let our memories fade to dim recollections that exist like ghosts in the half light of our subconscious, our forgotten history, buried deep in the abyss of our unconscious where we have no recollection of them, believing them to be forgotten. And yet we delude ourselves because they can be resurrected in a moment by a scent, a sound, a sight. Our physical senses are capable of hijacking the now, flooding the present by what we thought was gone forever in the distant past. And so it would be for Jamie and Jo. In time the man they thought they knew would grow faint and eventually disappear until Jamie might see a red Porsche or taste truffle fries, or when Jo sees a movie when a philandering husband meets his Waterloo as his infidelity is revealed to a cheated wife. Alone again, Jamie could feel the pressure of stress building within her. Going to the bathroom she reached for her old friend the razor and cut a couple of new lines in her forearm, just enough to allow small rivulets of blood to drip down into the sink, washing away the humiliation. She watched the red stain slowly slip down the bowl and felt the familiar caress of calm come over her.

Jamie used work as the salve to the mortification she felt at being so betrayed, so foolishly taken in. She was conscious of a visceral embarrassment at her gullibility and at how naive she had been in being prepared to turn a blind eye to so many warning signs. The evidence had been before her for eighteen months, every moment a déjà vu of life with her father. What she found particularly galling was her realisation that she wasn't really happy in the relationship and hadn't been for many months, a fact that had only finally dawned on her in Mexico when they had been away and she'd had an extended period of solitude with the time to think. She automatically assumed the fault for this was hers, a result of her character. She felt she must be flawed, that something in her make-up and behaviour attracted this type of man and this form of treatment, and Frank's manipulation of her merely endorsed her poor view of herself, further eroding what little self-confidence she had. After all, she was the common denominator. It was she who had ignored the facts and clues and it was she who was now paying a heavy emotional price for burying her head in the sand, for the excuses she had made to justify Frank's behaviour. The week passed slowly without a word from him, despite Jamie calling his number a few times in the couple of days after he had left the apartment. She left messages for him to call her until the call that told her the number no longer existed. She assumed he had changed his phone and adopted a new number, and perhaps a new persona.

On New Year's Eve Cath asked Jamie where she was going to celebrate the midnight moment. Jamie had not said anything at work about what had happened and what Frank had done, largely because of the shame she felt, but she could not lie and so she told Cath the whole story, painful as it was to admit her failings within the relationship. Cath was incensed.

"That's ridiculous," she said. "The guy's a complete asshole, a user and none of that is your fault. It was he who took advantage of a decent person and you didn't give him permission to do that. He chose to, and with that other girl, so you're not alone. I'm not having you spending the night by yourself so come to my place. We're having a bit of a party and you can stay the night as well, as long as you don't mind crashing on a mattress on the floor, or on the couch if no one else is using it. Get to me at about seven and don't dress up. Oh, and don't bring anything. Just yourself, so no bottles or food. There will be plenty of that there already."

"That's so kind. Amazing. Thank you."

"*De nada*. We'll have fun. Don't waste energy thinking about him. As I said he's an asshole and not worth it."

Jamie felt a wave of gratitude and affection for Cath's empathetic generosity and spontaneously stepped forward and hugged her, holding her tight as tears came to her eyes at last. She had held in her emotions and just fed voraciously on her anger, an anger that was exacerbated by being directed not only at Frank, but also at her own part and failings in their story, for which she had to accept some responsibility. After a few moments Cath stepped back and held her at arm's length, her thumbs caressing Jamie's upper arms in a universally recognisable act of comfort.

"You're going to be okay," she said. "It's just going to take a bit of time, first to process what has happened and then to move on from that. It's almost like a bereavement where someone has passed away. You'll get there, just you wait and see. Now it's time to go and close shop for the day because I want to go home. I'll see you later. Make sure you're there or I'll come get you." She smiled and gave Jamie another quick hug before turning to shut down her computer and grab her purse before heading for the door. Jamie dried her eyes on a tissue and then tidied her desk and left the building a short time later.

The party that night was the antidote Jamie needed to lift her from the ennui she had sunk into, drained of energy or inspiration. Cath's place was crowded with the noisy throng of the young celebrating the public holiday and the annual moment of hope for a better world and a better year to come. Drink flowed and plates of lasagne and salad were demolished in an atmosphere heavy with joy and the smoke from numerous spliffs. Jamie still found it odd to see people smoking weed openly without fear of any form of retribution. She had occasionally taken it when she had left home and moved up to London, and then again when Frank had offered it to her, but she was not a habitual user and didn't really want to become one. For this particular evening and moment it seemed appropriate to indulge herself and she happily shared puffs from proffered joints. Midnight came and was celebrated by what appeared to be a group hug-in as people moved from one to another, like bees visiting flowers, hugging and gifting chaste kisses on cheeks. One or two committed couples kissed passionately and gazed into each other's eyes as lovers do, wrapped in their passion for each other as they contemplated their future together in the new year ahead of them.

With the witching hour passed, the party carried on for an hour or so until the weary guests started to say their farewells and drift away into the cold night. It had started to snow again, quite heavily, and Jamie was glad of the offer to stay the night and not have to brave the cold and the elements outside. She also didn't want to be alone, not on this night of all nights, when the lonely feel the intensity of their solitude in the midst of a togetherness from which they feel excluded. She helped Cath and her partner Jenny clear up some of the mess from the party, loading the dishwasher and setting it running before tackling the task of putting seemingly dozens of empty bottles into large plastic sacks ready to be taken down to the bins in the yard at the back of the building in the morning. Once the apartment looked a bit more habitable, Cath pulled some blankets and a pillow out of a cupboard and handed them to Jamie before she and Jenny headed off to their bedroom. Jamie made herself a bed on the couch before going through her nightly bedtime ritual of make-up removal, face washing and teeth brushing, the everyday normalising routines that give our lives a comforting rhythm. Turning off the lights, she lay down under the covers and contemplated the year ahead of her which surely, she whispered to herself, could only be better. Perhaps she should not risk a relationship for a while and just enjoy her freedom. She was young yet and there were many forms of companionship that did not bring with them emotional ties and commitments, the invisible chains that could tether her to someone else's whims and needs, a dock she no longer wished to be moored to. In any event, it felt impossible to her that she could trust any man again, so some time out from the dating scene would mean the removal of a stress in her life.

Sleep finally came, dreamless and deep. It was the smell of fresh coffee that woke her. Rolling onto her back she opened her eyes to see Cath quietly preparing breakfast.

"Hi, good morning," she said.

"What time is it?" Jamie said, rubbing the sleep out of her eyes.

"Nine-thirty," Cath said.

"Oh my goodness, I'm sorry. I overslept."

"Hey, so did we so no problem. Coffee?"

"Yes please, that would be amazing. Thank you."

Cath poured some coffee into two mugs and brought them over to Jamie who had propped herself up against the cushions. She handed one to her and then sat down in an armchair next to the couch.

"What are you doing today?" she said.

Jamie looked out of the window. It was overcast and she could see snow on the trees, their branches moving slowly in a gentle breeze, occasionally shaking off small lumps of snow.

"I've no idea," Jamie said with a small laugh. "I'll go home and do a few chores and then go for a walk probably. I hadn't really thought about it. Everything's a bit upside down at the moment so it's hard to make plans. I'm finding I'm making them with the best of intentions but somehow I'm leaving a trail of them all undone. I seem to be becoming an intentions litterbug. What a mess. Welcome to a spinster's life, but I'm not having a pity party here. It's actually what I want, some time to myself, with no strings, just being free to have fun and not feel I've got to please or think about someone else for a change."

"Jenny and I have talked and we don't think you should be alone today. We're going for a hike over at Larch Mountain so would you like to come with us and hang out for the day? There's a beautiful waterfall there and with this snow it's going to look amazing. We've got spare clothes and hiking boots here you can use and we'll drop you back at your place this afternoon."

"That would be wonderful," Jamie said without hesitation. She flooded with relief at not having to spend the day with only her thoughts for company.

After showers and breakfast, the three of them set off in Cath's car for the drive to Multnomah Falls. Jamie had read about them in a Portland guide book she had bought when browsing through the many floors in Powell's Bookshop in their huge downtown store, but not having a car she had not been able to get out to the falls or the surrounding countryside. She had suggested she and Frank visit it a couple of times but each time he'd said irritably that he'd already seen them and didn't want to again, so she never brought up the subject again for fear of his reaction. She had learned not to cross him or annoy him, and so her focus was always on pleasing him, letting him set their agenda whilst burying her own opinions and wishes if they disagreed with his. Inevitably he had an opinion on every subject, and so Jamie found she would let him start conversations so she could gauge his mood. Once she had read the wind of his state of mind, which was generally unpredictable, she would just agree with everything he said or wanted to do, which was usually always for his benefit. He would only ever agree to do something she wanted if it suited him and didn't inconvenience him.

The hike and the Falls were as beautiful as Cath and Jenny had promised. They followed trails in the Columbia River Gorge that took them through forests heavy with mist. Fallen trees and the branches and trunks of those living were cloaked in vibrant green and thick moss, interspersed with lichen that flourished in the pristine damp air. The snow had not really penetrated the dense canopy above. Jamie spotted the tiny, delicate umbrella of a fungus standing proud of its mossy bed. Fragile and pale blue in the half light, it was almost translucent, its gills under its minuscule canopy showing through, capillaries as thin as a strand of hair. Yet another of Mother Nature's breathtaking creations. The falls themselves dropped more than one hundred and eighty metres as the Multnomah Creek tipped over into the gorge in two consecutive cascades. A bridge across the gorge directly in front of the slim plunge of water gave a front row seat and an uninterrupted view of the veil of water being whipped into mist by powerful updrafts of air from the pool at the base of the drop.

By the time Jamie was dropped off at her apartment she felt exhausted. The combination of the late night and a day of fresh air, with a layer of emotional stress from her discovery of Frank's two timing, had taken its toll. His case was still in the entrance lobby and she assumed he'd not had the courage to come to collect it for fear he might meet her. She would have welcomed a confrontation to vent her anger, and also because she had so many questions that remained unanswered. Being unable to face him and tell him what she felt frustrated her and she knew much of the stress she was feeling must come from that pent up emotion, but she began to realise that perhaps courage was not one of his strong points. After a light supper and glass of wine, she changed into comfortable pyjamas and settled in front of the television to watch a movie. When she woke up later she saw she had missed the whole thing and so she turned the television off and went to bed and slept the sleep of the exhausted.

The rhythm of the working week resumed the next day when Jamie's alarm woke her, the clarion call to a new year of work and life. The habitual gathering of colleagues for a drink on Friday evening was something she had not attended for some time because of the atmosphere it created with Frank afterwards when she got home. He would sit silently watching the television when she got back and would barely acknowledge her, so it just became easier to make her excuses at work that she and he were going out somewhere and she had to get back to get ready. It was such a pleasure to spend time with people who had now become friends and she returned home with the warm feeling of being part of a community at last. She pushed open the door to the entrance lobby and noticed that Frank's case had gone. He must have collected it sometime during the day knowing she would be at work. Jamie opened the post box for her apartment with the new pass code she had put in when Frank had gone, took out a handful of letters and went upstairs. She dropped the letters and junk mail on the kitchen work top, made a smoked salmon salad, poured some wine, kicked off her shoes and dropped onto the couch to enjoy her light meal. With her feet curled comfortably beneath her, she opened her laptop and checked on her emails and messages but could not concentrate on them and so she gave up and turned on the television to watch the late-night news before going to bed.

The morning came cold and overcast with light snow falling in brief flurries, harbingers of the heavy fall to come from the yellow-tinged, pregnant sky. Jamie lay in the warm bed for a while as she resurfaced from her deep sleep and its dreams. A large bird sat on a branch high in the tree that she could see through the window. Feathers fluffed up against the cold, it had a hooked beak and large white spots in two lines down its wing feathers, which were folded on its back. She assumed it was a raptor of some sort resting before a day of hunting. Watching it moving its head around as it surveyed its frozen world, she was glad of the warmth of her apartment. Coffee beckoned so she got up and pulled on a pair of thick socks and a dressing gown before setting the filter running to fill the rooms with the aromatic scent of the start of an American day. Taking her mug and picking up the mail from the counter where she had dropped it the evening before, she sat down on the couch and started flipping through the envelopes, tossing the junk mail in a trash basket by her side. One envelope caught her eye with its large lettered red banner announcing 'Final Demand,' written boldly in capitals across the top. The logo of the North West Pacific Bank through which Frank and Jamie's joint credit card was arranged was in the top left corner. Frowning in puzzlement, she slit the envelope open and pulled out a sheaf of papers which she unfolded on her lap.

In one glance her blood froze as she was overwhelmed with panic. Her heart racing, hands shaking uncontrollably she could not focus on nor understand what she was trying to read. She shut her eyes and took deep breaths, trying to calm herself and still her palpitations, telling herself it couldn't be true despite the words on the pages that were fluttering in her quivering hands. Slowly calming down from the peak of her panic, she began to read the letter and other papers in full. Addressed to her alone it advised her the bank was on the point of appointing a debt collection agency to seize her possessions unless the outstanding debt on the card was repaid in full, and immediately, by which they meant within seven days. Turning to a statement of account the bank had enclosed she saw the outstanding debt was $24,654. The shocks came in legions, overwhelming her senses, leaving her feeling faint, her ears buzzing and accentuating the beat of her racing heart. The account was in her name alone and was not a joint account. The only payments that had ever been made had been the minimum required by the credit card company each month, the very payments she had been making. From what she could see Frank had paid nothing, and even the small monthly payments she had been sending to his bank account had not been paid over for the last four months. In the last month a payment for over $8,000 had pushed the card over its credit limit of $15,000. The bank appeared to be a bit upset about this, as was Jamie. She felt used, abused and foolish as the harsh light of reality and understanding shone on the truth that lay on her lap. It appeared from what she was looking at that she had funded their entire relationship. The rent on her apartment, their trip to Mexico, every grocery and utility bill, every restaurant or café meal. Had she paid for meals and jaunts with other women? Jo perhaps? She felt completely lost, alone and adrift with no foundation to which to anchor herself. The whole relationship, if that was what it could be called, was a fantasy. Who on earth was the real Frank? Jo called him Johnny but was she anywhere nearer the truth about him than Jamie? Were there others similarly duped, either now or in the past?

Jamie felt the need to get out of the apartment and just do something, so she quickly dressed, went out into the cold morning and walked between piles of heaped snow along cleared sidewalks, letting her mind wander over the past eighteen months. Little things she remembered turned from hardly observed moments into clues. She had never been to his house or where he lived before he moved in with her. In retrospect, that was odd and how long did it really take to refurbish a house? He appeared to have no real friends, only a small handful of acquaintances. How many people go through life without forging some bonds and connections? She suddenly remembered the red sports car on the second time they had gone out, when they went to the beach on Sauvie Island. It must surely just have been borrowed for that weekend to impress her, with a lie to the salesman that he was intending buying it. She had seen it on that Monday morning as she rode past the showroom in the bus, but she had then forgotten about it, or just chosen to ignore it, and he had never appeared in it again. She had told herself there were so many innocent reasons as to why that car was there in that sales lot that morning. His near obsession with meeting what he termed the important people at her exhibitions, the monied and influential, was now worrying. What were those private deals and negotiations really about? Was he duping them too?

As for the bank debt she now had, she had never seen any correspondence from the bank or the credit card company and now she understood why Frank had always been home from work before her. He must have censored the mail, removing any envelopes from the bank before she could see them. She remembered she had asked him why the card only had her name on it and he had explained her question away by saying something about that was their practice and her name had been the first on the application form and so they had followed with that onto the card itself. He also said they did that because they wouldn't be able to fit both their names on it. He said to her he had generally kept the card rather than giving it to her because it was he who was paying for what they spent on it above her very small contribution, and therefore quite naturally that gave him a degree of control over its use. She only ever had it when she went to Whole Foods or Fred Meyer to do their grocery shopping, always having to give it back to him when she got home.

"We'll only pay for our joint expenses with it," he'd said. "If you use your personal card for your personal expenditure, I'll do the same with mine." Now it was obvious it must have doubled up as his personal card too.

That had seemed logical and fair to Jamie and so she readily agreed to the arrangement. Frank had a quick answer and reason for everything, and every one of them had seemed quite plausible at the time, but Jamie could still not come to terms with her guilt at not having worked it out as being a strange and very one-sided relationship. Had she really been that desperate for companionship that she was prepared to accept everything and ignore the obvious facts in front of her, no matter how illogical? Was she that fearful of risking the relationship she thought she had found? Was she really that frightened of being alone, of becoming a member of the diaspora of spinsters-in-waiting spread throughout the world, that she should allow herself to be subjugated to someone else's every whim and opinion? She had so many unanswered questions, her mind was spinning and it was in that concentrated thought process that she stepped out into the road in front of a car she hadn't seen.

The driver stamped on the brakes and the car stopped a couple of feet from her in a blast of angry horn and flashing lights. Jamie jumped back and mouthed an apology to a shocked and angry driver who gesticulated at her as he drove on past her.

"What was I thinking?" she muttered to herself as she turned back on the sidewalk and walked off the adrenaline that had poured into her bloodstream, leaving her tremulous and shaking, slightly nauseous and tired. The enormity of the debt she was now clearly solely responsible for, despite not having created the majority of it, was overwhelming, as was the sense of unfairness. She had no idea where to turn for help, or what to do. Obviously contacting the bank on Monday would be a good place to start but before then she wondered whether Jo had been similarly duped. Taking her phone from her pocket, she dialled her number.

"Hi," Jo said, picking up immediately.

Jamie went through the motions of the habitual greetings we all use as our preamble to our main conversations, whether those greetings are sincere or not, and then she cut to the chase.

"I'm calling because I've just had a bit of a shock. I got a letter from a bank saying I owe them a lot of money on a joint credit card Frank opened with them. It seems he arranged it so he's no part of it and it's all in my name."

"You too?" Jo said. "I got a letter like that a couple of days ago and I'm still in shock. I should have called you about it but I'm really not thinking straight at the moment. I seem to owe them about seven grand. I don't have that kind of money and I just don't know what to do."

"North West Pacific Bank?" Jamie said.

"That's the one," Jo replied, and Jamie could hear her start to cry softly, hearing and feeling her palpable and very real desperation and fear. "Johnny said we should open a joint credit card to cover joint bills but he said I'd only ever have to pay the minimum monthly amount. Oh god, what am I going to do?"

"Me too," Jamie said. "That's exactly what he said to me. Look, let's meet up and talk. Want to join me for a coffee this morning?"

"That would be amazing," Jo said. "If you don't mind that is. I feel so alone with this."

They arranged to meet in half an hour at a café Jo knew, so Jamie summoned an Uber to make her way there. The ride gave her time to gather her thoughts and to reflect on how she had got to this point, when everything seemed to be going right. But had it? She must have known in her heart that her relationship with Frank was hardly normal, but she had ignored her instincts, so perhaps she was the one to blame for the mess she was now in.

Jo was already at the coffee shop when Jamie arrived, sitting on a low, comfortable couch with a glass of water on the table in front of her. Her eyes were red from crying and she was biting her bottom lip whilst twisting and untwisting a strand of her loose hair around a finger. She smiled when she saw Jamie and half stood to greet her before collapsing back down.

"Coffee?" Jamie said, pointing at the glass of water.

"Yeah, Americano please," Jo said.

When Jamie returned with the coffees she put them on the table and sat down on the sofa next to Jo, close enough so they could talk quietly without their conversation being overheard. She instinctively reached out and put her hand on Jo's, which were clutched together in her lap. As they talked, it quickly became apparent to Jamie that they were dealing with a pattern of behaviour, a parasitic modus operandi that stole a lifestyle out of other people. It was also clear to both of them that they had no idea who Frank actually was. Where did he work, or did he even work? How could they get to the truth of who he was?

"I can't believe we are the only ones," Jamie said. "I bet he's done this before. I think he's a serial user and I think we should go to the police. What he's done is stealing, surely?"

"But that makes it public if we do that," Jo said. "It's so embarrassing. I'm ashamed. What am I going to say to people? Oh God, and then my parents."

"Yeah, I understand but we are both broke now, big time. I was ashamed too but now I'm just plain angry and I'm not going to sit here and let the little bastard get away with it. Not without trying to do something, anyway."

Jamie and Jo met at the downtown police station after work on the following Monday where they each told their story. Whilst sympathetic the detective said there was little they could do without evidence since neither of them really knew Frank's true identity. The police needed more and he asked them to go away and think carefully about what they could gather, a paper trail that might lead to him. After parting outside the station, Jamie had gone back to the apartment and spent the evening going through what little she could find, but everything came back to her. Frank had clearly been careful to avoid leaving anything that might connect him to her so there was nothing of him in the apartment now she had got rid of his possessions. Brushing her teeth before going to bed, she noticed the end of the handle of Frank's small hairbrush sticking out from behind some of her make-up bottles on the shelf above the sink. She must have missed it when she had thrown all his things into his case, but now she wondered if it might be useful to the police. If neither she or Jo knew who he was, perhaps the police might if they could match up his fingerprints or his DNA. It was possible the police had a record of him from his past. She went to the kitchen and pulled a couple of sandwich bags from a roll in the kitchen drawer and, putting her hand inside one of them, picked up the brush and dropped it into the other which she then sealed shut. She had never touched the hairbrush so the only fingerprints that could be on it would be Frank's, or Jo's if she had used it on one of the occasions she had been at the apartment. She rang Jo to ask and she confirmed that she had never used it so it would only have his identity on it. On her way in to the Museum the next morning, Jamie took a detour to the police station and dropped the bag off with Detective Benson.

"Thanks, that's great," he said. I'll get it to forensics and I'll call you if we get a match. If you don't hear from me you'll know we don't have anything on him."

Jamie's phone rang that evening as she was washing up her supper things.

"Hi, is that Jamie?"

"Yes. Detective Benson?"

"Yeah. Look, just a call to say good news, we have a match from the hairbrush. It appears your Frank, or Johnny or whatever he's calling himself at the moment, is actually James Wright and he has history. He was born in Miami in 1985 so he's about thirty-two. His parents were on Welfare for years but there are no police records of them, apart from comments in his files with Social Services who were involved with the family because of some of his behaviour when he was at High School. The notes show that they were good parents but seemed to have a delinquent for a son. He has a long history of fraud, even as a juvenile when he conned the parents of school friends out of money. He did a bit of time in a juvenile institution but then disappeared for a while, turning up in Phoenix under the alias Chris Peterson. He ran a scam there for a few months, befriending elderly people. He would appear on their doorsteps and offer to do chores for them. You know, tending their yards, going to the stores and doing shopping for them. Stuff like that. In time he'd win their trust and would offer to help do their bills and banking for them. These were usually elderly people who had no understanding of how to use technology and so they were grateful when someone offered to help them with it. They treated him like a son and he milked them. He eventually got caught and was prosecuted and did three years in a penitentiary there, but then disappeared again when he got out on parole. He next turned up in San Diego and was again caught scamming old people, but also pulling the same stunt as he did on you two. He was indicted but then skipped bail before trial. The bail had been put up by one of the elderly people he knew who he had not yet defrauded. He must have gone to them for help somehow. They just could not believe someone as nice and kind as him could be guilty of anything. They're a bit poorer now. There's a warrant out for his arrest and bail bond agents are looking for him but so far he's stayed under the radar. Do you have any idea where he might be?"

At their first meeting Detective Benson had said there was not much chance of a prosecution without more evidence. The bank's statements and letters to both of them could not be linked with Frank, and there was no evidence they had been coerced into opening their accounts with the bank. They had both willingly, it seemed, signed the application forms. Detective Benson had said they needed more. It seemed they now had it and surely a case could be built from that?.

"No idea at all I'm afraid," Jamie said. "Neither of us ever went to where he lived and he never told me the address of his house. If he has one. We either met in cafés or restaurants or at our own apartments. He told me his house was uninhabitable because he was having huge renovations and building works done on it and so he suggested that he should move into my place. I assume he went to Jo's on a part-time basis when he had told me he was away on business, or visiting his parents in San Francisco. He said they were very wealthy but old and infirm so I never met them."

"Okay, well I see from his case notes here that both his parents died a few years ago. He has an older sister who still lives in Florida and we'll check with her whether she's heard from him, but from the notes we have she seems to have disowned him so I doubt she has. We're on to it and have put out a national alert for him. I assume he was never violent to you?"

"No, never, and I think Jo would say the same. He was just difficult if he didn't get his own way. I'm sure she would have told me if he had been to her."

"Do you know where he works or what he did for a living?"

"No, I have no idea," Jamie said. "He told me he had skills in technology that meant he worked for the Government on secret projects and could not discuss them with me or tell me any more. I assumed he worked for the Secret Service or FBI or something like that. You know, the CIA perhaps. I didn't question it any further because I just accepted I wasn't allowed to know."

"Well, I can assure you he doesn't work for the Government," Detective Benson said with a small laugh, "although the Government would love him come and stay for a while. There's a room with his name on it."

"So, in the meantime, what do we do about these credit card debts?"

"Pay them quickly, I'd say. Do a deal, or lawyer up. I ain't a lawyer but I don't think the credit card Company will care about your guy or what he did to you. They won't see that as their problem. I should think as far as they're concerned, you signed the papers, you own the debt. As I just said, I think I'd start with trying to do a deal. Close the account and then get an extended time for paying it off. Make sure you destroy the card so it can't be used again, or block it if you don't have it. It's probably blocked anyway. Closing the account should do that for you for certain. Sorry, but I can't see it any other way. And don't expect this Wright guy to have any money to give you when we catch him. I've seen this sort of grifter before and I can tell you, they spend it as they get it and never have any of their own. They use yours until you run out and then move on to the next mark, or sucker as they think of you. I'm sorry to say it straight like this. It's always someone else's money they use, never theirs. They don't care if they are going to get caught, and some delude themselves by assuming they never will be. They don't worry about what might happen and just want to have it all today. You hooked up with a bad one here I'm afraid and if you ever get the chance to speak to him I think you'll find his only interest in you was what he could get out of you financially. Any affection he showed you will have been an act to keep you on the hook until you were no use to him anymore. He will have forgotten you now and is probably already grooming his next hit."

Jamie hung up, put the phone down on the couch next to her and buried her face in her hands, the tears coming at last, tears of frustration and anger as she faced her ruination and downfall. Her dreams were in shreds, just so much detritus in her garden of hope.

Picking up her phone again, she did the only thing she could think of and sent a text message to Charles in England.

'Are you awake yet? Can you call me when you are? It doesn't matter what time it is.'

She was not expecting a reply and went over to make some camomile tea before going to bed. As she waited for the kettle to boil, her phone shrilled its FaceTime call. Rushing back to the couch she jumped onto it and picked up the phone to see who was calling. Relief flooded her when she saw it was Charles and his smiling face appeared on the small screen.

"Hi Jamie, so good to see you."

"Oh god, I'm so pleased to see you. I hope I didn't wake you."

"No, not at all. I've got the day off today but the early morning habit doesn't stop so I was up and reading a book. Are you okay? You look as though you've been crying. What's up?"

It poured out of her in a seemingly endless stream, the whole sorry saga. Despite her embarrassment at having been so taken in, the more she talked the easier it flowed. The therapeutic balm of the confessional calmed her, as though her admitting all would transfer the problem to someone else, for them to mend and hand back all fixed. We each carry our own backpack of problems about with us, that little burden of worries that sits on our back. They come with us wherever we go and for some it is a mission in life to find someone to give the backpack to so they carry the burden for them for a while, or better still, solve its contents of problems and make them go away.

"I'm terrified I'm going to be made bankrupt and deported or something. Sent back. I'm not ready to do that. I love it here and am not finished with it and now it feels as though it's all over, already."

"Wow, I'm so sorry," Charles said when she finally stopped talking, exhausted. "So how much is outstanding on this credit card?"

"Over twenty thousand dollars," she said.

Charles smiled. "How much over twenty thousand? What's the exact figure?"

"It's $24,654," she said, picking up the letter from the bank and reading out the figure that glared at her off the page. "That was a few days ago so there may be a bit of interest. I'm going to call them in the morning and see if they can give me extra time to pay it off, you know, a fixed monthly amount. D'you think they'll buy that? I want to close the account as well of course."

"Well," Charles said, "banks are not exactly known for being big hearted so I doubt it, and even if they did, their interest rates are horrendous, particularly on defaults so I doubt any monthly payments you could afford would work as I think the debt will just keep mounting. So, I think that would just delay the issue, and you'll have it hanging over your head the whole time. So, here's what we're going to do. I'll transfer you the money today and you just pay the whole thing off in one hit. No deals, no begging at the bank and no more tears. Okay?"

"No way!" Jamie said. "That's not why I called and I can't take your money. That just transfers the debt from one place to another. It doesn't solve the problem. I only called to talk it through with you. There's no one else I can talk to like this."

"Look, here's the thing," Charles said with a smile. "I'm pretty well paid by the bank and last year was a bumper year for me so they were a little pleased and my bonus reflected that. Seven figures and it hit the bank just after Christmas so I won't even notice this. I want to do this for you."

"I don't know what to say," Jamie said. "I know, we can call it a loan and I'll pay it off over a couple of years."

"Well, here's the rub, I can pretty much predict I shall get the same again at the end of this year. I have a couple of huge deals going on, major international takeovers that are going to happen in the next twelve months and they're pretty much in the bag because the takeovers are not hostile and so they're uncontested. They're going to happen. When I say I won't even notice it, I really won't and this is the least I can do for you. I know how important being over there is for you and I don't want you to lose that. I still feel bad I didn't help you at uni so this will go some way towards making up for that for me. It's probably not entirely altruistic because it will make me feel better and will give me a lot of pleasure. Send me your bank details now and I'll do the transfer right away. This book's at a boring stage so this will give me something better to do this morning."

Jamie started crying again, crying with relief and with an overwhelming sense of being loved. This is what it feels like to be loved she thought, that thing I have been chasing all these years.

"Don't cry," Charles said. "It's going to be okay and I want you to promise me you'll always come to me if you're in trouble. Will you do that for me?"

Jamie nodded her head, unable to speak through her tears and choked throat, afraid anything she said would just come out as a squeak.

"Let me know when it arrives," Charles said. "I'll do it as a dollar transfer to save you trouble at your end. It will probably take three or four days to get to you."

Jamie started to cry softly again. "Thank you," she whispered. "Thank you, thank you. I don't know what else to say."

"There's nothing to say. It's a pleasure and I'm just happy I can help you. Just get a good night's sleep and let's talk in a couple of days. Try to forget him. He's not worth the energy and you're only hurting yourself by being angry with him. Sleep well. Love you."

"Love you too," Jamie replied with a small wave of her hand.

Ending the call, Jamie sat back into the sofa, emotionally exhausted but not quite ready to go to bed. Reaching for the remote she turned on the television and chose a travel programme about some once-upon-a-time minor celebrity everyone had probably forgotten who was making a last-ditch attempt at resurrecting his career. It was like watching a drowning man grabbing at a floating twig as the presenter was filmed walking and talking his way around some of the Greek islands. It was just wallpaper and background to her thoughts as she retraced the steps she had taken since she had first arrived in the country.

# CHAPTER 5

# JACK, DECEMBER 2020

"Are you okay? You seem a bit down this morning."

"Yeah," Jamie said. "I'm okay. Just sick of this Covid virus and not having a normal life, but then everyone's feeling that I should think. We're all in the same boat, not that it helps how we each feel I suppose. I should just feel lucky neither of us has caught it."

I first met Jamie early last year. It all started with a meal. So why am I telling you her story? I suppose it's to show how our behaviour and how we treat people has consequences, some lifelong. Acts that to us are neutral and innocent can nourish a soul, or cause untold damage. When we become parents there are no guidelines or lessons from which to learn how to bring up our children, other than our very personal experiences and memories of our own childhood. Unconsciously we pour our faults and our own dreams and ambitions into our children, and we do that with every act and word. From that children build a perception and a picture of their self, their self-worth, their place in society and the world they inhabit when they become adults, so the impact on them is lifelong. We influence the relationships they will go on to have, long delayed unintended consequences that affect who they might choose as temporary or life partners and ultimately how they might repeat our mistakes and successes with their own children, or how they might choose to bring them up a different way. We tell ourselves we won't make the same mistakes our parents made, blind to the fact we'll just make different ones. We just have to hope our children will forgive us. Our potential to wreak havoc and damage through our unique version of nurturing is a force that is hidden from our own eyes. We cannot see the impact and affect we are having on young lives and minds that have no choice but to be in our complete control. Jamie's experiences and outcome shows how some like her are damaged by their past, but ultimately can recover. Or do they ever? We have to pass a test to drive a car and yet we can take charge of the most precious thing, a helpless life utterly dependant on us, and the only test we must pass is the successful completion of a sexual act.

"Hi Jack, how are you doing?" Cath said when I answered her call. "I haven't seen you for ages, not since you guys split. Are you okay?"

"Yeah, I'm fine," I said. "Well, kind of. I'm sorry I haven't been in touch. I've been hiding away a bit I suppose. You know, licking wounds and all that since Isla left. It's not terminal, just bruising and I need to be a big boy and deal with it. Somehow it's just been easier to hunker down, but I'm not sure that's helping much."

"It never does, although I can understand doing it. I did the same once when I got the big dump. I felt like I was a piece of trash that had been thrown out. So, we need to change that. Are you free on Saturday evening? I'm having a few friends around for dinner and it would be great if you could be there."

"Yes, I'd like that, thank you. It would be great to see you both. It seems forever since I last went out so it's good to have something to put in the calendar."

My girlfriend and I had agreed to go our separate ways a couple of months before and since then I had been going through a bit of a self-imposed hermit period, hiding away from the world, tending my emotional wounds in a prolonged self-indulgent wallow of pity. No matter that we had both agreed quite amicably it was the right thing to do, falling back into the unaccustomed single life again after so long together was painful and I was having difficulty adapting to it. I think that may have become part of our problem in that our lives together had become too comfortable, too much of a habit, too formulaic perhaps. There was nothing new in it to break the routine of waking up, doing a job, coming home and falling exhausted into bed to sleep. Do all couples morph from the heady days of passion and the adventure of discovery about each other, to then slide into a contented companionship, one that somehow becomes devoid of novelty and excitement? Is it impossible to sustain the passion and the excitement, or do all partnerships just osmotically and irresistibly seep into a quasi-sibling relationship, unnoticed while we fall asleep on the job of maintaining that intoxicating exhilaration? Is that how we slowly drift into a state of just taking each other for granted? It is part of the human condition to want more, to want a new high, a bigger hit from any addiction, whether that be physical with drugs and alcohol, from our emotions where love and desire are potent narcotics, or for more material wealth. These are all drugs that we chase ever upwards for more and more, always seeking higher hits each time. Like all highs, there's a natural limit, an unbreachable ceiling that all stimulant takers must reach, and once there, we addicts often plateau. It's just too much effort to strive for more, and so complacency sets in, and perhaps taking each other for granted is a lazy way out of the effort of keeping a relationship alive, the vegetative state that requires little energy. The realities of running a life together set in, with divisions of labours, shopping lists and chores to be shared, the mundanity of real life rather than the romanticised version that disappears shortly after the honeymoon. The mystery fades as we learn all there is to know about each other, with no surprises left to be discovered. Perhaps that's the primary function of having children. We are tempted into creating them when we need something new in our partnerships, something we can focus on together. Little do we know that the tiny something new we gaily bring into our relationship is going to overwhelm and dominate our every moment for the rest of our lives, leaving no room for that foolish romantic stuff. It's the alluring call of the sirens of our genetic lineage and legacy that draws us onto the rocks of exhaustion and responsibility.

After Isla left I sensed I had lost a part of me and consequently felt somehow diminished as a person. I had got used to her in my life, of going places with her, the sound of her in our apartment. When we went to parties or gatherings, there was a comfort in knowing she was there, even if not by my side. Our eyes would meet across a crowded room and we'd smile a smile only we would understand, that inner, private world lovers inhabit together that excludes everyone else. Gradually, towards the end of our journey together, my eyes would find her in that crowd and I realised she was no longer looking for me. Her eyes were elsewhere. She was growing independent of me and I couldn't seem to find a way to fix that, to draw her back to me. When Cath's call came it was the spur I needed to pull myself out of my self-imposed lethargy and introspection, that self-indulgent place I knew I had retreated to so I could really wallow in self-pity. I arrived at the dinner to find there were about ten of us around Cath and Jenny's long dining table, and Jamie was one of that group. She sat at the far end from me and although we chatted briefly before and after we sat down to eat, our meeting was not particularly memorable to me. I wasn't looking for a new relationship and, whilst she was attractive with her large soft eyes that I noticed were devoid of noticeable make-up, she was not particularly welcoming. Indeed, she seemed aloof and distant, cool without quite being bored or rude. I remember she was slim and feminine with a room-brightening smile if she chose to use it, but our conversation didn't scratch any surfaces and after we had all left, I forgot about her.

Towards the end of the evening, as we all sat around the destruction that was the surface of the table, a breaker's yard of cutlery where dirty dishes jostled for space with fast emptying wine bottles, Cath stood up and tapped her glass with her fork.

"Okay guys, there was a motive in getting you all here together tonight. Jenny and I have a little announcement to make. We're getting married, and we want you all to be there, so you need to clear your calendars for a Saturday a couple of months from now. We've got invites for each of you here to take home with you, so you all have to block out that weekend as soon as you get back tonight. We really want you all to be there for us. It's going to be out on the beach at Manzanita so you're all going to have to get your shit together and get accommodation sorted before it all goes. No excuses taken by us."

We all clapped and cheered, raised glasses and drank toasts to shouts of "About time," "We've been waiting," and "What took you so long?" Cath and Jenny had been exemplars of how to build a lasting relationship and their friends had whispered shared thoughts about their making it permanent since single sex marriages had been legalised in Oregon six years ago. Now it was to happen and there was a tangible sense of goodwill towards them both that evening.

On the morning of their wedding the sun rose clear and bright into a blue sky dotted with puffball clouds. I got up early and left my Airbnb to go down onto the beach for a barefooted dawn walk on the sand, paddling in the sea. Very few people were up at that hour, and those who had braved the early morning were mostly walking dogs. The small town itself was still asleep with nothing yet open so I came back down the road, past the golf course close by on its outskirts. A couple of Mule deer were calmly grazing on the fairway by the road. They glanced up and watched me warily as I carried on walking past them and then, presumably assessing I was no threat, put their heads down and carried on doing the green-keepers' job for them. We were to gather for the wedding ceremony on the beach near the town at mid-day which gave me time to shower and get back for a late brunch in a beachside café. I sat at a table on the sidewalk, reading the newspaper over a couple of cups of coffee after my meal before making my way down to the beach. Early arrivals to the wedding party were congregating and talking in small clusters. I knew many of the guests and walked from group to group, catching up on news of their lives before taking a seat in the middle of the rows set out in front of the small flower bedecked gazebo on the sand. The far-off water line of the outgoing tide was fringed with white surf where the small waves broke on the beach, giving an idyllic backdrop to our view of the happy couple when they arrived hand in hand in front of the wedding officiator.

The humanist ceremony was simple and heartfelt, the central couple oblivious of the breast cancer that was to ravage Jenny's body and mind and take her away from us all, still hidden in her future, out of our sight in that part of our journey none of us can see or predict. What different life choices might we all make if we had the gift of foresight, but then where would the adventure and excitement be without the thrill or shock of discovery? We applauded the newly married couple and threw rose petals over them as they made their way back to the town through their guests.

An al fresco lunch had been arranged in a small hotel on a hill on the outskirts of the town. As we gathered in the gardens near the tables that were laid out beneath the trees, I spotted Jamie walking uncertainly across the lawn towards the collection of guests who were gathered in small groups, all intent on their conversations with well-known acquaintances. Closed ranks of friends are the shy outsider's worst nightmare at any party, that impenetrable boma of backs. How to break into a group if you don't have the self-confidence to fake it? I could see from Jamie's expression that she was uncomfortable and feeling very out of place. Her hair was partially tied back and she wore a delicate garland of little white flowers in it. Small earrings hung from her ears, dancing their syncopated steps with each stride she took. The light material of her floral dress billowed and flowed around her slender legs, accentuating their outline and her delicate femininity. She moved between the groups, coming to a stop in front of a low balustrade where she stood gazing out to the sea, her arms folded and holding a glass of champagne. I excused myself from the people I was standing with and made my way over to her.

"Hi," I said. "Great view, uh?" Tree tops lay beneath us, a carpet of green that flowed down the hill towards the sparkling blue ocean in the distance. Sunshine reflected off the water and the white yachts and fishing boats glistened as they bobbed about on its surface.

"Yes, it is," she replied quietly, in a neutral tone that shouted out that I was stating the obvious and needed to up my game if I was going to get her attention.

"Pretty obvious, I suppose," I said sheepishly.

"Certainly is," she said with a small smile, still looking out at the sea.

We stood next to each other silently as conversation stalled in an awkward vacuum of my embarrassment. She didn't seem open to the idea of trying again so I nodded and walked back to talk to more friends until we were called to sit down for lunch. I joined the hunting party as everyone wandered between the tables in search of their place, peering across chairs and tables until each found the small card with their name on it denoting their designated seat. As others began arriving at their prandial roosts on our table, I stood chatting to a woman on my left who turned out to be Jenny's aunt, who clearly doted on her niece. She was retired and lived in the sunshine of Florida so didn't get many opportunities to see Jenny. Engrossed as I was in our conversation, it wasn't until I pulled my chair back to sit down that I noticed my lunch companion to my right was Jamie, who was already seated.

"Well, I bet you feel the lucky one," I said to her. She raised a quizzical eyebrow. "Sitting next to me after our long chat over there," I added with a grin and a nod towards the balcony. "I'm Jack and we met at Cath and Jenny's a couple of months ago. When they announced their engagement?" I realised I was babbling to fill the vacuum of her silence as she gazed at me with her big eyes, her hands folded at rest in her lap.

"I had a puppy like you when I was young," she said. "All bouncy and chaotic. Jamie." She held out a hand and we shook as she smiled.

"So you do speak," I said. "That's going to liven up lunch no end."

"Yes, when I have something to say," she replied.

We were like duelling fencers, thrusting and parrying whilst not trying to give anything away, any opening or insight into our bruised souls. Not that I knew Jamie's was so damaged at that first meeting. That was all to follow as for those first moments together we each danced around the detail and hurt buried in our histories.

"So Jamie, tell me about yourself. I assume you're from Britain?"

"Is it that obvious?" Jamie said. "Yes, I arrived here about eighteen months ago. I applied for a job at the Portland Art Museum when I graduated from university in London, and luckily I got it and have been working there ever since."

"Big move. Did you leave family behind, parents?"

"I don't really have parents, just a brother," she said.

This seemed to me to be a very strange way to answer my question but I decided to let her cryptic reply lie unchallenged. Instinct told me now was not a good time to ask for an explanation or elaboration.

"So what about you?" she said. "Where does Jack come from? Were you born here, in Portland?"

"No, like you I'm an immigrant," I said. "I was born and grew up in Asheville. That's in North Carolina. It was a job move for me too. I'm in IT and there were a few start-ups here that didn't want to do the San Francisco or Silicone Valley thing. Instead many have opted for or moved here where rentals and costs are lower, and a better way of life too. Not so crowded out and not quite so hot given how the California climate seems to be changing and heating up. Those forest fires down there are something else. Also, there are too many people in California now. Mind you, it's getting hotter here too and we're also now getting the fires. I joined a company here about four years ago and then two years later set up my own consultancy business which is what I do now."

"I've not been to San Francisco yet," Jamie said, "but from what I've heard I'm glad to be in Oregon. I'm loving it here now, although it took a bit of time to settle in, with one or two hiccups along the way, but I suppose that's inevitable in a new place. I'm fine now and getting out and about a bit more, seeing the countryside, meeting a few people. I love it here at the beach, and it's so close to the city. So easy to get to. I'll definitely come back."

And so the to and fro of inquisition and discovery started and continued. In the weeks that followed the wedding I had occasional twinges of shame that I had paid no attention to Jenny's aunt, but I was so engrossed in my conversation with Jamie, the time over lunch either stood still or accelerated. I have no idea which it was because suddenly it was over and the party started to break up as people left for the journey back to the city or for an evening in the town for those staying the night by the beach. I was staying over until the next day but wasn't sure what Jamie's plans were and didn't want her to infer the wrong message if I asked. Whilst we had chatted amicably enough, and scratched a tiny bit off the surface of our respective lives, there was still a reserve about her, a distance she obviously wished to maintain that made me feel the slightest indication of the wrong kind of interest in her would put her to flight. She would run for cover, it was obvious. I assumed there was a love of her life somewhere in the background, a boyfriend who had not been able to make it, and she was giving off the 'I'm attached and happy' aura, crafted to keep predators at bay. Eventually I decided I had nothing to lose and Jamie could think what she liked because it wasn't going to affect me or change anything, so I came out with the million-dollar question.

"Are you staying over? What are you doing tonight?"

Jamie said nothing, just stood perfectly still looking at me, weighing up her answer before delivering it.

"Yes, I'm staying the night and I have no plans for tonight. I'm just going to stay in. I have a great book on the go at the moment."

A door slammed in my face, or a lonely cry? I had no idea so, throwing caution to the wind again, I jumped in with both feet.

"A bunch of us are meeting for drinks and a meal this evening so if you want to join us you're more than welcome. It has to be a better option than a Saturday night alone in a room, surely? And there's no agenda from me. It just seems a shame to be alone when there's no need."

Jamie shrugged her shoulders almost indifferently. "Okay," she said. "Why not. Where are we meeting and what time?"

"Are you okay with Thai food?"

"Yes, love it," Jamie said.

"Great, we're meeting at The Mighty Thai. It's on Manzanita Avenue, you can't miss it. Six o'clock."

"Okay, I'll be there. Thanks," Jamie said before turning away to say farewell to Cath and Jenny who were posing for a few photographs with friends. I watched her leave the gardens and wondered at what was behind her slight coolness. Why the brittle carapace around herself? She was cautiously and defensively friendly, but there were no invitations to step closer. She had answered my questions, but only superficially, skimming the surface of her history when it became personal, but expanding and informative about neutral subjects such as art and her job. I asked myself what it was that had piqued my interest in someone who seemed to wish to remain so private, so aloof and distant, but I had no answer other than the clichés of men loving the thrill of the chase and wanting the unattainable. Perhaps it was that very detached coolness that presented the irresistible challenge. In truth, looking back, I know I wasn't so much on the hunt or chase, or wanting the unattainable as just intrigued by her for some reason I still cannot comprehend. I know I wasn't ready for another relationship then. My bruises were too deep at that time, and if I had attempted any superficial dating or relationship I think I would have just been playing a game of comparison between a date and Isla, and I didn't want to be doing that. Therein lay disappointment and it wouldn't have been fair. It didn't occur to me I might find an improvement on Isla but I suppose the dating game often doesn't come with logic. I think my interest was nothing more than that, just old-fashioned interest. Some platonic conversation and feminine companionship for the afternoon and evening with no particular agenda or objective in mind.

I remember I purposely did not sit next to Jamie at the large table the gathering used for that evening meal. I arrived at the restaurant before she did and, once again seeing her slightly lost expression as she came through the door, I felt a bit responsible for her being there having invited her, so I walked over and greeted her, bought her a drink and introduced her to some friends before drifting off to catch up with others I had not seen for a few months. At the end of the evening, as we all milled around in the choreography of our hugging and kissing farewells, I found myself next to Jamie again. One of the benefits of alcohol lies in its role as an antidote to inhibitions and its ability to instil courage, and so I smiled at her and leant forward to kiss her on the cheek.

"Had a good time? Better than a book?"

"Yes, it was fun. Thank you for thinking of me. It was kind of you."

"No problem. It was great you were here and I'm glad it worked out for you. Have you got your phone on you?"

"Yes," she said, hesitantly and suddenly a little brittle.

"Okay, take my number and if you want to meet up and have a drink or whatever, you know, just hang out, you can call me. No pressure, it's up to you but it would be fun to see you again. You're an enigma."

"An enigma?" Jamie said as she copied my cell number into her contacts on her phone. "How d'you mean?"

"Well, I think if I explained you'd no longer be, so I'll leave you to think and guess. See you around and I'm glad you made it tonight. Better than alone in that room back there I hope?"

"Yes, it was," she said with a slight frown and a small wave with her hand as she turned to say her own farewell to Cath and Jenny.

Three or four weeks passed and I forgot about Jamie. Business was booming for us and I was immersed in work and clients' needs. I got on with my reinvigorated life, which included a bit of light hearted dating and dinners that eased me back into the social scene without committing me to anything. Strangely, since the wedding party, thoughts of Isla rarely came into my head, and if they did they didn't tear at my heart as they had done. I began to accept she would be with someone else. It was inevitable and she was perfectly within her rights to be with whoever she liked. We no longer had obligations to each other and had lost that intense intimacy, those private conversations in each other's arms in bed, the exchanged glances at dinner parties, the encrypted messages no outsider could interpret. The difference now was the loss of those shared moments and emotions no longer hurt. The past is the past and I realised what I had been feeling recently was an irrational jealousy of whatever relationship I imagined she was now having with another person. And I had been telling myself I was in some form of mourning. All those intimacies and secrets we once shared belonged to someone else now, and my torturing myself about that was futile. How could I be jealous of what I could not have, and indeed had agreed not to have? Would I really want to be back with her? No, definitely not, so my faux jealousy could be no more than hurt pride. The illogicality of that made me smile to myself and was perhaps the kick I needed to shake off my immediate past, a past I could not change or influence.

The contact from Jamie came through a text message from her.

*'Hi, Jamie here. Don't know if you remember me from the wedding. There's a country music gig early evening on Saturday at Topaz Farm on Sauvie Island. Beer, Tacos, Music. Want to go? Quite understand if not.'*

I waited an hour or so before replying, not wishing to be seen as either over-eager or just plain desperate. Secretly I was delighted to hear from her. Jamie had an allure about her and she was someone I wanted to spend time with.

*'That would be great. Meet you there or do you want me to pick you up?'*

She said she'd like to be picked up and gave me her address and a time, so I met her at her apartment and we drove out to the farm where we joined Cath and Jenny who Jamie had obviously asked to come too. Perhaps she felt the need for safety in numbers but for my part I didn't mind since I was just happy to be there in the warm early evening with bands playing away people's cares. Adults and children danced unselfconsciously on the grass in front of a trailer that had been converted into a small stage. Cath and Jenny had brought rugs and I went and bought us all beers and tacos at the bars set up in some of the barns. One had animals in pens in it for children to pet and feed. Nearby, large, enclosed and low roofed sheds had long trailers outside them with thousands of small plant pots with green plants growing in them. Intrigued I walked over to get a closer look to discover each was a young marijuana plant. On the assumption each would generate a tax charge when finally sold, the State was nurturing its own fortune in those sheds Was it too cynical to think the Governor had legitimised cannabis for the simple reason the tax revenue stream was irresistible and the change of legalisation probably had nothing to do with an altruistic liberalism?

Over the following weeks, Jamie and I would regularly meet for dinner in the evenings, trying out the many different restaurants and their very varied and international cuisines. We fell into an easy pattern of casual platonic dates, often hiking for a couple of hours at the weekend. Generally I collected her from her apartment and dropped her off there after we had eaten or been out for the day. Occasionally we just met in a bar for a drink and companionship. It was on those evening dates that I noticed she drank quite a lot more than I did, though she never seemed to lose control or appear to be drunk or incapable. I always walked her to the front door of her apartment block, said good night with a chaste kiss on the cheek and left. I began to think our friendship would always remain just that, almost a sibling relationship. I became resigned to that because I enjoyed her company and our many conversations. For the time being our friendship was special to me, and too important for me to want to jeopardise. There were no restrictions about not dating other people, but for some reason I had no desire to do that. It is part of the human condition to look for signals, a primitive mating intuition that some transgress or are blind to, but I instinctively felt Jamie would have baulked at any physical advance. I suppose this was my own response and interpretation from her giving no signals at all that she might be attracted to me. There were no messages semaphoring that my wanting more would be welcomed.

The first hint of a thaw happened one Sunday morning. Both being at a loose end that day, we arranged to meet at the regular Sunday Market in the centre of the city. I arrived at the open-air café that was our meeting point and was sitting sipping a coffee when I saw her walking under the trees towards me, smiling. We had brunch and then got up to wander around the stalls. Falling into step beside each other, Jamie nonchalantly slipped her hand into mine without any fuss or ceremony, as though it was the most natural thing for us to do. She didn't acknowledge it with a smile or a glance, but just continued to walk with me, perusing the varied wares and foods on sale in the many pop-up stalls, chatting about what we were looking at.

"Shall we get a few things for lunch?" she said. "We can have it back at mine."

"Yeah, why not, that would be great," I said. "Those cheeses look amazing and the stall over there sells quiches and stuff like that."

"Perfect," she said. "I've got salad and can put something together for us. I'll get some salami and cold meats as well."

And that is how I found myself spending the afternoon in Jamie's bed. At that time I had no idea whether she had planned it or whether it was just how the cards fell that day, but I do know it came from her, not from me, and I didn't want to break the spell by asking her. We had a bottle of wine between us with our meal, or rather I had a glass in anticipation of driving home and Jamie had the rest. Rain set in and so rather than going for a hike as we would normally have done, after our light meal we retreated to the couch together armed with coffees and had put a movie on the TV when Jamie leant over and put her head on my shoulder. It felt so normal, as did the rest of the afternoon and evening. We talked late into the dark and this time with depth to our conversation, exhuming subjects that lurked beneath the skin. It's strange how obligations seemed to stem from us having moved our friendship into the physical realm, where we somehow acquired a moral imperative and obligation of complete honesty to each other. I told her about Isla and how we had agreed to part, and that it had taken some time for me to get over our separation. Jamie told me about Frank, his controlling and ultimately devious ways, the shock of discovering how she had been duped and the financial debt she had been left with and how she had been saved by her brother's generosity. Her explanation of her relationship with Frank and her subordination to his every whim explained to me for the first time her coolness for so long after we first knew each other. Of course at that opening of ourselves to each other I didn't know the rest of her story, and for that afternoon I thought Frank alone explained her detachment and her fierce independence, her insistence that she was the sole arbiter and decision maker about every aspect of her life, from the clothes and make-up she wore to the friends she chose to have and insisted on continuing to see. I had never argued the point with her and was more than happy to give her the freedom she seemed to want. It suited me that she was independent as it allowed me to focus on work without any sense of guilt. I also remembered my wise grandmother's comment to me when I first started dating.

"Jack, I have grey hair for a reason, and that's called experience. Now you're seeing girls I want you to remember, the tighter the rein the faster the horse bolts. You cannot hold a girl in a cage. You have to trust. Now and again, that trust is going to be broken and you might get hurt, but that doesn't make it right to take control of their lives."

Her astute words had always stayed with me and so I had no problem with Jamie's assertive control of herself and her life. I could quite understand why she was like that, especially as she didn't know the real me as we lived through those weeks of trust building all couples have to go through in the heady days of discovery. That hard won, but so easily lost, thread of trust that binds any partnership is the glue that holds a couple together. Trust takes time to build, layer upon layer like an onion, but it can take a mere second to destroy. We really have to know someone to trust them, and that too takes time.

Jamie's abiding emotion after she had discovered the truth about Frank was anger, tinged with humiliation, but not the pain of loss as I had felt it. I'm not sure whose reaction was the healthier, but as our time together over the following weeks and months passed and I learned about her father's attitude to her, about his complete lack of any feelings for her, I came to feel her anger at Frank was a mask for her real rage and hurt, which was more directed at her father. I didn't feel this was something she could admit to herself because we are supposed to love our parents, aren't we? Frank was the scapegoat for that destructive resentment, albeit a deserving one.

"Have you ever asked yourself how you came to be with Frank?" I asked her. "Could you not see a similar pattern of behaviour developing?"

"Yes and no," Jamie said. "Looking back and facing the facts, I know I saw them but I ignored what was in front of me, the red flags waving frantically at me. Like my feelings about my father, I was sure I could make Frank love me for what and who I am. Even now I know a part of me thinks my father and I could still put a connection together, a true attachment, and I so want that. It's hard for me to give up hope for that."

"Have you ever wondered whether his lack of affection and attention is what makes you keep your distance from people? Emotionally I mean. Even with me, after the time we've spent together. It's as though you daren't let anyone in or get too close to you. At times I have thought you'd got over it but then it happens again. You never seem to notice what you're doing or how it might come across. I'm not trying to criticise or feel sorry for myself, just saying how it comes across. It's part of you and I accept that because the rest of you outweighs that for me."

"No, I haven't thought that. I didn't even know I was doing it, but I suppose you're right and I'm really sorry. I find it really difficult to trust anyone. I mean if the one person you should be able to trust without question constantly lets you down or rejects you, what hope have you with other people? I just assume everyone's going to let me down, the only question is when they're going to do that, so it's just much easier not to get too close or involved. That way I can't get hurt."

"So do you think I'll do that? Let you down somehow?"

"Well, no and yes. I don't know. I can't be sure. The answer is no when we are talking and together like this, but up until now it was yes, and I imagine tomorrow in the cold light of day a little part of me will think that. I can't help it. It's just the way I am."

"I suppose it's a form of protection. Easy for me to say it makes no sense and we all have to trust people, but I haven't had to go through what you've had to put up with. I know Isla and I broke up but that wasn't either of us letting the other down. We had just drifted apart I suppose, and so it would probably have been inevitable and means we weren't meant for each other long term. There was no breach of trust by either of us."

"Just be patient with me. I like being with you and I don't want to lose that, but it's going to take me time to get used to this and to trust someone else, especially after Frank."

"Well, I hope I've shown so far I'm not a Frank."

"Nor was he when we started out. That's the problem. So often what you see at first isn't what you get later. He was quite the opposite when I first met him, but once he moved in here he changed and I think the real person came out. The user."

At that stage Jamie hadn't told me about what she had done to get herself through university. That came later, after she received the email that shook the foundations of her world. We had continued to take our relationship slowly as I didn't want to put pressure on her by making demands of her time. There was no hurry and I was still at the stage of feeling it was fun but wouldn't be the end of my world if it finished. I was probably fooling myself to protect my own feelings should Jamie suddenly decide she'd had enough and needed to break free before I did that to her. I had stayed over at her apartment one Saturday in the early fall last year. Getting up in the morning while Jamie dozed that delicious half-sleep that we can indulge ourselves with on the weekend, I had put some coffee on to drip for us and then went out to an artisanal bakery a couple of blocks away. I bought a couple of freshly baked croissants for our breakfast and some still warm crusty bread for later in the day. I strolled back to the sounds of the fading dawn chorus as the birds finished marking their territories with their song before flying off to get on with their foraging for the day. Letting myself into the apartment quietly in case Jamie had fallen asleep again, I kicked off my shoes by the door and breathed in the delicious scent of coffee signalling that the essential ingredient of every morning was ready. I put my head around the bedroom door to check whether Jamie was awake. She was sitting up in the bed, her laptop open on her knees, tears streaming down her ashen face.

"Hey, hey, what's wrong? What's happened?"

Jamie said nothing as she started sobbing again, burying her face in her hands. She turned the computer around on her knees so it's screen faced me, and I sat on the bed to see what she was looking at. It was an email from her brother, Charles.

*"Hi Jamie. I'm emailing you because it's the middle of the night for you. We can speak later. I'm afraid I have to tell you Dad has cancer. It's not too good.*

*Pancreatic cancer apparently and he's not in good shape. Give me a call when you get this. It doesn't matter what time. C X"*

I climbed up onto the bed next to Jamie and held her in my arms as she leaned her head on my chest.

"I'm so sorry. That's really tough for you. You'd better call him when you feel okay to. I'll get you some coffee."

When I returned with our mugs Jamie had recovered. Still sitting up in bed, her eyes and cheeks wet, she had her head turned and was gazing out of the window at the turning leaves on the trees. Spots of rain dotted the glass. She turned to look at me with a wan smile.

"You okay?" I said.

"Yes, sort of. It's complicated."

"I'm sure it is," I said. "It must leave you feeling a bit mixed up. Torn?"

"It's so much more than that," Jamie said. "How many times in the past few years have I hated him. I've frustrated myself to destruction about not being able to give up hope. I wish I could but I never seem to be able to. Over and over I just continue to hope that he'll change, that he'll notice me. I've hated myself for not having the sense to just give up hoping and I've hated him for what he did to me and made me do. I'm so tired of hating but I don't know how to stop."

"Made to do? What d'you mean?"

Jamie turned to look at me, her eyes sad and fearful. She bit her bottom lip and her eyes welled up again.

"I need to tell you something. I'm just afraid to. Please promise me you'll hear me through and not run away. Please. Just do that for me?"

179

"It can't be that bad. Why would I run away?"

"Promise?"

"Okay, of course. I'll not run away."

Jamie turned to look out of the window again. I gently took her chin and turned her back round to face me.

"Go ahead," I said.

"I've told you what a cold bastard my father was to me. He never wanted a daughter, only sons. He treats my mum like shit but she supports him and agrees with him on everything. She always took his side and never stood up for me. The other person I should have been able to trust was never there for me. When I got my offer into university I was so excited but, because in his opinion I wasn't going to do a proper degree like law or economics or something like that, he said he wasn't going to pay anything towards my three years there. That was it, I was on my own as far as he was concerned. Effectively disowned. Well, that's how I felt. He paid for Charles of course when he went. I think he thought that by refusing to help me he would bring me to heel and I'd change my course and pick a subject that he wanted me to do, one he wouldn't be embarrassed about down at the Golf Club. I think for the first time in my life, something inside me dared me to say no and to defy him. I stuck with my choice and went to do History of Art in London. To pay for it I borrowed as much student loan as I could, and also took a job waitressing in a restaurant in the evenings and at the weekends. But what I made was never enough and because of the amount of work and reading I had to do for my course, I couldn't justify more hours than I was already doing. The bills and debts just kept mounting, especially because London is so expensive, and I could hardly feed myself. Thank God the restaurant gave me a meal each shift, but I knew if things carried on as they were I would have to drop out and go and get a full-time job. I've no idea what I would have been able to do if I had left my course."

Jamie turned away again and chewed on a hangnail.

"So what did you do?" I asked gently. "I mean, you finished your degree and graduated, yes?"

"Yes, I did," she said. "This is the hard bit, the bit that frightens me and haunts me." She fell silent again.

"Just say it. I promised I wouldn't run away. I meant it."

"Okay," she said before taking a deep breath. "I met a guy who said I'd make a lot of money as a model and an escort in the evenings, so that's what I started doing. You know, dinner with businessmen, keeping them company in the evenings when they were travelling with their work and staying in London. That gave me a bit more than I was getting as a waitress but not much and so, well, you know, I did more. And it wasn't modelling." Jamie turned and looked at me, her hand over her mouth.

"More? You mean you had sex with some of these men?"

"Yes," she said, breaking down and sobbing again, pulling away from me. We fell silent as I took in the enormity of what she had just done in speaking of her past, the courage it must have taken to make such an awful admission, the risk she had just taken.

"Well, I don't think it's something either of us wants to crack a bottle of champagne over but I assume none of those men meant anything to you?"

"They disgusted me. Sad perverts who had to buy it because I assume they weren't satisfied with what they were getting at home. Or maybe they were too much of a bunch of complete losers to be offered it. And who's fault was that? No, I hated every single one of them, and not just because of the sex, but because of them using women like me as they did. I still do. It's worse because I found out my father was one of them when I went to a hotel room for a job and found it was him in there who had booked me. I used a different name for that part of my life so he had no idea it was me, and I was only given his room number. I'm so sorry, I should have told you before but I was scared you'd walk away, and anyway, I've been trying to forget about it all. I've never told anyone else, apart from my brother. If you want to go, I'd understand."

"Jamie, it's okay. There's a big difference between sex and love. Love is about all the intimacies, feelings and desire. What you did was just an act and anyway, it's in the past. Neither of us can undo that. Who am I to judge you and judge what you felt you had no option about doing? I've never been in your position. There weren't too many middle-aged women looking for a good time in Asheville, and anyway, there was no need because my parents helped me through college. I was very lucky."

"You're just saying all that now. I've only just told you this. Once you've had time to think about it you'll change and be disgusted."

"Jamie, you were a victim, but not of your choosing. We are here, now, and it's only the now we can deal with, and the future we can plan for. If you hate your past so much why not go back and change it, undo all that happened?"

"Because I bloody well can't, that's why," Jamie said forcefully. "God what wouldn't I give to be able to do that."

"Exactly, that's correct. You can't change it so what's the point thinking about it? By doing so you're now choosing to continue being a victim, and that's very different from being forced into being one."

"God, my bloody father. It's all his fault. Do you wonder why he makes me so angry, why I hate him?"

"Are you angry with him right now?"

"Yes, I am."

"Do you think he knows you're feeling that right now?"

Jamie thought for a few seconds. "No, of course he doesn't," she said.

"That's my point Jamie. I'll bet he has no idea you're feeling this anger right now, in this moment. He doesn't know how it's affecting you and dominating your life, and he never has done any time you have felt it. The only person who does is you, so the only person being hurt by it is you. He certainly isn't being. And you've chosen that because only you can choose to be angry. You could choose not to be. You can choose not to think badly of what happened. The thoughts and memories will of course come but you can choose to ignore them, or just accept them as part of a past that isn't happening now. It's gone and can only exist in your mind with your permission."

"That's easy for you to say, but it's hard to do that."

"I never said it would be easy, but being hard is not the same as being impossible. If you don't change how you think about it, only you will suffer the consequences and be damaged by that. No one else will, and definitely not your father. As you just agreed, he has no idea what you're thinking. It's your choice. All your thoughts and how you think about them are your choice. All this anger and resentment is yours and you're the one nurturing it and feeding it. Not him. Anyway, more importantly, shouldn't you call your brother now?"

'Yes, you're right," Jamie said. She pulled the computer back onto her lap and dialled Charles up on FaceTime as I went back into the kitchen.

"Hi," Jamie said when he answered. "I've just read your email. It was a bit of a shock."

"I know, I'm sorry, it must have been." Charles said. "Are you okay? I'm sorry to tell you by email but I wanted to let you know as quickly as possible and I thought writing to you before talking to you would give you time to catch your breath and think about it."

"Yes, I'm okay although it hit me harder than I would ever have expected, considering everything that happened. Somehow it mattered and I'm not sure why. What about you? You're living it there with Mum. Are you coping? Do you want help? I can come over if you want."

"No, I'm fine although it's not easy. Mum's terrified about the future and is just lost so she's struggling."

"Poor Mum, I can imagine. He's run her life for so long the real her has gone. That person disappeared long ago. How did all this come out?"

"Well, he'd not been well for a few weeks. He'd lost a lot of weight quite quickly, had stomach pains and had been feeling nauseous and very tired. At first they thought he might have developed diabetes but when he started to go a bit yellow, attention turned to his liver. The medical team were suspicious and investigated further, which is when the first mention of the pancreas happened. The diagnosis was then quite quick, as was the prognosis. His cancer started in the pancreas and then spread and is stage four. It's in his liver, hence the tumours there. A scan showed it's gone to his lungs as well. His doctor was also concerned he might develop blood clots, especially in his legs. It seems the cancer is inoperable as it has spread too far and so chemotherapy and radiation are the only options for him, but only to prolong life for a while. The outlook's not good and he has been given an estimate of no more than six months to live."

Charles stopped speaking, almost as if to draw breath. The room fell silent as I came back in with more coffee. Jamie patted the bed next to her and I sat on it by her.

"This is Jack," she said, turning the computer towards me so I appeared on the screen. I could tell Charles was Jamie's brother immediately. Their shared genetic history was obvious to see. I moved closer to Jamie so he could see us both in the same shot. "I showed him your email so he knows about Dad."

"Hi Jack, good to sort of meet you. So, are you two an item?" He grinned as he asked the question.

Jamie and I looked at each other and smiled together.

"I don't think we've discussed that, or formalised it yet," I said. "We're just having fun and going day by day. Hey, I'm sorry to hear about your dad. I'm no medic so I have no idea what's involved for him. It doesn't sound too good though, from what you've just said that is."

"Well, you're right, it's not good I'm afraid," Charles said. "They've said six months but looking at the way he's been declining I don't think it will be that long. He's wondering whether there's any point in going through chemo and all that treatment if it's not going to make any difference to the outcome. If he does choose to have it he might just make the six months apparently, but if he doesn't, he'll go a lot sooner. Jamie, if you want to see him you should get over here soon."

"I'm not sure I want to see him," Jamie said. "I'm not sure there's any point. Has he said he wants to see me?"

"No, not yet," Charles said. "Do you want me to ask him?"

"There you go, says it all doesn't it. Even now he's not remotely interested in me so why should I bother? And no, don't ask him. It has to come from him, not because he thinks I asked him for that."

"Okay, I won't," Charles said. "I've got to go. I said I'd help Mum sort out some papers and…"

"How is she?" Jamie said, interrupting him. "I know you just said she was terrified when she got the news, but is she holding up?"

"She's okay, sort of. She's taken it quite hard and I think she's more frightened about herself and the prospect of being alone. As you just said, Dad's done everything all her life so I think she feels pretty helpless. Anyway, I'll keep an eye on her so I'll keep you posted on what's happening. Let me know what you decide about coming over or not, but don't leave it long if you decide to come. I'm not sure how much time he has."

Charles disappeared off the screen and Jamie closed the laptop and put it to one side.

"I'm going to have a shower and get changed," she said, "and then let's go for a walk. I need some fresh air to clear my head."

While Jamie went through her morning rituals in the bathroom, I cleared up the kitchen and tidied away the wine glasses and empty bottle we had left out the night before. As I worked my way through the apartment doing a superficial clean, I wondered how I would feel if I had been given the same news about either of my parents. I knew I'd want to go to see them as soon as possible, but my relationship with my parents was very different to Jamie's with hers. Whereas her upbringing was founded on the quicksand of mistrust and abandonment, mine was built on the bedrock of trusting love and affection, and bottomless support and encouragement. For the first time I truly appreciated how lucky I am with what I have and have had when compared to what some people have and think is normal.

When Jamie came out of the bathroom, I made some scrambled eggs and bacon to go into our croissants. We ate our breakfast together before I showered and shaved and then we set off in the car to Mount Tabor Park where we climbed to the top of Mount Tabor. We found an empty bench and sat on it to take in the view of the city. Mount Hood stood proud in the distance, it's white sloped beauty masking the volcanic urges and dangers beneath it. As we sat in silence, hands entwined, I wondered whether it would follow its sister Mount St Helens one day with its own self-destructive, cataclysmic eruption. Our conversation had been neutral on our walk, with our looming companion the elephant in the room of the morning's news silently shadowing us. I decided to leave it that way to allow Jamie time to process the enormity of what she'd been told. Of course, the elephant's bulk cannot be ignored and ultimately has to be confronted and I decided I would bring up the subject when we sat down for lunch.

"Do you want to have lunch at Ya Hala? Have you been there before?" I asked.

"No, never heard of it," Jamie said.

"It's a Lebanese place. Great food. I love Middle Eastern and this one's a particularly good one. It's not too far from here."

"Okay," Jamie said distractedly. "Sounds good." She appeared listless and devoid of interest in the world about her.

We made our way down off the top of the mountain on a different trail to the one we had used going up, passing families enjoying the weekend. On the lower-level paths, young children rode their little bikes or scooters, some bedecked with trailing ribbons and

Disney themed bells. Others had small baskets with a favourite soft toy peering in terror over the top of the rim. The children's oversized helmets made them look like thumb tacks on wheels. Weaving and wobbling through the strolling walkers, there were occasional coming together moments, bruised shins and expletives, followed by the inevitable tears as small people were picked up off the ground to be held close, or chided by those who subscribed to a less sympathetic way of bringing up their children. Two ways of parenting, contrasting approaches with contrasting outcomes. Parenting has consequences, mostly unintended because so much of it is reactive and has its genesis in how we ourselves were brought up, the only lesson and benchmark we have to measure our actions against. We learn to perceive ourselves through the prism of an adult's eyes when we are in our formative years, and those influences surface in our adult forms as we go out into the world and interact with it through our work and friendships. Jamie had her own unique perception of herself, which flowed into and fed her voracious low self-esteem that constantly sought endorsement of her lack of worth. Her belief was that she must be deserving of her father's disdain for her. To her it was her fault. This was reinforced by Frank's treatment of her, which to her mind was clearly brought on by her own actions, or by something that lay within her character. I could see the longer term effect on her in her difficulty with letting her feelings go, and also in her inability to trust. Then, and even now, she often maintains that physical and emotional distance I sensed when we first met. It is still there in our relationship today, whatever that relationship may be. Our actions have outcomes and unintended consequences beyond our control, no matter that we were the origin of those resultant behaviours.

Reaching the restaurant we took a table outside on the sidewalk.

The earlier grey clouds had lifted and the dying year's wan and weakening afternoon sunlight bathed us as we looked through the menu and made our choices. With Jamie semi-trapped with me, I took the bull by the horns and addressed the unsaid that had lain between us since leaving the apartment.

"So, when are you going to see your dad?"

"I'm not," Jamie said. "Why should I? What's the point? Why should I go all that way just to be ignored and humiliated again? He's not going to change, not now, and I sure as hell don't want to look as though I'm begging, letting him think he's won." Defensive and on the edge of aggressively angry, she was building a wall of callousness and indifference she could hide behind, and which would provide her with the self-justification she would need to support her decision.

"So where does that get you?"

"Well, for a start it gets me not having to see him. I've been fine with not having him for a couple of years now, so nothing changes for me."

"Good point," I said. "Nothing changes and you stay stuck where you are, over here hiding from the issue over there, not facing it or dealing with it. Letting it chew you up all the time, dominating your life and the person you are becoming. You don't see that in yourself, but I do. Perhaps you're just frightened of facing him, rather than angry with him. I'm sure you're that as well but this is more than that."

"I'm not scared of him," Jamie said indignantly, her face reddening with anger. "I just don't want to see him, not after what he did to me for all those years. You weren't there and didn't see it so you can't make judgements about how I feel or what I say about him. And then, as if that wasn't enough, when I found him in that hotel bedroom, that was the last straw. I can't get that picture or moment out of my mind. It was a complete nightmare. It wasn't you who found him or had to put up with what he did, so really easy for you to say go back, forgive and forget, make it up. He lied to us all for so many years, all my life in fact. He wore a virtuous badge so large you couldn't see him behind it. That's actually what he bloody well did, hid behind a facade of uprightness. He's a complete fake."

"Jamie, Jamie, I'm on your team here. I'm not the enemy. I do understand you have every right to feel as you do but I just don't want you to live with regrets. You're angry because I'm forcing you to face an unpleasant issue and decision. Why not go and tell him what you feel? A chance to lay the ghost and get some closure on this for yourself. My concern is for you, not him. I'm worried that if you don't go and face him, it will haunt you all your life, as it does now. Even after all this time, as you talk about it, it still seems so raw to you. I don't think you've moved on at all if that's why you came here. Remind me again, why did you leave Britain and come here?"

"To get away and start again I suppose. To get away from him and the memories, leave it all behind."

"Well, clearly none of that happened, did it? It's just geography with the same issues in a different place. Perhaps you were running away from yourself rather than from him but you can't run away from a shadow. It follows you. Have you thought about that? I think if you don't go back this will always haunt you. You obviously haven't left the memories behind which tells me nothing has changed. You wouldn't be feeling or reacting like this if you had. If you want a future without this ghost on your shoulder you need to face it. The only way of doing that is to have it out with him, deal with it and then move on and leave it all behind. If you don't you're going to carry on as you are, hiding behind drinking too much, injuring yourself and pushing people away when you feel they are getting too close. One day you're going to look around and find there's no one there. No friends, no family. They will all give up and stop trying."

Jamie was leaning forward listening intently, resting her chin in one hand and looking fixedly at me across the table. Her look would have been inscrutable if it were not for the nascent tears floating in each eye, bow waves of emotion, wet drops hanging pendulously on her lower eyelids, ready to cascade onto her cheeks. Perhaps I had said too much and been too harsh, but it seemed to me if not now, when would be a good time for some tough love, a few home truths. I had not planned what I had said and could only guess a combination of the moment and pent-up frustration at her inability or unwillingness to seek help and move on had opened a hidden floodgate within me.

"What do you feel about him, about your memories of him and growing up with him?"

"Disappointed," Jamie said, almost without hesitation. "So many little things come back to me. Moments I had forgotten or perhaps not noticed at the time. I remember I was going to a school dance, what you'd call a prom here I suppose, except in our case they were importing boys from a nearby boys' school. It was a big deal, the first big dance I went to. We were in our last year at school and we had come back a week early for Christmas so I was at home. I had a long dress, my first, and I was upstairs and had got dressed and ready. As I came down the stairs he was standing in the hall at the bottom. He looked up at me as I slowly came down and I got this really uncomfortable feeling he was undressing me with his eyes. I immediately felt that was impossible, it was my crazy thinking and of course he wouldn't be doing that. Now I'm not so sure, and that hurts."

"Then you need to tell him that. From what Charles said, you may not have too much time to do this and if you don't, that hurt will never go away. Only you can cure this and lay this ghost. No one else can do that for you."

"I suppose you're right," she said. "I suppose if I don't go I'll be running away forever, but I admit, seeing him terrifies me. Will you come with me? I don't think I can do this by myself." She reached across the table and took my hand, holding tight in supplication. It was unlike her to make a first move like that, which emphasised the need and fear in her was significant enough for her to go against her natural instincts.

"Well, I wasn't expecting that," I said. "Yeah, why not. I've never been to Britain so okay, let's do it."

"God, thank you, thank you," Jamie said, burying her face in her hands again.

"Call Charles in the morning and tell him you're coming. If nothing else he'll feel he's not facing this at home alone. And you'll need to tell your Mum too."

Jamie flinched and shook her head and sat back in her seat defiantly.

"You don't talk about her, do you? Why's that?"

"Because she stood by him, especially when she found out it was him in that hotel room. It was all my fault as far as she was concerned and she seemed to blame me."

"Isn't that what wives and husbands are supposed to do? Stand by each other."

"Not at the cost of their children, no. She was always like that. I've told you, she always took his side against me, never stood up for me. She just allowed him to bully me. He had all the power. I was the helpless one as a child. She was the adult and she should have protected me so no, I don't feel the need to talk about her, or even to her. She abandoned me and I can't forgive that."

"But again, if you don't find a way to forgive her, only you will suffer. Like him, she doesn't know you feel that, although I suppose she can guess it. I say again, she doesn't know we're having this conversation about her now. Only you know that and as with your dad, only you are paying the price for your anger with her. Like with him, you need to talk to her about how you feel. You need to hear her side of the story too. Why she was like that? You need to ask her directly. What's her side of the story in all of this? Perhaps she felt she had no option for some reason. Self-preservation? You need to hear that reason to make some sense of all this and to be fair to her. Another reason for going back now and using this as an opportunity to reset your thinking and your future happiness. It's your last chance. Hate is corrosive and it will drip into your mind, not theirs. Perhaps this is the one positive to come out of your dad's cancer and this is your opportunity to grab that. You have to go back and face this."

"I know, you're right. I'm just terrified to do it. Please come with me."

"Okay, I've said I would and I will, but on one condition. When we get back, you need to go and see someone. I think you need to get some help. Some therapy. I can't do that for you or help you in that way. I'm not qualified. You need someone who's independent and objective and who's trained to deal with this sort of stuff. All I've got is my own experiences and instinct, and that's just not enough. For all I know I could make it worse for you."

"We'll see how I am when we get back. I'll probably be fine by then," Jamie said.

"That's just kicking the can down the road," I said. "I reckon without help you'll get back and still be drinking too much, self-harming as you are now and not really dealing with it, and not dealing with the causes of why you are doing these things to yourself. They're not normal. So no, it's not a case of you seeing how it is when you get back. You contact someone now and fix some dates for when you get back. Get them in the calendar before you go."

"I don't know," Jamie said. "It's such an American thing to have a therapist. It almost seems there's something wrong with you if you don't have one. Perhaps I should get a therapist to help me work out why I don't want a therapist." Jamie smiled for the first time in our conversation.

"Nope, the deal is I go with you if there's a date fixed in your diary before we get on the plane. It's non-negotiable because I don't want to see you doing all these things to yourself if we are to stay together. It's not right and it can only get worse. I think you'll agree your drinking and self-harming habits are not normal and a clue to there being something wrong. I don't want that for my future if it's going to be with you."

"Okay, okay, I agree," Jamie said with a smile of resignation, holding up the palms of her hands towards me. "Thank you," she said. "I suppose I should have done all this long ago."

Our order arrived, pricking the private bubble we had immersed ourselves in, oblivious of the bustle of the passing traffic and people walking past us outside our insular moment. Jamie needed no more persuasion to make the journey to facing her past and our conversation quickly reduced in intensity, moving to the logistics of making the trip. There were calls to be made, a visa application for me to be organised, holiday to be booked at work although Jamie felt she might be able to take a couple of weeks as compassionate leave. The Museum had a very paternalistic, family-oriented employment policy and her contract allowed some leeway in times of need. For me it was less of a problem. Having my own business I could take whatever time I wanted and my partners could cover for me. In any event, I had holiday time due and I could do a lot of my work remotely so it wouldn't be a particularly big deal for me.

"I can always fly back earlier if you feel the need to stay on there for a while."

"Aren't you afraid that once I'm there I might not want to come back here?" she said.

"Yes, of course, but that doesn't change anything. If that's your decision then we were never meant to be. Anyway, I would never want to hold you against your will. I'd feel I had a trapped animal in a cage. That's not a relationship, that's being a zookeeper. You need to be with me because you want to, not because I'm holding on to you. Yes, it's a leap of faith for me, and yes, I'd rather you came back, but that's going to be your decision and I'll respect whatever you decide to do."

"I don't think I'll be staying there," Jamie said with a smile. "I love it here and feel very safe and settled."

# CHAPTER 6

## OXFORD, JUNE 2019

Thankfully, the Delta flight out of Portland was a direct flight and we didn't have to route through Seattle or any other intermediate airport. We got to the airport early and I sat on a seat near our gate while Jamie went off to look at the very few shops on the concourse and to get us each a coffee. Next to where I was sitting, the children's play area with its small slides and colourful obstacles to climb resounded to the laughter of half a dozen noisy children letting off steam. Their apprehensive looking parents watched over them, I assume each dreading ten hours in a tube with little wrecking balls, probably wishing they had chosen a celibate life. One little toddler managed to escape out on to the main concourse without his parents noticing. He set off at speed, his diaper filled trousers waggling behind him as he duck-waddled off for the far horizon where we had just come through the security gates. I was on the point of going to retrieve him when both parents appeared from the play area like demented frogs in a blender, arms gesticulating, shouting his name and frantically looking everywhere. I prayed they weren't going to be sitting anywhere near us on the flight, that visceral terror every bachelor feels before boarding as he eyes up stressed families in any Departures Lounge. I think any male would say all children should be heavily sedated before boarding, but I don't think that's a kite that's ever going to fly.

Jamie returned with our coffees and sat down next to me.

"How are you feeling?" I said.

"A bit nervous," she said. "I have no idea what I'm facing, what it's going to be like when I see them. Thank goodness Charles is picking us up from the airport."

"Well, they can't kill you, and what's more, this time will pass. It will be the initial meeting that's going to be awkward. It's inevitable. How long is it since you had any contact with them? You can't expect to just stroll in and pick up from where you left off. Once that first time is out of the way it will get easier and anyway, Charles and I will be there to help you so you won't be completely alone. If you think about it, you have absolutely nothing to lose."

"I know, and thank you for coming with me. I really don't think I'd be getting on the plane if you weren't here. I'd be running for the exit by now. I'm going to try to get lost in a couple of movies on the flight to stop me thinking."

"I downloaded some good ones onto my tablet so we can watch them together."

They called our flight and the next part of our incremental journey started as we stood up and joined the line waiting to show boarding cards and Passports at the desk. The flight was nearly full but fortunately we seemed to have lucked out with a child free area in the back section. I breathed a sigh of relief as the doors were closed and the pre-flight announcements started, guaranteeing that last moment passenger from hell didn't appear, laden with overfilled carry-on bags and two feral semi-housetrained children as they made a beeline for the empty seats in the row behind us, passing terrified passengers already in their seats and willing them to just keep on walking. Like all uneventful flights, time passed slowly through the night until the landing routine started with the hurried snack an hour and a half out of Heathrow Airport. The tedium of the long hours of entrapment in uncomfortable seats were history and now I wondered where the hours had gone. Two movies, an indifferent meal crammed onto a small tray and some snatched moments of sleep ate up the time until the plane entered its final descent path from the east, bringing us in over London. Jamie gave me her window seat and leant across me as we shared the view out of the window down onto the city below us. She pointed out some of the landmarks to the right of the plane as I marvelled at the random arrangement of buildings and streets. The city was so in contrast with our geometric layout back home, with our well-defined blocks and grids of streets. I was looking out at an aerial view of a very different heritage and older history.

Immigration and baggage collection are the same the world over, to be endured and negotiated patiently. We met again in the baggage hall after Jamie and I separated for me to go through the aliens' entry point. At the Immigration desk I was politely asked the standard questions about the purpose and length of my stay by the ubiquitously bland Customs Officer who showed no emotion and hardly looked at me. Are they trained to be like that or is it they see so many people in any one day they become indifferent to us all, relegating us to being just another piece of baggage to be processed and passed on down the line to the Arrivals Hall? She did manage to welcome me to Britain as she handed back my Passport whilst looking over my shoulder at the next passenger to be processed, waving them to step forward.

Charles was standing behind the crowd of people hanging over the barriers. He spotted us as soon as we came through the automatic doors into the hall and waved at us so we could find him in the sea of eager or anxious faces. We weaved our way between couples and families hugging each other, the sound of greetings in a myriad of languages in our ears. The world has shrunk and become cosmopolitan, and nowhere is more evidence of the global village it has become than the Arrivals Hall of an international airport. Charles and Jamie hugged for a long time before he was able to release himself and shake my hand.

"Hi, welcome," he said. "How was the flight?" He took our trolley and pointed down the hall. "We're this way." He started to walk through the crowds with Jamie next to him so I fell in behind them and followed.

Once we were in the car and not negotiating crowds, ticket machines and Charles trying to remember where he had left his car, conversation became easier. I sat in the back seat with our hand luggage on the seat next to me and gazed out of the window whilst trying to ignore the fact we were on the wrong side of the road and everything was back to front having lost eight hours of my life in a new time zone.

"So, how are they?" Jamie said.

"They're sort of okay, except Mum's struggling with the fact Dad has decided not to have chemo or any other treatment. He's agreed to palliative treatment if it's necessary, but he doesn't see the point in putting up with all the side effects of chemo and radiotherapy when all it will give him is a few more extremely unpleasant weeks. He says he'd rather just get on with it. He made the decision yesterday and so I thought I'd wait until now to tell you in person rather than have you thinking about it on the flight."

"He can do what he likes," Jamie said without feeling, but speaking volumes of the tension within her. I leant forward and put a hand on her shoulder. She put her hand on mine and turned and smiled at me, her face softening. "I'm okay," she said, "just not looking forward to this. Thanks."

We chatted about neutral subjects for the rest of the journey, and now and again Charles or Jamie would point out landmarks to me as we passed by them on the freeway. Passing Oxford we took an exit onto narrow country lanes until we came to an old village, the kind that sends we Americans into ecstasy over their quaintness and eccentricity. The beautiful stone the buildings were made of glowed softly in the summer sunshine. Back home we have so little of any age, we are immediately attracted to these very old buildings that shouldn't by right be still standing. How can anything be that old and still functioning and upright?

"We're nearly there," Charles said over his shoulder.

"Wow, this is beautiful. Is this where your parents live?"

"Yes," Charles said, "We're on the edge of the Cotswolds here. The house is just the other side of the village. It was the old Rectory, where the vicar used to live, but the Church sold off all their big Rectories, in the fifties and sixties I think it was. They then housed vicars in smaller, more modern houses, probably to save money, but also because I don't think they felt it was appropriate for vicars to be living in large, grand houses. Anyway, here we are."

We had just left the outskirts of the village, driving over a narrow stone-walled bridge, when we swung through pillared gates on one of which a slate announced this was The Old Rectory. The entrance opened out onto a wide gravel drive that lay in front of a large, imposing three story, red brick, square fronted house. Clearly Jamie's Dad charged top dollar as a lawyer. Large, wide sash windows were framed by a luxuriant wisteria that covered most of the lower part of the building, its pendulous flowers hanging like bunches of pale blue grapes. Two dormer windows in the red tiled roof sat in perfect symmetry, with large chimney stacks in parenthesis either side of them. High, red-bricked walls extended from each side of the house like outstretched wings, giving the frontage a pleasing balance. The flower beds in front of them were filled with flowers and flowering shrubs, all in bloom. In the centre, the tall white front door was flanked by pillars under a small stone canopy, creating a porch that jutted out to give a modicum of shelter to anyone standing there. The whole building whispered solidity, wealth and privilege, and the enduring class structure of British society I had heard about but had never seen or understood. We have a class structure but I think it is more meritocratic, celebrity and materially based than one founded on breeding and the luck of birth into an old and established moneyed class.

The tyres scrunched the gravel as Charles swung the car around to park it in front of the house. The front door opened and a slim, grey haired version of Jamie stepped out and stood waiting for us to finish parking. She was dressed in a dark skirt and white blouse, an elegant silk scarf knotted loosely at her throat, its tails lying on her left shoulder. She stood nervously with her hands clasped together in front of her, almost in supplication it seemed to me. I noticed the edge of a small white handkerchief showing from one of her hands, which she suddenly lifted to wipe an eye. We got out of the car and Jamie turned to face her.

"Mum," she said.

Her mother's hands flew to her mouth and her face creased, almost in pain. Neither of them moved towards the other for a moment and then Jamie relented and walked to her and held her as her mother sobbed into her shoulder.

"It's okay Mum, let's just go in." She put her arm around her mother's waist and led her through the door into the house while Charles and I retrieved the bags from the trunk of the car before following them in. The front door led into a large, stone floored hall with a wide carpeted staircase leading to the upper floors. A variety of pairs of wellington boots stood in a row by the door, umbrellas and walking sticks with deer horn handles propped up beside them. The walls had framed prints of birds and hunting scenes on them. A large mirror hung next to a rack with outdoor coats and hats on it. Wide doorways on either side of the hallway opened into what appeared to be a large, spacious and light living room on the right and an equal sized dining room on the left with a long, highly polished dining table and chairs in the centre. A sideboard stood against the far wall the other side of the mahogany table, bearing two large silver candelabra and a tray with cut glass tumblers on it. Jamie and her mother had gone into the drawing room and were sitting on the sofa. I was about to follow Charles down the hallway to what looked like a large kitchen at the end but Jamie beckoned me to join her and her mother so I put down the case I was carrying and went in. The room had a large bay window with a long window seat in it overlooking part of a yard at the side of the house with shrubs and a small lawn. Light streamed in through the windows, brightening the room. A grand piano stood in a corner and I noticed silver framed photographs of the family on it, carefully arranged in front of a large vase filled with flowers that gave off a deliciously fragrant scent.

"Mum, this is Jack," Jamie said, turning towards me.

"Good to meet you, Mrs Wilson," I said, walking over to her and holding out my hand to shake hers. She remained seated but took my hand and we shook our greeting.

"Hello," she said, "Please call me Joan."

"Sure, thank you," I replied. "Joan it is."

Jamie indicated I should sit down in one of the armchairs, which signalled to me that she was not yet ready to be alone with her mother.

"It's great to meet you," I said, and then continued to fill the awkward silence that filled the room. "Jamie and I've known each other for a few months now and she asked me to come over with her so she could show me a bit of England. I've never been before. I love what I saw of the village here when we arrived."

"That's nice," she said smiling weakly. She was clearly very uncomfortable and finding the reunion difficult, which was understandable given the history.

"So, how are you Mum?" Jamie said.

"Oh, you know, alright," Joan replied. "It's just this is all so unexpected. It really has come out of the blue. Dad was so well and then suddenly he just started losing weight fast, and getting pain. It's been such a shock."

"Where is Dad?" Jamie suddenly said. "Upstairs?"

"Oh no, he's in the hospital at the moment. He was in a lot of pain yesterday and so I took him in early this morning. I've not been long back. There was no point in my staying as I would have just been sitting in a corridor waiting, and I knew you would be arriving so I left him and said I'd see him later. Tomorrow or the day after perhaps. They have him on a light morphine drip at the moment while they plan what to do for him, so I imagine he's asleep. He had a bad night with the pain and he needs the rest. He's decided not to have any treatment like chemo or anything."

"Yes, Charles told us," Jamie said. "What do you feel about that?

Did he ask you what you wanted?"

"Oh no, he didn't. You know your dad." She let out a small laugh. "It was what he'd decided and there wasn't much conversation about it. I did try to persuade him to have it but he said he wouldn't and that was the end of the matter. I want him to have the treatment because, I don't know, there may be a chance it might work. I read that some people do get through this type of cancer and I said all that to him, but he wouldn't listen. I wasn't sure when you'd want to see him but he knows you are coming over."

"So not much change in him then," Jamie said. "Can we go tomorrow, in the morning perhaps? I'm really tired from the flight. I didn't sleep much and I'd rather be fresh and awake. I think I'll go up and have a shower and unpack and then just spend the afternoon here. Perhaps we can go for a walk and I can show Jack the village."

"Of course," Joan said. "I'll call the hospital and say you'll come sometime in the morning. Dad has his own room so you can go anytime really, although he'll probably sleep and rest in the afternoon so the morning will be better. Your room's all ready and there are fresh towels in your bathroom for you both. Have a rest if you want and then we can have some tea this afternoon. I've baked a cake for you."

"Thank you," Jamie said, getting up and turning to me. "Come on, I'll show you our room."

Jamie's bedroom was on the top floor, in the roof of the house. A large double bed was in the centre against the back wall, opposite and facing the dormer window that looked out on the drive below. There were two bedrooms on the floor, with a bathroom between them. I assumed the other bedroom was Charles' room because the case he had taken from the trunk of his car and carried upstairs with him while we chatted to Joan was on the bed there. We unpacked our bags and each showered before putting on clean clothes and going out to explore the village. Little shops offered a mixture of opportunities for potential shoppers, from basic groceries to shops aimed more at tourists who Jamie said flooded the villages in the area. As we walked through the narrow streets I could see Jamie was intrigued to find any changes since she had last been home. At the far end of the village was a quaint little tea room and seeing it, Jamie said, "You have to have a cream tea. You cannot come all this way and not have one."

"What's a cream tea? Whatever it is, it sounds fattening."

"Come in and you'll find out. They're delicious, and don't worry about the calories. You can burn them off."

She pushed the door open, which knocked a small hand bell hanging at the top of the frame, setting it tinkling. The interior was laid out with small tables and chairs, each table covered with a white tablecloth and with its own small pot filled with wild flowers. The room smelled of fresh baking and the aroma from scented candles that flickered on the counter. Cakes and buns lay in rows in a glass cabinet on it and behind that was a large coffee machine, two large kettles and a couple of refrigerators. A door led into a small kitchen at the back. As we sat down at an unoccupied table in the small bay window the waitress came over to us, smiling.

"Jamie, hi, how are you? God, when did I last see you here?"

"Hi Laura. It must be three years or more. How are you?"

"I'm fine, thank you. Are you living in London? You went to university or something there didn't you?"

"Yes, but I live in the States now. This is Jack by the way." She nodded towards me and I smiled at her.

"The States! America? Oh my, that sounds pretty exotic for sleepy old here. London's an adventure for me, but the States. Wow, that's amazing. When did you get back? Are you moving back home? Sorry, hi Jack. I didn't mean to ignore you. It's just I haven't see Jamie forever." I nodded and smiled at her.

"Oh, we flew in this morning. My Dad's not too well so I came back to see him and Mum, but we're booked to go back in a couple of weeks."

"I'd heard he wasn't well," Laura said. "I heard them talking about it in The Feathers last night. I'm so sorry. It doesn't sound too good from what I've heard. Wish him well for me, and your mum. He's often in here for his morning coffee. The Church wardens often meet here. Talking about coffee, what can I get you both."

"I think we'll have a cream tea between us, with a pot for two though. One each would be too much for the first day back I think, unless they've got smaller since I've been away." Jamie laughed and Laura smiled and nodded.

"No, they haven't got any smaller I'm afraid. No one here knows how to spell diet, let alone follow one. Wow, America. That's incredible. I'd love to go there one day. I'd better have babies and get all that out of the way first though, hadn't I?" Laura laughed as she turned and went back to the kitchen to put together the tea.

"I often worked in here in the school holidays," Jamie said. "The summer holidays were great because of the tips from the tourists. I worked part-time but Laura has been here full-time since she left the local school. It makes me realise how different backgrounds produce different horizons, ambitions and expectations. A chance of birth and I could be Laura, happy to stay within the confines of a small community with the sole ambition of marrying and having babies.

Nothing wrong with that, it's just I want so much more from life."

"I can see that," I said. "No different to small town America where a small minority escape and the rest stay behind. What did she mean by The Feathers?"

"Oh, that's what one of the pubs in the village is called. It's short for The Prince of Wales Feathers, which is a bit of a mouthful so it has always been shortened. That's quite usual here with pubs with longer names. It's probably the most popular of the three pubs in the village."

"So, how are you feeling? You've met your mum now and I know that wasn't easy. Were you okay with that?"

While we were on our own I was keen to grab the opportunity to move Jamie off the neutral subjects of the village's finer qualities, the tourists and her holiday employment career. I knew both were smokescreens and avoidance techniques designed to ignore why we were there and what lay ahead for her.

"I don't know what I feel? I think hugging her was an automatic reaction. I felt sorry for her but that didn't make me feel any less angry with her. I've told you, I was the vulnerable one. I needed her protection because I was the child and she didn't give me that, and that hurts. Having said that, I could see how fragile she is at the moment and I didn't want to make her life any more of a misery than it already is."

"Well, as I said before, you need to ask her why that was, why she didn't stand up for you. Have you never wondered if there was a reason for that? I'm not saying there was a reason, or that I'm trying to defend her for what happened, but I do feel you need answers if you're going to bury this once and for all. A mother doesn't abandon a child for no reason so there's obviously something in the background."

"I know, I know. I should talk to her, and I will," Jamie said.

"You're right, I should at least give her the chance to tell her side of the story."

"And when you do speak to her, you need to keep calm and not let that anger take over. If you feel the red mist coming down, either take a deep breath and stop, or even just walk out of the room for a few minutes. If you don't, I reckon she'll just go back into a shell. She's walking a tightrope of fear from what I saw of her just now. I don't know whether she's terrified of losing you forever, or of what you might say, but she seems pretty much on the edge to me and I think she needs help. You're going to have to be the adult in this, because I don't think she can be. She seems pretty beaten up. She's the other part of the equation in this trip and I think you have to ask yourself whether you want to at least try to build a bridge with her, as well as with your dad. She might be just as much a victim here as you are. He's not the only problem you're worrying about because you have issues with both of them, not just him. Otherwise, what was the point in coming?"

"You're right, but it's so hard to put what happened out of my mind. I need to think of her as being separate from Dad, a different problem. And yes, I do want to build bridges with them if I can, or at least, with Mum. That hope has never died and perhaps it never will."

"Here it is," Laura said as she appeared at our shoulders and started placing the tea things on the table from the tray balanced on her hand. Tea pot and a matching milk jug, China cups and saucers with dainty little teaspoons rattling as they landed on the table, side plates all neatly arranged with practised ease. In the middle of the table she placed the centrepiece that Jamie said was a scone with little pots of jelly. When I asked what kind of jelly it was Jamie corrected me.

"It's jam," she said. "Strawberry jam. If you ask for jelly here you'll get jello and that doesn't go too well with toast or a scone. And this is the clotted cream."

Next to the plate with the scone was a large pot filled with a lump of thick yellow cream. Jamie picked it up and held it close to my nose to make sure I could study it well. I learned the public were divided as to whether the cream or the jam went on the scone first, but that seemed irrelevant to me since they were both going to the same place. It also ignored the more important point which was the combination looked to me like a heart attack on a plate. It would be hard to imagine how more calories and cholesterol could be packed into a mouthful. I suppose replacing the jam with more of that cream would do the trick. It was of course delicious and, I felt, dangerously addictive.

"This is great," I said, "but if I want to avoid blocking every artery and tube in my body in the next five years, I think I'd better steer clear of this end of town."

"Yes, a cream tea's probably a dietician's worst nightmare, but it's so worth it. It's funny what you miss when it's not there. Back in Portland I have at times fantasised about these cream teas. English pubs is another thing I miss, although so many are closing which is sad. Along with the church for those who are religious, the local pub has for generations been at the heart of communities and villages like this. Even in the cities they are focal points for people. They are somewhere in our neighbourhood we can drop into by ourselves and know we will generally see someone we know and with whom we can share a drink and conversation. The publican knows all the regulars, and is often the local newspaper with his finger on the pulse of what is happening in the village or town. It's like your bars, but different somehow. It seems to me the point of bars in America is often the drink whereas with pubs the main point is the community and companionship. The pub is something people almost belong to, like a club without a membership fee, and the local as we call it is often the centrepiece of the community's lives."

Finishing the tea we settled the check with Laura and walked slowly back through the village to the house where Joan was preparing another tea for us, this time with homemade cake, served on China plates, each with a miniature fork. How many teas in one afternoon is enough in Britain, or is eating it the national sport? Jamie had told me on the walk back that we'd have to have another, including the cake, so I was prepared for the assault on my stomach, whilst resolving to run every day whilst on the trip to make sure I didn't have to buy new, larger jeans before going home. Charles joined us in the drawing room while we had the tea. He had been working while we were out in the village and said he had hoped to be able to stay for a couple more days but had to go back to London in the morning after breakfast to join a last-minute meeting. Jamie looked disappointed but we were scheduled to go to the city in a few days and were staying at his house when there which reassured her. She and her brother were clearly very close, a tight knit partnership, perhaps born out of the necessity of facing a common enemy. While Joan went to the kitchen in the early evening to prepare supper, we stayed in the drawing room with Charles where the conversation turned to the coming morning and Jamie's visit to the hospital.

"You'll be okay," Charles said. "You're a different person now, grown up and no longer the child you were. And you've come into yourself, an adult. He can't change that about you. I don't know whether you'll find him changed. Because I see him and Mum a lot, I probably don't see any differences in them but I suppose there must be. You'd be a better judge of that, having been away for so long."

"I assume I'm nervous because I don't know what to expect when I see him," Jamie said. "I've dreamt of this moment so many times and imagined what I would say to him if I saw him again, but now it's about to happen I have no idea what I'm going to say, or even how to start a conversation. He's a stranger to me, not the man I thought he was. How's he going to react? He never liked me and you were always his blue-eyed boy. I don't mean that against you, it wasn't your fault. First, you were a boy and I know he was disappointed I wasn't a boy too. He told me so. Even my name was a reminder of that. You were always so good at everything. You were academic, a sportsman and you went into what he feels is a 'worthwhile' career in the City, something he could be proud of and tell his golf mates about. What did I do? I was the frivolous one, throwing paint on paper and doing silly drawings, and I suppose to him I still am that disappointment."

"I know," Charles said, "and I feel bad about that but you know, he really wasn't that great with me either. I was captain of the rugby team in my final year at school and we finished the season unbeaten. That had never happened at the school before so it was a big deal. He never came to watch one match. Not one. That would have interfered with his regular game of golf with his muckers at the weekend. Mum came, but not him. So I do understand a little of how you feel."

"I know," Jamie said. "I should be stronger, but it's hard to be when I think of him, of how he totally dominated me and controlled me. I was just an unwelcome expense to him, an overhead he could have done without."

"Remember, he can only control you now if you allow him to," I said. "No is a very small word but it's what you need to be able to say, if not to him then to yourself. Don't let him get inside your head and don't be afraid of him. He's not going to hurt you. He can't do that without your permission."

"It's a bit too late not to be hurt," Jamie said. "That's all happened already and you're right, I may not be able to control him but I can myself and that's what I have to keep in mind."

"And keep an open mind," I said. "Don't go in there looking for a fight. Just take this as your one chance to tell him how you feel, what it was like and did he know that."

"Who'd like a drink before supper?" Joan said, coming back in from the kitchen. She was wearing a bibbed apron and brought with her the faint scent of the kitchen and cooking.

"That would be great," Charles said. "I'll organise it. Is wine okay? Red, white or rosé?"

We all opted for the rosé and took our glasses out into the yard, or garden as Jamie corrected me. We went through wide and open doors from the kitchen onto a broad terrace at the back of the house. A large sweeping lawn, bordered by scalloped flower beds led my eye to an orchard, behind which were open fields. Trees in the orchard had young fruit hanging off them and I could see a couple of squirrels were chasing each other through the grass and up and down the slender trunks. Comfortable garden chairs with deep cushions were arranged around a low table and we sat around it, sipping our drinks in the warm evening air, serenaded by the end of the day birdsong. Conversation was light and easy as we caught up with each other's news and Jamie told Joan about her job and life in Portland. Every now and again Joan would go back into the kitchen to check on the meal, but would return eagerly to question Jamie about the detail of her new life. Jamie made no mention of the financial and emotional disasters Frank had caused, a story that could only worry any mother. When supper was ready we helped lay the table on the terrace and lit large candles that flickered in their vases. We carried on our conversation as we ate, until Jamie and I began to lose the fight to stay awake, defeated by the combined forces of wine, a lost night's sleep and jet lag with the eight-hour time difference taking its toll.

"Off you go," Joan said. "Go to bed and we'll see you in the morning. I'll clear up."

"Yes, go," Charles said. "I'll help Mum."

In the morning we admitted to each other neither of us could remember our heads touching the pillow. Sleep came fast and deep for me and was only interrupted by the early morning sun pouring through the window and falling on my face. I lay for a few minutes in that blissful half-sleep of the morning, my eyes closed but fully conscious whilst trying to remember where I was in the unrecognised surroundings. The birds in the trees and garden were in full voice, calling and singing to the new day. Crows were cawing loudly but were out of sight to me, so I assumed they were on the roof above us. I looked across at Jamie, lying on her side with the sun yet to reach across to her. Her face was serene and calm in her sleep, her breathing quiet and shallow. I quietly got out of bed, put on some running shorts and trainers and slipped out of the silent house to run off some of the previous day's excesses.

I went through the front gates and turned left, away from the village where I had gone with Jamie the afternoon before. The narrow road slowly rising ahead of me was bounded by stone walls covered in part with lichen and moss. Large ferns grew out of gaps in the stones, their fronds reaching out to me as I passed them. An avenue of trees grew in the fields the other side of the walls and formed an arch over the road. I could see sheep grazing quietly in the fields. Reaching the top of the hill, the open countryside lay around me, giving me views across rolling fields that were laid out in a haphazard grid of more irregular stone walls and hedgerows. A light mist lay in the small valleys and depressions and in one field two deer quickly lifted their heads and watched me intently as I ran down the undulating and empty road. An owl sat on a wall ahead of me but flew off silently as I approached its perch. Used to fields that were measured in square miles rather than acres, the quintessential British quaintness of the small fields made me realise why tourists visited the area. What history lay hidden in the stories those fields could tell, of generations of families that had worked them over the decades? There's a timelessness about our planet as it follows its endless journey of change and adaptation. Our short lives would be meaningless to it if it were not for the scale of havoc we can each wreak in our three score years and ten of life. Our footprint is disproportionate to our minuscule size. Wherever we are we should leave nothing more than our small footprint and take away nothing more than the dust on our shoes, and yet the very earth that supports us is littered with the detritus of our quest for wealth and advancement. Not satisfied with trashing our home, we are now leaving our junk on other planets. I can no longer look at the moon without visualising the carcasses of vehicles and other expensive trash we have left up there. The lush lichen growing on the walls and trees I was running past was a testament to the clean air of that small rural corner of the country, but how long will that last in the face of our ability to spread pollution?

Rather than risk getting lost in the maze of lanes that wound their way between the fields, I stayed on the road I set out on and after half an hour turned and retraced my steps back to the house. As I went through the front door I could hear murmured voices from the kitchen where I found Charles and Jamie talking quietly.

"Hi Jack, good morning," Charles said. "I'm off to London so I'll see you at the weekend. I'll come back but you guys call me if you want anything or if you need any help." Turning to Jamie he said, "Good luck today. You'll be fine, I'm sure." He hugged her and once again she held onto him tightly. Turning to me he shook my hand and slipped quietly out of the room.

"You okay?" I asked, mopping my face with a small towel Jamie handed to me.

"Yes, I'm fine," Jamie said. "I slept really well and that's helped. I need to get today out of the way and now it's arrived I just want to get on with it."

"Do you want me to come with you?" I said. "That's not a request, just an offer."

"No, thanks. I need to do this alone I think. It's going to be awkward enough and I think you being there would be a distraction. If there's any chance of him talking I think he and I need to be alone. I don't want Mum there either so I'll just get her to drop me off at the hospital and collect me when I call her. She can go and have a coffee and do some shopping. Will you be okay here by yourself?"

"Yeah, I'll be fine. I need to do some work and catch up on emails and stuff and if I finish that I shall just go out for a walk. Have a cream tea or something equally healthy," I added, laughing. "You can call me when you're on your way back and I'll meet you here."

"Thank you for understanding. It helps a lot."

"No problem. And Jamie, you need to go without any expectations. Don't go with hope of reconciliation or fear of failure, just go with an open mind. This visit is for you, not for him. You need to lay this ghost and get some sort of closure for yourself out of this trip. You're not here to try to cure or change him. That's for him to do, not you, so be a little selfish about this and get out of it what you want. If that is a reconciliation then great, but don't necessarily go there hoping for or expecting that. Just see what happens and we can talk when you get back if you want."

"I will definitely want to talk about it," Jamie said with a short laugh. "Fear not."

"Good morning," Joan said, coming in to the kitchen. "I hope you both slept well. Have you been for a run Jack?"

"Good morning Joan. Yes, I woke early and couldn't get back to sleep so thought I'd burn off my first British cream tea. It's so beautiful around here. I feel as though I've stepped back in time. I saw deer and an owl and a farmer was herding sheep with a dog in a far-off field."

"We're very lucky here with the countryside around us but I'm afraid we rather take it for granted. We must take you further afield so you can see more of it." She turned to Jamie. "Are you ready to go?"

"Yes, I've got everything." She came over to me and kissed me lightly. "See you later."

"Yeah, will do." I squeezed her arm lightly and then gave her a hug.

# CHAPTER 7

# JOHN RADCLIFFE HOSPITAL, OXFORD

Joan swung the car off the road into the hospital car park, the building's rectangular blue and white facade looming over them. She parked the car and she and Jamie got out and started the walk through the cars to the main entrance.

"He's in the short stay medical ward," Joan said. "It's on level five and he's paid for an amenity room there. Just ask for him at the desk, which is just in front of you when you go into the ward. I sent a message to him to say you would be coming this morning so he's expecting you. I'll be in the café here with my book so there's no hurry. Take your time. You two have a lot to talk about and I'll see you when you come down."

Joan kissed Jamie lightly on the cheek and went off into the café as Jamie walked over to the lifts, reaching them as one arrived. She stepped in, pressing the button for the fifth floor before leaning against the back wall to make way for a couple of wheelchair patients to be pushed in with her. The lift stopped at the floor she needed and, stepping out, she followed signs to the ward where she announced herself to a nurse sitting at the ward's reception desk. The nurse looked at the computer screen to check and then directed her to the room her father was in. Standing outside it, Jamie took a deep breath and tried to calm her shaking hands, pushing them deep into the pockets of her jeans as she gathered her courage. Knocking quietly on the door with the toe of her shoe, she pushed it open with her shoulder. Her father was lying in the bed, resting half upright on heaped pillows, his eyes closed. An oxygen tube snaked across his grey, sunken face, aiding his laboured breathing. His thin, bare arms rested on the bed and she could see blue veins knitted under the translucent skin on the back of his hands. A cannula in the crook of his left elbow was connected to a tube that ran down from a bag of fluid hanging from a stand by the bed. How shrunken and diminished we are by age and failing health, shadows of the people we once were, our dignity and vitality shipwrecked on the rocks of the accumulation of our years.

Jamie closed the door behind her and tiptoed across the room to an armchair next to the window the other side of the bed. From there she could face him with the light behind her, a silhouette she could hide her expressions and emotions in. She sat for a while, watching his chest move rhythmically with his shallow breaths. His stomach seemed to be swollen and she wondered if that was caused by the damage from the tumours in his liver. Now and again his hand or fingers twitched slightly, perhaps in response to his dreams. Jamie felt grateful for this quiet moment which she found calming. He looked vulnerable, weak for the first time in his life, and she realised there was nothing there for her to fear. This was a shell of the man she remembered, a husk that could be winnowed away by the slightest breeze, leaving only a harmless old man. She turned her head to gaze at the view out of the window, knowing she could now look at him objectively, detached from any emotions about him, neither love nor hate. She had never felt so liberated, so free of her memories and past. They were just that, memories, no longer the nightmares she had allowed them to become. Now her connection with him was merely biological and no more than that, and for the first time in her life with him she felt in control of herself. All she wanted was an explanation, if she could wring that out of him. She knew the what of her childhood but not the why, and some answers might help fill the gaps, the final empty spaces on a painting by numbers image that had yet to be completed.

"So, you're here."

Jamie turned to look at him, unsure how long he had been awake and watching her. His face remained expressionless, his gaze steady. He coughed and winced with pain.

"Yes, you were asleep and I didn't want to disturb you. I got here about a quarter of an hour ago. How are you?"

"Not too good. It's terminal and they're sorting out palliative care for me so I can go home and have it there rather than in a hospital. I've also got an infection, hence the antibiotic drip." He lifted his left arm to show her the drip.

"Charles told me you don't want chemo or any treatment."

"No, I don't. I don't see the point of it when it just prolongs what is already an unbearable situation."

"What about Mum? Did you discuss it with her? I think she'd like you to have it."

"It's nothing to do with her. It's my decision. I'm the one going through this, not her, and that's what I want. Anything different is just delaying the inevitable and she's going to have to face that anyway, just a bit earlier this way. She'll get used to it when I'm gone."

Jamie saw no point in discussing the subject of treatment any further with him, knowing she had no hope of changing his mind and getting him to see it from her mother's point of view. His attitude was just another example of him putting himself first, no matter what that might mean to anyone else.

"Okay," Jamie said. "So, what are we going to talk about now I'm here? What are we going to say? I think I'd like to start by asking what you were doing in that hotel room?"

"I could ask you the same question. What the hell do you think you were doing there? A common prostitute. That's not what we brought you up to be. It's disgusting. It wasn't me doing anything wrong. That was you. Mind you, if I'd known I could have paid to watch you with someone."

Jamie felt the shock of what he had just said as though he had slapped her in the face. Her anger begin to boil and she felt a red mist of rage descend and envelop her, threatening to breach her promise to herself to stay in control of her emotions and suppressed rage. How dare he? How dare he deflect away from himself and on to her, with no hint of shame? She sat for a moment, concentrating on her hands folded in her lap to buy herself some time to calm down. She felt he was just playing another game, one where she would lose control of herself again and thus the conversation and the argument. This was not a game to her, and if it was going to turn into one, as it always had with him, so be it but she would make the rules this time.

"So you want to dodge my question. Make it my fault, as you always did, and be disgusting at the same time," she said, icy calm now. "Let's just play that out shall we, and then I'll come back to my question. If you remember, you refused to pay one penny towards my university degree. How did you imagine I was going to pay for it?"

"Well I…" he started but Jamie held up her hand.

"No, stop. I've not finished. I'm speaking and you'll let me finish, or I'll walk out." She paused to gather her thoughts for what was an unrehearsed conversation, despite often having wondered and gone over in her mind what she might say to him if they ever met again.

"I suppose you thought I'd come to your heel. Again, like so often before. When I didn't, when I said to you I was still going to go, that I'd get jobs to pay for it and for my upkeep, you just shrugged and turned your back on me, in more ways than one. Have you the remotest idea what it might feel like to be abandoned by your own father? How devastating that feels, although frankly, I should have got used to it by then. Well, the casual jobs I was able to do that fitted in with my course were never enough and all I did was get into more and more debt. My credit card was stopped and the bank wouldn't extend my student overdraft. I'd already used up all my student loan for that year. London's not cheap. So, I started being an escort, but not one with any strings attached. One thing led to another because I was being chased to pay off my debts and under a lot of pressure with nowhere to turn, other than to give up and drop out. That would have made you happy, wouldn't it? So yes, I became a prostitute, and I hold you responsible for that. It was entirely your fault. Do you have the faintest idea what I went through, how hard it was? Those men disgusted me, and then I find you're one of them. How long had you been doing that?"

Jamie's voice was rising with another wave of anger so she stopped to take a moment to gather control and calm down. She felt detached, almost distant from herself, a light headed floating sensation, as though she was in a corner of the room watching two people talking.

Her father lay still on the pillows staring at her. His uncombed greying hair formed a small halo around his head, and she could see from the grey stubble on his face that he hadn't shaved for a couple of days or more. His sunken cheeks sagged and the loose skin under his eyes added to his hangdog look.

"I'm a man. I have needs," her father said. "You wouldn't understand and anyway, there's nothing wrong with it. Quite natural I think."

"Isn't that what marriage is for?" Jamie said, coldly. "You know, I promise to be faithful and all that. What part of I promise to be faithful didn't you mean? You have a wife. Doesn't that mean anything?"

"You may not want to hear this but your mother wasn't remotely interested in that side of life, so what do you expect me to do? Sit at home like a Trappist monk?"

"Yes, frankly, that's exactly what I'd expect you to do because there's that other promise about sickness and health. You marry to help and support each other, come what may. You can't just go around selecting which of the promises you've made you're going to keep, ignoring and breaking the ones that don't suit you."

"You're delusional and have absolutely no idea what you're talking about. And you say I'm responsible for what you did. How could it be my fault? It was your decision to do that, not mine. You could have left university and gone out and got a proper job, done something useful. I didn't ask or tell you to do it so don't try and shift the blame onto me. You need to learn to take responsibility for what you do, and did."

"So that's it? That's all you have to say? That's what you think?"

"What else is there to think? It was your choice to go and do that stupid, and may I say worthless course, so you have to take the consequences of that. Not me. In fact I wouldn't have paid for any university course you did because you would have failed or dropped out, so why waste my money? What was in it for me other than frittering more money away on you after already paying for your schooling? You needed to go out and be a waitress or filing clerk or something, until you found someone to marry and become a housewife."

"What was it I did to make you hate me so much? Was it that I was a girl and not a boy? That was hardly my fault. I tried so hard to please you, time and time again, but you just pushed me away, ignored me. That broke my heart you know. So often I couldn't count, but I never gave up on trying. I never gave up hoping that one day you'd notice me, that you might even show you loved me. But you never did. For me you were an absentee father, a bachelor with a family. You were never there for me when I wanted you to be, and God there were times when I needed that so much. You have no idea. You didn't see that, or even me and so I just felt invisible, in your way. A nuisance. Are you even aware you never once kissed me or hugged me? Not once. Why did you have me?"

"I don't know what you mean 'love you.' I provided for you didn't I? Food, clothes, education, although that was a waste of time. Then there was that damned horse you rode all the time. What more did you want? You wanted for nothing. In any event, as a girl, your job is to get married and have children. The problem is they won't have my name. What use is that to me? I'm not remotely interested in someone else's name for my grandchildren. That doesn't happen with a son."

"You've said that to me before, so nothing new there. That's not love. That's being a chequebook father. That's not what being a father is about. Why can't you see that? And as for grandchildren, what's in a name? They are still one quarter you. They're still your grandchildren no matter how you might disown them for a name they have no choice over."

"Well, I can't think what else I could have been. This 'father' you're chasing after is a fantasy of yours. I don't understand what more I could have done to meet up with your idea of this pipe dream, this fictitious father. All I see is ingratitude frankly. You cost a lot of money and I didn't see you going without anything, and I see no benefit or gratitude coming back to me now, or ever."

"I repeat, that's not being a father, just paying the bills and then using that to control me, to make me feel I should be grateful all the time and, if I'm not, it all stops. That's just being threatening, holding me as a hostage to ransom. I'm not one of your overheads. Whether you acknowledge it or not, I'm your daughter. A person, not a utility bill. You ask what it is to be a father? What was I looking for? It's to put me first, ahead of yourself, but of course you never did that. It's being that one person I can go to for help and guidance and not be judged. It's being that one person I can trust, always. The person I can say anything to and not worry about what you might think of me, no matter what I may have done. You were supposed to be the bedrock of who I am, my very foundations, that seam of strong, unconditional consistency running through my life, my being. The person who gave me the strength and confidence in myself to face the world. You were none of those things. You were the person who made me know I was a disappointment, that's all you ever were. I tried so hard. I hoped and hoped and I cried so many times. That affected me, I know that now. If I couldn't trust you, who could I trust and so I don't trust anyone, and that's so sad. There's always a part of me that holds back, especially with men. That's the true legacy of your 'fathering' and it's only today that I've come to realise that. You were never a father to me. You were a sperm donor."

'Well, if you don't trust anyone you'll never be hurt or disappointed so I would say I did you a favour. You should be grateful for that. Life is hard out there so I would say I helped you prepare for it pretty well."

"That's teaching by brutalising, how circus animals were trained. By the imposition of fear, not love. I'm not going to get anywhere with you am I?" Jamie said.

The penny dropped and she finally realised he was unchangeable. For some reason he didn't actually understand what she was talking about. Looking for more was pointless and she had been wasting her time and energy for years, chasing a dream that not only didn't exist, but couldn't. His outlook on life was an aberration but it was the one he had and held onto. It was clear to Jamie it was too late for him to be any different and that he obviously couldn't change, even if he decided he wanted to. She looked at her watch. She had been in the room with him for an hour and a half and it felt like five minutes. Time was for her to spend on herself, not to be wasted on a futile hope and conversation that led nowhere other than to more hurt and unhappiness for her. How had it taken her so long to see the truth in front of her?

"I have to go now," she said, getting up out of the chair and reaching for her jacket which she had hung off the back. "I need to get back to Jack and then get up to London in a couple of days." She walked to the door and turned to look back at him.

"Who's Jack?" he said, frowning.

Jamie looked at him, saying nothing for a few moments as she opened the door.

"He's what you have never been to me. Someone who loves me, and loves me for what I am. He stands by me and puts me first. You could learn from him, except it's a bit late for that now, isn't it? Thank you for this. It's been a revelation and a liberation. I now realise it's not me who is the disappointment. It's you. I hope they get your treatment sorted out. Mum can let me know how you're getting on. As for us, there is no us. There never has been and that's a loss for both of us. What's so sad is you can't see that. For me there's a future I can at last look forward to. For you there's just a legacy of failure. Your one positive achievement is helping me see that today, and that is all I have to thank you for out of your part in my life. I feel free and for that I am grateful to this day, not to you. I have a new life now, a life of hope in America and one you'll have no part in. The saddest part of that is your absence will mean nothing to me."

Slipping out of the room Jamie let the door close behind her and on his expressionless face. As she walked the corridors and got in the lift, she felt strangely elated. 'He can never hurt me again,' she thought. A paternal umbilical cord had been cut and she had wielded the scissors, and she felt good about that without any sense of guilt. She no longer felt an obligation to even like him, let alone feel love or loyalty to him. She stepped out of the lift and walked briskly back to the main entrance and to the café. Standing outside looking through the window she could see her mother sitting at a table by herself, engrossed in a book resting on the table which had two coffee cups on it. She looked fragile and diminished as she turned a page, lonely and isolated and above all, vulnerable. Jamie now needed another conversation, the other half of the intention of this trip. She went in and walked up to the table.

"I'm so sorry I've been so long. I had no idea of the time. Shall we go. You must be desperate."

"I'm fine," Joan said, closing her book and putting it in her large bag. "This is such a good book. It's about a young girl who's orphaned. Well, not immediately but her mother runs off and the father's a bad sort so she ends up bringing herself up. You should read it. I've nearly finished it so I'll give it to you."

"You should get a Kindle Mum. You wouldn't need to have such a huge bag to carry your books around in. They're so easy to use. I'll show you mine when we get home if you want."

"People keep telling me that but I'm old fashioned. I love the feel of a book in my hands, turning the pages, the feel of the paper. Anyway, they're expensive and I don't think Stephen would want me to spend money on one. Perhaps I will try one someday. I might surprise you all yet."

Putting her bag over her shoulder she followed Jamie out of the café and then fell in step next to her as they walked to the machine to pay for the parking before making their way back to the car. As they walked, Jamie slipped her arm through her mother's, they were putting on their seat belts when Joan turned to look at her.

"Are you alright?"

"Yes, I'm good. No, I'm not just good, I'm much more than that. I'm free at last. Let's get home. I want some coffee and then we can talk."

# CHAPTER 8

## THE OLD RECTORY

A large rectangular island filled the centre of the kitchen at the house. Four tall seats were grouped at one end of it and I was sitting on one of them with my laptop open in front of me. While Jamie and her mother were out at the hospital I had used the time to catch up on emails from friends and work. A couple of clients were experiencing functionality problems with their systems and I arranged for someone to visit them to fix the issues they were facing. I heard the front door opening and Jamie's laugh drifted down the corridor.

"Hi," I called out. "I'm in the kitchen." I closed the computer as Jamie and her mother came through the door.

"I'd kill for a coffee," Jamie said. She seemed elated and happy.

"Well, lucky you, I've just made some fresh." I got down off the seat and went to the wall cupboard where the cups and mugs hung in rows off hooks under a shelf. "Cup or mug?" I said, holding one of each up for her to see.

"Mug please, I need lots!"

"Joan, how about you?"

"Oh, yes please, but just a cup for me I think. I had a couple at the hospital but another won't hurt."

As I busied myself with heating milk in a small microwave and pouring the coffee, I listened to Jamie and her mother chatting about what to do with the rest of the day. They elected to go into Oxford to have a late lunch and do some shopping. They suggested I go with them so I could see the city and the colleges there. I had heard of the university and had read a travel guide I bought when I knew I would be going with Jamie to her home. The guide said the city was called the city of dreaming spires, apparently getting the name from a poem.

"That would be great," I said. "I'd love to go. I read about the city before coming over and was hoping we might be able to fit in a visit."

"It's incredibly expensive to park in the city now," Joan said, "so we'll drop the car off at the Park and Ride and catch the bus in. Also, the car parks fill up so it's always a nightmare to find a spot free."

After a light lunch in a small restaurant, we walked through the old part of Oxford. It was beautiful and seemed to me to ooze history from every stone. The ancient stone buildings bounded streets both broad and narrow, and when we entered some of the university buildings and grounds, it was like stepping into an oasis of calm, an escape from the bustle of the roads and City outside. On a business trip to New York a couple of years ago, I found I had some spare time between meetings and so went to the Frick Collection on Fifth Avenue. I had exactly the same sense of calm there, the peace after the storm. The traffic on Fifth was frenetic and noisy, and then I stepped through the doors into the building, the former residence of the industrialist Henry Clay Frick where the collection is housed. Like the transition from night to day, the world about me changed in an instant, and I was in a place of tranquillity. I wandered through the rooms and a large, bright gallery towards the back of the building that stretched before me under its wide glass ceiling that allowed light to cascade down, filling it with brightness. Looking at the magnificent paintings hanging on the walls I was lost in wonder at the range of talents and genius on display. For a short while the cares of the working day were swept away, bringing a moment of respite to a busy life. At one point, the quiet was disturbed by the restful tinkling of water coming from a small fountain that lay in a little atrium in the centre of the building.

In those quadrangles and college gardens in Oxford I felt that same serenity and sense of peace, bringing a moment of perspective and realisation that there is more to life than chasing our tails and our avaricious dreams. I imagined contemplative students and professors calmly walking through those spaces, books under their arms and deep in thought. The reality was more likely to be a case of stressed academics and undergraduates, each immersed in their own busy world, racing from one meeting or lecture to another, constantly chasing deadlines, as we now all seem to do. It was probably only we visitors who had the time to enjoy the peace of the hidden inner sanctums of those ancient, historic buildings. For me it was a step back in time and a step into a world I had never experienced or seen. America is too young a country for buildings with such history and perhaps that's why so many of us hark back to our forefathers and their flight from other countries to set up a colony, and ultimately a painfully won independent country. We all harbour an interest in our roots and our forebears. Perhaps that's a counterpoint to the temporary nature of our lives, bringing a sense of a longer purpose to our short time on earth as we play our brief part in the continuum of life and evolution.

We arrived back at the house in time for another tea, which I had now come to realise didn't just refer to a drink but more to a daily ritual, a sacrosanct routine that is not to be missed. While Joan busied herself in the kitchen making the tea and putting out the rest of the cake she had made, I sat in the drawing room with Jamie, aware that none of us had brought up the subject of her visit to her father that morning.

"So, do you want to talk about this morning?" I said. "You don't have to and I understand that, but I just want to know you're okay."

"No, I don't have a problem talking about it," she said as Joan came into the room with a laden tray. She hesitated half way across the room when she heard Jamie speak, uncertain whether she should stay or leave the room.

"It's okay Mum, you need to hear this too."

Joan looked relieved and set the tray down on the table before sitting on the couch next to Jamie.

"Do you want me to leave you two alone to talk?" I said, feeling somewhat self-conscious about being part of what was essentially a family matter and conversation.

"No, not at all," Jamie said. "I want you to stay. How did it go? I suppose that depends on whose point of view we're talking about. He hasn't changed, has he?"

Joan shook her head and said quietly, almost to herself, "No, he hasn't."

"When I got there he was asleep so I sat for a while until he woke up. He really doesn't look well so I assume it's getting worse a lot faster than they anticipated but that's probably because he's not having any treatment. Anyway I asked him why he had always disliked me and he didn't really have any answers, and he definitely had no idea of what that might mean to me. I know he's always been selfish and put himself first, even to ignoring your wish for him to have treatment Mum. He pretty much said it was none of your business what he chose to do or not do. He blamed me for what I did at uni, you know, to pay for it, and he said he would never have paid for me to go to any university anyway because I'd inevitably fail. As for finding him in that hotel room, he said he'd done nothing wrong and it was a perfectly normal thing for a man to want to do. He said something about having needs. God knows, that was more information than I needed, but it was his sheer lack of shame about it that got me. It truly was perfectly normal and okay from his point of view. One or two things he said I really don't want to repeat, but they were disgusting. Staggering when I think about it. Nothing has changed in him and the only thing I think I really got out of this morning was my own understanding of what you've gone through all these years Mum. I'm sorry it's taken this long to know that, and for how I blamed you for so much without thinking about it from your point of view. I should have been more help to you. More understanding."

Jamie took a sip of her tea and looked at her mother who was quietly crying, dabbing her eyes with a small handkerchief. Frail and vulnerable, she sat forward on the edge of the seat, a small bird ready to take flight at any moment.

"Don't cry, Mum. It will be okay."

"I hope so," Joan said. "It's been going on for so many years and I've never been able to talk about it. It's just all a bit overwhelming really."

"I know, it is for both of us. On the basis that at last I knew I had nothing left to lose, I told him what I felt, how he had hurt me so many times over so many years and what a failure he had been to me as a father. He has no use for a daughter and only ever wanted sons. I get that now, and I get that says everything about him, as a man and as a father. It has nothing to do with me and I didn't cause that. I think the most shocking thing to me is I felt I might as well have been reading him a shopping list. There was absolutely no reaction from him. It's as though he's emotionally dead, a complete shell, hollow inside. I had never thought that about him before but I can see it now. Perhaps it's not his fault and there's something wrong with him, something he cannot change. He certainly can't be what I want him to be. It literally isn't in him. How I wish I'd known that long ago. Life would have been so much easier, but I didn't and there's nothing I can do to change that."

"I'm so sorry," Joan said. "When you were born he just said you were not what he wanted. He said it was my fault you were not a boy. He didn't bother to come and see you in the hospital, or me for that matter. He never even held you when you were a baby, not once. I only ever stayed with him because of you and Charles. He said to me if I ever tried to leave him he'd make sure I didn't get a penny, and that I'd never see either of you again. I was terrified of him. He's a lawyer and knew about these things and how to make them happen. I'd seen him do it for some of his clients. He wasn't the man I thought I was marrying, the one I first met, and he still isn't. It must have been a complete act before we were married. He started to change fairly soon after our wedding. It was gradual, bit by bit, until I was trapped and totally dependent on him. I wasn't even allowed my own bank account or credit card. It was years before he let me have one. I know I failed you but I was so frightened that if I took your side, on anything, he'd throw me out, or just make my life hell. More of a hell than it already was. There are no words that describe how guilty I feel about it all, about not supporting you and not fighting him for you."

"Mum, Mum, I understand that now, and you mustn't feel guilty," Jamie said, moving over to sit by her mother and putting an arm around her thin shoulders. Joan leant her head over onto Jamie's shoulder as she dabbed at her eyes with her handkerchief.

"Well, I do," Joan said, "and I think I always will. I don't feel I was a good mother to you and that hurts so much. I'm so sorry. I don't know how I can ever make that up to you. It's too late I suppose and I worry you'll never forgive me. I felt I had lost you forever when you went to America, that I would never see you again. I was terrified I'd die without having moments like this. I don't fear death itself. What I fear is what I leave behind, the vacuum in your lives, you and Charles. Of the pain that will cause you, but that is part of your life, for you to deal with, as I had to."

"I can see that but I don't blame you, Mum. Charles and I are adults now. I suppose I did blame you for a long time. I couldn't believe you stood by him after what I told you had happened, which is why I stopped contacting you and went to America. I ran away, in part I think to hurt you, and now I feel bad about that so we can both share feeling guilty. I should have been stronger, but I wasn't and I regret that. But there has been one huge positive from today in that I somehow cut the cord, if one can have a cord to a father or a man. I realise I feel nothing for him, that he's a stranger to me and I can step back and look at him objectively and feel no obligation to him, nor any wish anymore for him to love me or even just like me. That's all in the past and I want nothing from him now. I feel completely liberated, free at last. I cannot tell you how good that feels. I suppose if I'm honest with myself, I came here looking for revenge, to hurt him as he hurt me, and what I got instead is peace of mind. So much better and anyway, trying to hurt him would be a waste of time too because I don't think he understands that either. I realise he's devoid of any emotion, and if he does show it, it's an act. So strange when you think how charming he can be."

Jamie picked up her cup of tea and sat back. She leaned across and held her mother's hand, a moment of true affection, a mother and daughter moment, a bridge over the rapids of a torrid past grounded in pain and misunderstanding.

"Of course, the other even bigger positive for me is finding you again Mum. I cannot tell you how happy that makes me."

Joan burst into tears and Jamie slid back across and took her in her arms, so I stood up and took the dirty cake plates and my half empty cup to the kitchen to give them both some privacy, a moment to mend a five-thousand-mile-long broken fence that stretched across an ocean and a continent. I stepped out through the open doors into the afternoon sunshine in the garden and walked slowly around the lawn as I reflected on what Jamie had just said. From my perspective, I think it was the outcome I hadn't dare wish for, and hadn't believed would happen. Jamie was obstinate and so obdurate, saying that she was only coming under sufferance. I had really felt there was a danger the trip was only going to be a waste of time, but also more damaging because she was paying lip service to reason. It is extraordinary how life can change on a dime, how a light bulb can go on in our head and completely alter our lives, our way of thinking. In Jamie's case the outcome and change were positive. It could so easily have been destructive and long lastingly damaging for her, leaving her with a lifetime's burden of guilt and unrequited hope. I was in the orchard following a path that had been cut in the long grass when I looked up and saw Jamie walking across the lawn towards me. When she got to me she reached up and put her arms around my neck and hugged hard.

"Thank you," she whispered in my ear.

"What for?" I said. "I've done nothing. You did it all. You faced him and I'm proud of you. That was definitely not an easy gig, I'm sure."

Jamie leaned back and held my eyes intently.

"For making me come. For not taking no for an answer, and for being here with me. I could never have done this without you. I know there's a long way to go from here, for me and for us, but I really feel I've taken the first step to change. I know I have to change and I dread the effort of that in some ways. You're going to have to be very patient with me," she said, laughing lightly but with a tremor of uncertainty.

"Let's call it teamwork then," I said. "One day at a time and let's see where it takes us."

Joining hands, we turned and walked back up to the house to help Joan prepare the evening meal and to make some inroads into a bottle of wine.

# CHAPTER 9

# PORTLAND OREGON, 20TH JANUARY 2021

As I finish telling you Jamie's story, I look across the room and see her sitting curled up in an armchair with a book, a lamp by her side throwing a subdued, dimmed light onto the book and her face. The book arrived a couple of days ago and she opened it this morning, taking it out of its Christmas wrapping, a late gift from her brother, with a loving note attached to it. President Biden's inauguration passed peacefully earlier today and I for one took a deep breath of relief that the Capitol and our democracy held firm on this momentous day in our history. Jamie and I watched the ceremony on the television. The coverage included images of Donald Trump climbing up the steps to the Presidential plane as the about to be ex-President, turning to wave at a non-existent crowd, a last gesture of bravado in the face of his complete denial of the reality of his humiliation, and final exposure as the spoiled child he is perceived to be. For the first time he seemed diminished somehow, emasculated by the shame of impending impeachment debates, and the wave of very public opprobrium over his part in the storming of the Capitol. He looked strangely vulnerable as he made that wave, but I felt no temptation to summon up sympathy for him. He was undeserving of that, immersed in a deep pool of narcissism that blinded him from the truth of what so many really think of him.

"I've only just thought of this," Jamie had said as we watched, "but he reminds me of my dad. He's never once mentioned the hundreds of thousands who have died from the virus, never offered condolences to the relatives. No sense of remorse for the very obvious mistakes in the way he personally and his government have handled the crisis. It's as though the dead are just numbers on a page to him and he cannot relate each one of those numbers to a person who lived and breathed, who had a family, a life. It was the same with the Mexican border issues when children were held in camps separate from their parents. He just didn't understand what that might mean to those poor kids. There's no empathy, just like Dad. It's uncanny. Even when he speaks and is rude to people, insulting them to their faces at meetings or at one of his press conferences, there's no connection to how they might feel about him belittling them in front of other people. And nothing is ever his fault, it's always someone else. As for the lies, again, exactly the same as Dad."

The city here is a ghost town now. It isn't just about the pandemic. The right and left-wing demonstrations about police brutality that we had every day and night for so long, many descending into violence and anarchy, have now stopped, but the town is bruised by that. People are fearful, wary. The initially peaceful demonstrations attracted ugly opposing forces and interests from the extreme left and right, together with conspiracy theorists, each bringing their own subversive agenda to the fray. I feel fortunate to have a business that can operate in the virtual world and so, whilst business is down for us, we are surviving and breaking even and we have a future. For four hundred thousand of our fellow Americans, and untold numbers more to come, there is no future, only a trail of grief-stricken families mourning the loss of loved ones, so many of them unnecessarily dead. This is our generation's Vietnam on home soil, but by many multiples and with an enemy even more invisible than the elusive Viet Cong.

Jamie and I moved out of her apartment in August, deciding we'd try living together but in a new place. We rented a house in Alameda District, a fresh start with memories locked behind the old front door at the apartment. We left them behind to fade under gathering dust. Jamie kept her word and started seeing a therapist when we came back from England and it seems to have helped her to understand herself and why she feels as she does. She still struggles with trust and closeness, but at least she now knows where that comes from and why she feels like that. She now has to work on coping mechanisms that will help her to deal with her feelings, ones that do not see her resorting to alcohol or self-harm as avenues of escape from her thoughts.

"I don't think you can necessarily get rid of those feelings," I said, "but surely knowing you have them, and understanding where they come from, gives you the chance to choose to ignore them and act differently, to override them?"

"I hope so," Jamie said. "When we came back here I thought I'd dealt with it in that conversation with my dad in the hospital, so I very nearly broke my word to you and didn't see anyone, but I knew that would be wrong and unfair to you so I went, and I'm so glad I did. There's no magic bullet that puts the wrongs of the past right. It's a process, and I can see why for some it's a long one. One of my concerns when I started with the therapist was that she might become a crutch for me and I wouldn't be able to give her up. You read about people who have been seeing one for years and years and I really don't want to be that person."

"Well I would say the mere fact you know that's a possibility will stop that happening and anyway, any therapist who has professional values is going to want you to become independent of them I would think. I'm glad you have gone so thank you. I think it has done you good. So far anyway."

"You're right. I brought it up with her at our first appointment and that's pretty much what she said to me. She said her job was to get people to be independent of her as soon as possible and she suggested we would perhaps need no more than six sessions together to do that. And yes, I can begin to feel benefits. I still feel the need to self-harm or reach for the bottle but now I recognise why I do and she has helped me learn how to deal with that and not give in to it. It's like any addiction really. I think I'm drinking less too, aren't I?"

"Yes, I suppose we don't go and buy wine as often as we used," I said with a laugh.

Perhaps this home we share is our first tentative step towards a long life together in an upside-down world, and in an America that has found itself under what we all pray is the healing balm of a unifying President. We have shouted to the world from the rooftops for so long that America is great, but it isn't really. It has as many problems and is as imperfect as any other country, so who are we to tell everyone we are their role model and that we are the leaders of the free world? We have no right to say any of that. Has our country ever been more divided than it is now? The Civil War split a few secessionist States away from the Union in a brutal and costly bisection based on more limited agendas than what separates us today, but now there is division everywhere we care to look, in every aspect of our lives. Politically, economically, socially and racially, it is as though a cleaver has fallen down the middle of our society. The poor are poorer and growing in numbers as the gap between them and the rich grows ever wider, forming a dangerously unbridgeable chasm. The homeless are taking over the streets as the wealthy forge relentlessly upwards for more wealth than they will ever need or be able to spend. It is surely not right that even middle-class middle-income families are taking to living in their cars or recreational vehicles because they cannot afford to pay rent. I warn friends of the dangers that lie shallow in the waters of this discord, and that the French Revolution grew out of similar divisions between privilege and the disadvantaged who have no appetite for mere cake. Conversations have to be had about a fairer distribution of wealth, which will probably have to come through taxation, the most effective instrument the Government has for redistribution of the country's spoils. Sadly, it seems to me that taxation and economic policies for a long time have merely enriched the already overly wealthy at the expense of the underdogs. Hardly a vote winner on the hustings and electoral rallies which no doubt explains why the status quo has always remained.

Our political parties and their elected representatives drive self-interest to new heights, to the point of moral bankruptcy, riding roughshod over the interests of the electorate in their remorseless quest for control. In this stampede for power, democracy is being trampled into the dust, subservient to Party political games that are deaf to opposing views, thinking and reason, hearing only the clarion call of re-election. Our two main parties often obstruct progress and legislation merely on the grounds that the other side proposed it, irrespective of the individual merits of each proposal. In our own powerlessness, we the people can only ignore government through anarchy, our weapon of last resort and used to such effect in the storming of the Capitol. Anarchy has consequences and the anarchists should be careful about what they wish for because the outcome is so often very different, especially when powerful but minority subversive interests take control as happened with the Black

Lives Matter movement. For some reason, sleepy liberal Portland became one of the epicentres of the conflagration that came out of a well-meaning and well-intentioned protest. Much of downtown was boarded up to protect businesses. Guns appeared on the streets and soon the violent protests were a nightly occurrence. Antifa and opposing members of the far-right group Proud Boys emerged out of the woodwork like so much woodworm, hijacking the agenda with the resultant riots and looting that rocked the town. Rallies in Peninsula Park in the north of the city cried their demands for the police to be disbanded in the face of their violent attempts to suppress the rallies.

We have allowed our system of governance to become what it has morphed into. Surely the country's founding fathers never intended the outcome we have. How politicians speak and behave, the words they use are surely part of what has fomented some of the recent anarchy we have seen on our streets and on the Capitol, feeding in to the more radical views that have given the opportunity to extremist concepts to germinate and flourish and become beliefs. These are fertile breeding grounds for the conspiracy theorists of the like of QAnon, who peddle their dangerous beliefs to a worryingly growing believing cohort. And so, in the face of so much irrationality and agenda driving media and social imbalance, Jamie and I largely shut off both the mainstream and social media conduits of information and news. Who to believe has become a big conundrum which sadly emphasises the growing mistrust of government and the Government, the very people we should be able to rely on.

Jamie and I now concentrate on our own small lives, and what we can reasonably control. If we should go on to have children, we fear for them and the world they will come into. Is it irresponsible of us to do that when we fear for their future? Jamie never went back to see her father in the hospital. She shut the door on him, locking it behind her and hurling the key into an *oubliette* from which it, and the memories it represented, could never escape. Or so she thought. I know he will come into her mind from time to time. A sound, a scent, an unkind word or deed. All triggers to instant recall of long forgotten moments. We never truly forget, do we? Our brains store every nano second of our lives, and it's not our brains that fail us. Our powers of recall do that. They need a catalyst to retrieve our past, and it is our senses that provide it, often at the most unexpected and sometimes unwelcome moments. Jamie's moments lie ahead of her and they will trigger thoughts and urges she will have to use her new-found skills to control.

Jamie and I spent the rest of our two weeks in Britain travelling between Jamie's mum at her home and London where she became my guide, showing me not only the parts of the city the tourists see, but much more interestingly, the real London they never see. She still had one or two friends who she had kept up with and who she made contact with. We met them for meals and in pubs, and Charles made the effort to spend evenings with us when he could get away from his busy work schedule. Jamie and Joan found each other again, or perhaps for the first time in their lives, and have remained in close contact since we got back. Joan was able to make one visit to us when she came out for Christmas last year. We showed her the city and its surrounds and included a weekend at the beach at Manzanita, which she fell in love with. We cooked meals on fires we built on the sand, and walked along the empty and wide beach, watching the occasional horse rider or dog walker. On one early morning walk on the beach, Joan and Jamie marvelled at the sight of two turkey vultures fighting over a dead fish that lay on the waterline. Since those days and that visit, the pandemic has grounded the whole world and so they have had to rely on FaceTime to keep in touch.

Jamie's Dad died in early August, just after our return to Portland. The cancer raged through his body unchecked, quickly overwhelming it. The afternoon before we flew back, Charles came to the house in the village to spend our last night with us before he took us to the airport in the morning. We laid the table in the garden for supper, the lit candles in large glass vases casting a warm light across it as the sun set and night came. Sitting around the table, candlelight flickering on our faces, I could see Jamie was happy and seemed to have acquired a sense of belonging, of being part of a family at last.

"Are you absolutely sure you don't want to go and see your father to say goodbye?" Joan said, putting her hand over Jamie's, which was resting on the table. "There won't be another chance and I wouldn't want you to have any regrets. I can ring the hospital and arrange it, on compassionate grounds perhaps."

"No, thank you Mum. I understand what you're saying but I made my peace the other day. Not with him. That's never going to happen, but with myself. I know futility when I see it and I know I'm not responsible for him, only for myself. I can't fix him, so I think I may have fixed me instead. I know there's probably still a way to go for me, but for the moment I feel fine. Jack has said I should see someone when we get back and I will. You know, a therapist. It's taken some time hasn't it? It never occurred to me I needed one but I suppose that's quite common, you know, the one in need being the last to realise. I can begin to feel like a real American and have one on my CV. We're too uptight to admit to needing one over here, aren't we?" She laughed as she looked around at each of us.

"Well, if you're sure, then I'm happy," Joan said.

"And Mum, when he comes home and the carers look after him,

don't let him bully you anymore. There's nothing wrong with the word 'No,' and I think it's time you started using it."

"I know. Probably easier said than done dear, and anyway, I know it's not for long now. Perhaps I shall just opt for the easy life for these last few months."

"Do you love him, Mum?" Jamie asked, the wine clearly loosening her inhibitions.

Joan didn't answer straight away. She looked into the dark of the garden and then up at the stars in the clear sky above us. She seemed lost in thought for a moment and we stayed silent, fearful of breaking into her concentration on a difficult and personal question.

"Do you know, I don't think I know the answer to that question. I did once, at the beginning, but now, I'm not sure. I think what I feel now is probably habit. I'm used to him and I've adapted, just to keep him happy, to give him what he wants because my life becomes unbearable if he doesn't get that. When you told me you had found him in that hotel room, I hated him. Oh my goodness, I hated him. I'd always had my suspicions, and I knew perfectly well he'd had affairs. Many of them, and you wouldn't believe it but some were with the wives of friends of his. Can you imagine? Why didn't I leave him? I told you already, I was terrified of him, of being thrown out with nothing, of never seeing you and Charles again, and so I made the compromises I needed to make to protect myself. I never forgave him, but I didn't let him know that. He carried on as normal after you told me what had happened in London, as though it was nothing more than a lunch meeting he'd been at. He really couldn't see what the fuss was about. So no, I don't think I love him anymore and I don't know when that died, but he's all I've got and I'm used to it and the life I have. It's okay and soon he will be gone and I shall make plans."

"The first of which is you must come out and see us," Jamie said.

"I would love that," Joan replied with a smile of gratitude.

When we boarded our flight home, little did we know what the following year held for us and the world. For me, work and the coming Presidential election were uppermost in my mind. If President Trump stayed in the White House our tax bills at work would remain low, which would allow for the additional investment we wanted to make into the business to take it to the next stage. But at what social price? The virus arrived and then the Black Lives Matter movement burst onto the scene. The Presidential election in November brought Trump's irrational protests of a rigged election with demands for recounts and investigations into fraudulent voting. Tens of thousands or more, perhaps millions, of his supporters believed him, striking at the very foundations of democracy.

When Jamie's dad died, I was tied up with work and in negotiations to take over another company, so I could not take the time to go with Jamie when she flew back for the funeral.

"I'm afraid I really can't come with you this time," I said. "This deal is at such a crucial point and I really have to be here for that. Will you be okay? I do think you should go to say goodbye to him."

"I'm not going back for him," she said. "I want to be there for Mum and Charles and that's why I'm going. I said my goodbyes years ago, and especially when I saw him."

She returned from the trip and we fell into an easy pattern of life, like so many couples who forge their own habits and ways of living together. The move to this house was a positive step for us both and we have enjoyed our new neighbourhood, as much as we can, given how constrained our lives have become. We took a weekend out and flew to Asheville where I introduced Jamie to my parents, always a big step in any relationship. They loved her and immediately adopted her as their daughter, elbowing me out of the way for her to be their weekend's focus of attention. For North Carolina, Jamie from England was something of an exotic species.

"Are you happy?" I said to Jamie.

She lowered her book to her lap and looked across to me.

"Yes, I am. I love it here and I really cannot see myself ever wanting to go back to England. This seems like home, at last. Thank you for helping make that happen."

I patted the cushion on the couch next to me and she closed her book and put it on the floor before walking over and sitting next to me, which was a big step for her. I put my arm around her as she leant in to me and we lay back quietly in that faux Nirvana lovers achieve, where no words are necessary and silence is all that is needed.

"I think we're going to be okay," I said.

"Yes, I think we are," Jamie said as she put her arm around my chest and hugged, hard.

# ABOUT THE AUTHOR

Born in India, David has led a varied life, pursuing a variety of occupations before finally settling on 'living the moment' as a career choice. Now a wildlife and travel photographer, he lists family as his passion, one he indulges from his home in Surrey where he can be found often festooned in grandchildren, who he pays to say they like him.

In this his third book, David draws on his experiences as a father, and his observations of the parenting by others of his generation and before, always aware that becoming a parent is a precious gift and a privilege. The story is born out of an interview he listened to on the radio over three decades ago, an interview of a girl at university whose story shocked him as a father, and one he felt compelled to tell even after so many years.

Printed in Great Britain
by Amazon